Finding Isabella

A. J. GARROTTO

TANGO 2

Tango 2 is an imprint of
Genesis Press, Inc.
315 Third Avenue North
Columbus, Mississippi 39701

ISBN 1-58571-005-9

Set in Omega

Manufactured in the United States of America

FIRST EDITION

I dedicate this book to my own two "Analisas," Monica and Cristina.

Also to my friend and colleague, Carolyn Woolston (who writes as Lynna Banning for Harlequin Historicals), for midwifing me through the early stages of editing; and my agent Jennifer Piemme.

I am grateful to Karla Hocker, my editor at Genesis Press, for her encouragement and expertise in helping me fine-tune the final text.

Bill Cryer, my fly-boy friend, taught me what I needed to know about his beloved Beechcraft Bonanza J35.

Always, to Esther for putting up with her dreamer husband.

Finding Isabella

Prologue

They called her "La Coneja," the mother rabbit. She had once been a vibrant student at the Colleggio Santa Lucia. Skin pure as olive oil, matching that of her adoptive parents, complemented intelligence that flashed with intuition and wit. She had set her sights on a career in journalism. In fact, at the time of her disappearance, she had a firm job offer from the Italian daily, *Il Mondo di Oggi*. That had been long ago, in another place, during another life.

She squatted on the dirt floor in the corner of her thatched hut. The coarse coffee-sack shift that only a few months ago had hung loosely about her skinny frame now bulged at the belly. This was her third pregnancy since they picked her up in the heart of Santa Catalina and whisked her to the first of many makeshift prisons.

To distract herself from loneliness and the oppressive Caribbean heat, she recited the story of who she had been...before her abduction. Had it all been a dream? she wondered, as her ability to recall facts and images gradually weakened.

Each time, the same man had raped her. That wasn't how he termed their couplings. At first, she had fought him off but he was too strong, too violent. Gradually, she gave up. With surrender, she lost all hope of returning to her former life as Lydia Vitale.

In this state of degradation, all she had to look forward to was being pregnant. Each new life that grew inside her affirmed that she was alive, if not loved.

For Lydia, knowing always that her keepers waited, ready to receive the newborn who bore her blood and likeness, was worse than labor pains. They won't even tell me if it is a boy or girl! Her babies never heard the lyrical lullabies learned from her adoptive mother.

Left in solitude to recover from the pain of childbirth, the discomfort of breasts swollen and aching for her infant, Lydia could only speculate about its fate. There was no way to find out. Her captors had cut her off from the world. Even the matrons who guarded her and monitored her daily activities excluded her from their little world of social gossip.

During long nights when sleep refused to relieve the frightening nightmares, the residue of many beatings and humiliations, she queried whatever spirits might care to listen, Are my babies with the man who fathered them? Perhaps they have been adopted by wealthy Santo Sangrians. Or— The thought ripped her heart. Sold into slavery...even murdered? She prayed they hadn't been put in the hands of filthy child molesters.

The greatest pain of all was knowing it would happen again...and again.

"As long as you can have babies," her captors told her, "you will serve your country by replacing those stolen from us."

By the time she realized she was pregnant for the third time, Lydia had stopped wondering about her offspring. She lived within herself, tapping into a diminishing store of happy memories, recreating scenes of her childhood home in the sunny hills of Tuscany.

Chapter 1

A sudden bump jarred Analisa from sleep. Outside the Bonanza J35, the Central California sky had blackened. Crystal flakes clung to the Plexiglas windows.

"I've switched on the transponder," her dad muttered. "That'll get red lights flashing at the radar stations."

"Where'd this storm come from?" Terror added an unnatural rasp to her mother's words. "It wasn't supposed to arrive till after we got back to Orange County."

Suddenly alert, Analisa asked, "Where are we, Dad?"

"Can't tell for sure. The VOR's malfunctioning. Should be over Gorman. We're drifting west." He switched his communication radio to 121.5, the Mayday frequency. "That'll alert Los Angeles Center." With his usual composure, he pulled a cloth rag from under the seat and leaned forward to wipe the inside of the windshield. His left thumb pressed the radio button located at the top of the steering column. "Mayday. This is Bonanza 547 Bravo." His cool, professional tone gave Analisa confidence that he had the problem under control.

"547 Bravo, this is Los Angeles Center. What is your problem?"

"I'm icing up and I'm—" He paused to clear his throat. "I'm losing control of the aircraft."

Icing! Analisa knew what that meant. He had described the process to her in detail. Butterflies swarmed in her stomach. The Bonanza had no de-icing capability. She visualized super-cooled water hitting the wings and freezing instantaneously.

"Claire, see if you can find us on the En Route Low Altitude Chart."

"Oh God!" she breathed. "Are we heading for Mount Pinos? John, that's almost nine thousand feet!"

"Maybe we'll get lucky and find a road or an open space to set her down in," he said. "One thing's sure. Radar's got a bead on us. Bells are ringing and red lights flashing all over the place. The emergency crews will probably be waiting for us wherever we set this baby down."

"What are our chances?" she said, as the Marconi family's long-faithful airplane surrendered the sky foot by precious foot.

"Do you believe in miracles?"

"Yes," Claire whispered.

Analisa clenched her fists and prayed. The weekend with her parents at Lake Tahoe faded so far into the past, it was as if it never happened. They had celebrated her finishing graduate school and landing a plum job with a San Francisco-based international marketing firm. In a week she'd be moving permanently from Anaheim to the Bay Area.

"547 Bravo, we have your location radar fix."

"See," John said. "What did I tell you?"

Analisa sighed with relief. "Thanks, God."

"You're at 7,000 feet and heading into—"

A sickening crunch jarred the fuselage.

"Shit!" Analisa's dad shouted over the noise. "Clipped a goddamn treetop! Hang on!"

"Oh my God, I am heartily sorry," her mother prayed. "I detest all my sins..."

It felt as if every snow-laden limb in the forest was taking a whack at them, upset that this alien aluminum dart had intruded upon their peaceful winter day.

"I love you both!" she heard her dad say.

Analisa's brain returned the message, "I love you too, Mom, Dad," but in the millisecond it required, everything became a colorless blur. She couldn't be sure the words ever came out of her mouth or that her parents had heard them.

The Bonanza emitted a death-agony roar as it ripped its way through snow-muted pines in search of a final resting place. Analisa had a vague awareness of wings ripping from the fuselage. She imagined irate branches lashing out and puncturing the gas tanks as the plane streaked by. "Please, Lord, no fire!"

Despite Analisa's horror, some part of her brain kept processing. She felt a sense of anticipation.

What's it like to die?

Will I be awake when it happens?

The questions came as flashes, pure, wordless consciousness, involving neither speech nor thought.

Is death the end of everything?

With a final, violent jolt, the plane came to a grinding stop. Analisa's seat belt tore away from its anchors, hurtling her forward into the backs of the seats occupied by her parents.

With whatever conscious thought was left in her, she envisioned being consumed in a thunderous fireball, scorching her flesh before it killed her.

Chapter 2

There was no explosion.

No fire.

Just silence.

And the frightening smell of aviation fuel leaking from twenty- and ten-gallon tanks just inches below where Analisa lay.

Then pain!

Pinned and barely able to move on the floor behind the pilot and front passenger's seats, Analisa gained courage to open her eyes. Her right leg veered at an unnatural angle beneath her in the cramped space.

"Mom?" she called weakly. "Dad?"

No response. She twisted her upper body in an effort to peer through the space between the seats. Her father lay crumpled over the control wheel, his head wedged against the shattered windshield. Streams of frozen blood matted his graying hair.

"Daddy!"

Analisa gasped when she saw her mother. Blood splattered the area where her head had struck the window.

"Mom!" A cry of fury, grief, despair.

Alone in the freezing interior of her father's J35, Analisa got a glimpse of her future. What she saw terrified her—a life deprived of the love and support of the parents she adored. And for herself, if she survived, an existence marred by crippling disfigurement and disability.

With great difficulty, she raised herself to get a better look at the twisted bodies in front of her.

"Goodbye, Mom. Goodbye, Dad."

Violent, uncontrollable sobs followed her simple farewell.

❀ ❀ ❀

It had been just over twenty years since Analisa's adoption. Now a far different person in a far different place from that of her birth, she had been abandoned, left motherless again. Old feelings of confusion and loss swept through her with all the same force she had experienced as a four-year-old. This time with magnified intensity. Unless help arrived soon, separation from her parents would be brief, their reunion swift.

She had only lost hope once before...at an early age in an almost forgotten land where the tropical climate forbade even the hint of snow or ice.

By the time she was four years old, Analisa had already been abandoned twice. Now grounded, crumpled, and half-delirious inside the Bonanza's shattered cabin, she gave flight to tattered memories of her birth mother, Martina Aguilada. Analisa never addressed this woman as "mother." From the beginning of her new life in America, she had reserved that honored title for Claire Marconi alone.

Analisa—born Isabella María—had just turned three when Martina nudged her awake early one summer morning.

"Wake up, *hija*."

The air inside the tiny cubicle she shared with her sisters and brother was heavy with a mixture of body odors and the smell of an evening meal of tortillas and black beans.

Isabella rubbed her eyes and scratched at a patch of unruly hair that was inexplicably lighter and curlier than her siblings'.

"Where are we going?" she asked, as her mother hurriedly dressed her.

"Shush! You'll wake the others."

"But where are we going, Mamá?"

"To Santa Catalina."

"Is it far?"

"You ask too many questions for a little girl."

A faded blue bus picked them up on the main road leading down the mountain toward the sea. The constantly swaying, lurching motion of the overcrowded vehicle made Isabella so nauseous that twice her mother had to hold her head out the window to let her throw up.

The makeshift shelter she called home had always seemed spacious to Isabella. Not until mother and daughter reached the capital did she get her first glimpse of real houses. The thick-walled, iron-gated homes with their gardens of flame red and yellow-orange tropical flora stood like palaces compared to the thatch-roofed and only partially enclosed hut her family shared. The city's first-time splendor distracted Isabella from the dark questions she had puzzled over all morning.

It wasn't to one of these Santa Catalina palaces that Martina delivered her daughter on that August day, but to a humbler dwelling, squeezed onto a small corner plot behind a larger house.

"Señora Dorada will take care of you." They were the first words her mother had spoken since leaving the bus. Her voice was controlled, pitched lower than the child had ever heard it. "Goodbye. Be a good girl."

"Goodbye, Mamá."

As the months passed, the affection-starved Isabella grew attached to her foster mother, a grandmotherly woman with limited resources but playful eyes and a welcoming heart for strays, both human and animal.

When a stroke crippled Señora Dorada's husband, she no longer had time to devote to an extra child. Soon after, Isabella said goodbye to the second woman she had loved...and lost.

Señora Dorada deposited her at Hogar de Niños Santa Rosa, an earthquake-damaged orphanage operated by white-habited nuns who seemed to float rather than walk.

It was Sister Anastasia who took Isabella aside one day and told her, "God has blessed you, child. He has found you a family. In North America. You will soon be adopted."

Isabella had no idea what "adopted" meant but asked no questions. If Sister Anastasia said it was a blessing from God, there was nothing to do but wait for it to come.

The nun handed her a color photograph of a smiling couple. "Your new parents have sent you a picture."

Isabella looked first at the woman. What struck her was the laughter emanating from her direct, welcoming eyes. Martina always seemed anguished and heavy-hearted. Next, she noticed the woman's wide mouth, bright red lips, and the whitest, most perfectly matched teeth Isabella had ever seen. The woman's smile created a long diagonal dimple across her right cheek, complementing the playfulness of her eyes. Her hair was brown with hints of red and gold. Bangs fell in parallel lines to meet perfectly arched eyebrows. A warm glow of anticipation radiated through Isabella.

The man in the photograph possessed a smile that gave his face a fascinating pattern of crevices. Isabella let her finger play along the deepest one that formed a crescent from cheek to chin.

"He looks strong," she whispered.

Sister Anastasia placed her hand under Isabella's chin. The nun's skin was like gravel from years of labor but more gentle than any the child had ever known. She tilted Isabella's face to meet her eyes. They sparkled with such light and life that Isabella thought they had to be heavenly skylights through which God watched over the lost inhabitants of the orphanage.

"You are a fortunate little girl." The nun's voice was a melodious hymn like the ones that floated through the open windows of the convent chapel after the children had gone to bed.

Isabella ran from the room and hid the photograph among her few possessions. Unsure of what this new turn in her life meant, she memorized every feature of those two faces and compared their images to every strange grownup who came into the orphanage.

To protect herself against yet another disappointment, she kept a tight rein on her expectation that the man and woman in the photograph would someday actually step out of the picture and into her life. Despite her fear, she allowed herself to play with images based on bits of information about this place called North America gleaned from the older girls who shared her dormitory. In her dreams, she was a princess, clothed in fine, frilly dresses and living in a magnificent house at the end of a gold-paved lane.

The weeks dragged on. Time became her enemy. When a fever or cough required a visit to the infirmary, she studied the faces of the pretty, manicured women who volunteered one day a week to help the sisters care for the children.

Despite Sister Anastasia's urgings to pray to the Blessed Virgin, the thin cords of hope unraveled within Isabella's spirit. She got used to being hungry most of the time and accepted the nuns and children of Santa Rosa as her family.

❦ ❦ ❦

The instant she saw them, Isabella knew her saviors had arrived. The people in the photo she had stashed between the wooden bed frame and the canvas pad on which she slept now stood in the middle of the playground, bewildered by the dozens of curious children crowding around them. She watched the grownups' eyes move from one upturned face to the next, knowing exactly where their search would end.

Isabella held her ground at the edge of the shifting chaos, waiting for the couple to scan her way. When they did, there was instant recognition. It's about time you came, her expression told them. I almost gave up.

To her dismay, the man and woman began to cry. A sharp pain darted through Isabella's chest and wrapped her heart in barbed wire. They are not pleased with you, a voice inside scolded.

In the next instant, Isabella's new mother swept her up in her arms. It had been so long since anyone had embraced her like that. She had forgotten the warm feeling, the softness of a woman's breasts, the sweet scent of fragrant hair tumbling across her face.

The tall, friendly-looking gentleman hovered behind his wife, fumbling with his camera. Tears streamed down his cheeks.

He reached over his wife's shoulder and touched Isabella's face, as if to assure himself she was real. His hand was warm and much softer than she expected from someone who stood two heads taller than her first father.

"I am your papá," he said in her own language, but with an unfamiliar accent.

❧ ❧ ❧

The week that followed her new parents' arrival was as different from Isabella's days in the orphanage as her language was from theirs. Instead of the crowded austerity of the children's shelter, with its meager meals and hard beds, she found herself alone with the couple in a hotel room. Everything was unfamiliar, including her name. Instead of calling her simply Isabella, they called her Analisa Isabella. And a different girl had replaced the dirty waif in plain white smock and cracked sandals. In the mirror she seemed only vaguely familiar. Her mother bathed her at night and dressed her in a new outfit every morning.

On the second day, they bought her the most beautiful pink sandals she had ever seen. Analisa Isabella missed her friends at Santa Rosa, especially Sister Anastasia, but she loved having a mother's attention again. She liked the safe feeling of being with a father she didn't have to fear, one who was gentle and kind and made her laugh. She enjoyed singing for them the only song she knew by heart. "*Qué linda la muñeca...*" It was about a little girl's beautiful doll and set to a melody the orphanage children sang to the Virgin on her feast days.

It took only a day or two to decide it was worth the daily baths and the sacrifice of her name to be with this man and woman who treated her with such affection.

The first night, it was hard for her to sleep. The bed was too soft. Being able to feel the wooden plank beneath her as she slept had always given her a sense of attachment to the earth. On the thick hotel mattress, she felt as if she was floating on a puffy cloud observing herself and the wondrous transformation taking place in her life.

The next night, somewhere between waking and sleeping, a shadow of terror passed across Analisa Isabella's soul. She felt sad about leaving Santa Rosa and ashamed of her readiness to go anywhere on earth with the man and woman. She tried harder than ever to recall Martina's face, to keep her image from fading completely. Finally, her deep inner sadness and confusion erupted to the surface, first as a low moaning sound, then bursting into full-throated sobbing.

Analisa Isabella's inexpressible mixture of emotions canceled her new parents' best efforts to console her. They took turns holding her and whispering mantras of love and encouragement. During that endless night, she learned her first English expression. "It's okay."

The next morning, she awakened with a smile. Her parents were asleep in the other bed.

I am Analisa Isabella Marconi, she said to herself, child of Claire and John Marconi of...of Anaheim in California, USA.

All she knew about that place was one thing, but it seemed important, so she spoke the word with reverence. Disneylandia. She climbed onto the larger bed and crawled beneath the covers between her mother and father. "It's okay!" she announced. "It's okay."

John and Claire awakened with the disruption and snuggled closer, sandwiching their daughter between them.

"It's okay!" they chorused.

And it was.

From that day forward, Analisa Isabella never doubted that Sister Anastasia had been absolutely correct. She was indeed a blessed and fortunate child.

Chapter 3

With the last gray-white daylight quickly fading, Analisa struggled to remain conscious. Search-and-rescue teams had to be looking for the wreckage and would not abandon their search until it was too dark to continue.

Suddenly, out of the swirling snow and diminishing light, David Gallego approached the nose of the aircraft. He smiled, seemingly unaffected by the cold and the strong wind that rocked what remained of the broken Bonanza.

Despite the storm, he wore only black pants, a short-sleeve black shirt, and no hat. The square of white plastic showing at his throat contrasted with his medium-dark skin and short-cropped black hair. It seemed perfectly natural for her best friend to be with her at the crash site. Dave was always there when she needed him.

A feet few behind him stood another man, a broad-shouldered stranger, a Latino, like herself, with dark skin and hair. He smiled encouragement to choose life, grab hold of it and clutch it to her breast as a precious gift.

"Dave! You've come."

"Hang in there, kid. Help is on its way." His voice was deep, comforting.

"It's too late. My parents are dead. I'm going to die." She lacked energy to inquire about his companion. "Why am I always saying goodbye to the people I love most?"

"You're not going to die," he assured her.

"I—I want to sleep, but...I'm afraid I won't wake up."

"Sleep, Analisa. I'll stay with you."

Dave came around to the side of the plane. He reached through the jagged hole where the rear passenger window had been and touched her bleeding chin. His hand felt warm, his touch healing.

"Dave," she whispered, "I love you."

"I know."

Loving Dave was the most satisfying part of Analisa's life. She was almost fifteen and just finishing her freshman year at Marycrest High when he landed at St. Boniface with the oils of ordination still fresh on his hands. The pastor assigned the new priest to be the teen club moderator—typical duty for an energetic twenty-five-year-old ordinand. A star point guard on the freshman basketball team, Analisa was the youth group's vice president. They hit it off immediately. Dave was friendly, approachable and, in her idealistic mind, the perfect male, cast in her father's mold. Born of an Hispanic mother and African-American father, Dave became an instant role model for the Latin American adoptee. Although she called it something else, Analisa developed a plain, old-fashioned major-league "thing" for the new parish priest.

What began as a teenage crush saw a series of evolutionary stages over the next nine years. By the end of Analisa's senior year, Dave had assumed an essential role in her life. She shared school problems, conflicts with boyfriends, her ascendant-woman differences with her mother.

Dave alone had access to her soul, that inner chamber of bright light and contrasting shadows. He had never betrayed that trust.

Another side of the bond between Dave and Analisa was a spark of unselfconscious aliveness and spontaneity that took hold when they were together. She enjoyed teasing him and was fully aware when she crossed the line into flirtation.

At times the boundaries blurred. Fortunately, God had blessed each of them with an instinctive good sense that allowed them to take their caring to the frontiers of forbidden territory—and stop. Only once had they almost pushed those limits too far. Analisa was nearing the end of her junior year at St. Mary's College, when Dave arrived on the Northern California campus for a surprise visit.

When she saw him standing on the chapel's tiled front steps, she screamed and threw her arms around his neck. "You should've warned me you were coming."

"Thought I'd surprise you." He kissed her lightly on both cheeks. "Father Tom told me to go away for a few days. Sort of like the Angels' manager benching a slumping hitter. I had nowhere to go on short notice, so I got in my car and said, 'Car, take me somewhere.'" Squinting in the bright May sun, he surveyed the white Spanish-style buildings nestled amid the oak-sprinkled Moraga hills. "It brought me here...to you."

Analisa blew a kiss toward Dave's VW which rested from the four-hundred-mile trip in a Visitors parking space. "Thanks, car! You did good."

They dined that evening at Mondavi's in nearby Rheem. Lulled by a generous Italian meal, they agreed they needed exercise.

"Let's walk the bike trail on St. Mary's Road," Analisa said. "We still have some daylight left."

Once they reached the asphalt path that followed the scenic bends and curves of the hilly roadway, Analisa said, "Okay, the truth. Why are you really here?" Dave's hand found hers and folded it within his own. Her body warmed to his nearness.

"I told you. I needed to get away. The car brought me to Moraga."

Analisa and Dave had touched playfully before, but they had never held hands like this. And, they had never been alone in so romantic a setting, so far from home. It felt good to entwine her fingers with his and feel so casual, free and...right about it. Stop! her Catholic upbringing warned her. You have no right.

Heeding that voice had gotten Analisa out of some tight spots in the past, especially since going away to college. But, this was David Gallego, not a lusting college kid emboldened by a few too many beers on a football Saturday night.

It seemed foolish to withdraw from him now, just to keep whatever was happening between them from approaching a previously sealed-off chamber.

We're friends, she reminded the voice. Still, she resisted the urge to snuggle closer to his side. She broke the busy silence. "Sorry, Dave, that's not good enough. How about the whole truth?"

"Whole? Hmm. Can I really tell you the whole truth?" Suddenly, he gathered strength and resolution. "All right. The truth!" He announced it as if it was the title of a poem. "I love being a priest. I think I'm good at it, but—"

"That's it?" she interrupted. "You drove four hundred miles to tell me what everyone in Orange County knows? I expected something with a lot more drama, some secret revelation you could share only with your best and most trusted friend."

"Give me a chance to get my 'but' out." They laughed and Dave relaxed his grip on her hand. "I was saying before you cut me off, I love being a priest, but...right now I'm wondering how long I can go on." He paused to give her a chance to respond. When she remained silent, he continued. "I'm a people person. I'm happiest when saying Mass, teaching a class, facilitating a meeting. And, I love parties, as you well know. The hardest time for me is when everyone has gone home, when there are no more functions to attend and there's nothing left to do but go back to my room in the rectory and close the door. "I hate it. The alone part. Maybe if I were a more spiritual person, holier, I'd deal with it better." They stopped walking and Dave turned to look at her directly. "Does that shock you?"

Analisa had let him speak, all the while letting her mind, not her heart, process his words. "No. It doesn't shock me." With her free hand, she caressed the inside of his upper arm. "You work hard at guarding your feelings, but you've never been able to hide them from me. I've always known you pay a terrible price for your ministry. Sometimes, when I look at you, I see so much...I'm not sure what to call it...I only know I want to cry when it's there. I think, 'How can this great guy who's got so much talent and is such an instrument for good be so personally unfulfilled?'"

Dave looked surprised. "Why do I suddenly feel naked?"

"Truth does that."

"Look. I'm basically okay. Really. I have a lot of compensations. Three squares a day, a guaranteed roof over my head, more discretionary spending money than most lay people."

"Why are you telling me all this?"

"It's been harder lately. There's an empty place in my life. Like I have this balloon inside me. For a long time, it was so small I hardly noticed it. Little by little, loneliness became the helium that expanded it. Now, it's stretched to the limit. I'm about to explode. It scares me. I pray, but the pain is still there when I finish."

Dave had to solve his own problem, but she'd do anything to help him, no matter what.

"This is embarrassing." He averted his eyes to avoid her direct gaze. "There is one thing you can do."

"Name it."

"Hold me?" The simple request came in a whispered, little-boy voice. "You're the only one I can ask. That's really why I came here."

Analisa stepped in front of him and, tentatively at first, let her breasts press against his chest. In doing so, she discovered that his chin touched the top of her head.

They were like a couple of middle school kids at their first dance, all arms and legs and little sense of an appropriate way to mesh their bodies. It was clear that Analisa needed to take the initiative. She laid her head against him and circled his upper torso with her arms.

Gradually, Dave relaxed and accepted her gift. She moved her hands up and down his back in a slow, gentle rhythm, lightly massaging the anxiety out of tense muscles. In comforting him, she found solace for herself. As she caressed him, he hardened against her pelvis. Flashing red lights inside her brain sent flight signals to her feet. Her toes reacted with a "ready" response. No, she decided, I won't run.

Dave responded to her massaging strokes by taking deep breaths and slowly exhaling. His lips grazed the top of her head, then played gently amid her breeze-blown curls. Neither of them spoke until they became aware they were now standing in total darkness. Occasionally, the headlights of a passing car cast reflected illuminations in their direction. Slowly, Analisa regained awareness of the realities that divided them.

Dave broke the embrace, without the slightest hint of remorse or rejection. "Thank you."

Her eyes filled with tears. The demon loneliness he had brought north with him, exorcised from his spirit, had invaded hers. The few inches that separated them were like the Grand Canyon, an unspannable void.

Dave walked Analisa to the entrance of McCarthy Hall, where laughter and music spilled from open dorm windows. "I think I can go back and face it again," he said. "Are you okay?"

"Yes." Analisa wanted so much for it to be true, but feared she might never be totally okay again.

Chapter 4

La Coneja's third baby seemed to know the world held out no welcome sign.

"It refuses to be born," the midwife whispered.

"So would you," muttered the wizened matron at her side. She tossed a bloody towel into a metal bucket at her feet.

Only Lydia Vitale understood that her unborn child was obeying maternal instructions. Every night during the third trimester, she had pressed her hands into her belly until she felt the form of the growing fetus. Knowing they'd never allow her to hold this child in her arms, she caressed it when no one observed her.

"Since they will not let us be together in this life," Lydia told her baby, "I want you with me in the next." She decided not to cooperate with nature when her time came. "It's the only control I have left."

By this time, Lydia was hemorrhaging. "She must be in terrible pain," the midwife marveled.

"But she shows no sign of it," her assistant said.

"You better tell them what is happening."

"They will not take it well." And they will blame me for the deaths of their *coneja* and her baby, the midwife knew.

❧ ❧ ❧

Marta Lopez, nicknamed "La Esfera" because people said her face was perfectly round, stood beyond Guadalupe Santana's reach. In a mood like this, he could be dangerous.

He raked his coffee-colored hair with stubby fingers and shouted, "The bitch! She was only twenty-eight! How could she die?" Lupe was the driving force behind a group called Los Dejados, "those left behind."

"We hardly kept your 'bitch' in fine style," Marta said. "We have every right to force restitution of our stolen babies. But no one listened when I argued for more humane conditions for our *coneja*."

Lupe had chosen Marta to be his "closest companion." Although the title left her short of being married, it gave her status. With it came the privilege of speaking her mind— to a point. Lupe had been a faithful lover, as far as Marta knew, except for fathering the Vitale woman's two living children and this one who had died at birth. The three-year-old who was now her own son had been the fruit of that union, the first of the "redeemed."

Why Marta herself had not conceived mystified her. Like Lupe, she was healthy and only in her twenties. Barrenness was hardly a national epidemic in Santo Sangre. Both Marta and Lupe had grown up in impoverished families. Foreigners had adopted her youngest sister, Mariana. Marta hated her mother, not because she gave away a sibling but for condemning her oldest daughter to stay behind, hungering for food, yearning for a future.

Marta spent long hours in the blistering sun selling tortillas at her mother's stand. In addition, she cared for the other children and went to bed exhausted, only to dream of eating something besides *frijoles*. Los Dejados had given her a cause to embrace, a concrete way to satisfy her need for revenge.

Mariana had been the last of the six children born to Marta's unmarried mother. Two different men had lived with them off and on and had managed between them to father the bedraggled tribe her mother barely earned enough to feed. Six months later, Mariana disappeared.

"How could I feed all of you?" her mother had explained under Marta's insistent grilling.

"So, you killed her?"

"What foolishness! Mariana is better off now, with a new mother and a real father."

"When can I visit her?"

"Mariana lives far away, in a place called Holland."
The first sign that the transaction had not been a cold business deal was the crack in her mother's voice. "She will be
brought up properly. You will never see her again, so you
must stop thinking about her."

The next day, Marta gathered her courage. "Will you
give me away too?" She needed assurance her mother did
not have similar intentions for her. At the same time, the
vague description, "brought up properly," had stuck in her
head, creating its own alluring fantasies.

"Of course not."

If Señora Lopez thought her daughter found reassur-
ances about her status in the family consoling, she was
only partially correct. It dried the twelve-year-old's tears,
but not her memories. Envy replaced sorrow. As Marta's
life became more hopeless, envy festered into hatred. If I
ever see my sister, I will spit in her face, she vowed as
solemnly as any nun ever had.

Shortly after that, the dreams began. In one version
Marta, too, was a fortunate adoptee. She looked and felt
beautiful. Her skin was smooth from daily baths and applications of youth-preserving lotions. She dressed in fine
clothes and brushed her straight black hair until it reflected
the morning sun.

Another, more frequent playing of the adoption dream
fed Marta's hatred of her sister. In this one, Marta was the
daughter of wealthy parents. She saw herself in a spacious
bedroom dressing for a ball. Her white strapless formal
featured a cascade of pink silk roses that curved across the
front from left breast to right hip. Silk slippers matched the
color and fabric of the roses. Perfectly applied lip gloss
gave her mouth a sensuous glow. Downstairs, a festive
ballroom full of elegantly tuxedoed young men awaited
her entrance. When she appeared at the foot of the spiral
staircase, the handsomest of these made his way toward

her, blond hair perfectly groomed, intelligent blue eyes flashing desire. Behind his steady advance and longing gaze, Marta sensed a secret shyness, a hint of adolescent insecurity camouflaged by the bravado of his stride. Every cell in her body anticipated the experience of whirling around the dance floor pressed close to his muscular body.

The dream always ended the same way, with Mariana appearing and spitting out, "Go away! He's mine! You belong in Santo Sangre. You were left behind, or have you forgotten?" The tirade sent Marta running from the room in shame, the derision of her peers pounding inside her head. The loudest laugh of all, the one that rose and echoed most painfully, was that of her once-adored little sister.

When Marta's eyes opened, she'd be alone on her hard mat. No waltz played in the background. Her sister had vanished. All that remained were her wretched life and the dream-sounds of rejection and ridicule.

Now, Marta was a grown woman. Lupe had provided a channel for her rage. He had also given her a measure of love and affection, which was more than she had received from her mother. Best of all, he let her keep the first of their *coneja's* babies.

She moved from the stove to behind his chair and bent to kiss him. She loved to run her fingers through his soft, bushy hair, which had an almost reddish tint when the sun hit it just right. "We made a symbolic statement by redeeming two babies." She slipped her hands over his shoulders and down his chest, pausing to play with his warm, sweat-moistened nipples. "We should get on with our lives. We can still make our own babies, you and me. At least, we can keep trying."

"I have no interest in symbolic gestures," Lupe growled. "What do two babies mean? The foreigners have stolen hundreds from our country."

Stung by his rebuke, Marta pulled back. "It's just—"
"Just what?"

"Perhaps we have gone...too far."

Lupe swung around to face her, knocking over the chair as he rose.

Marta stood her ground. "The woman did not have to die! If you had let me provide for her better, she could have given us more babies. She might have learned to like it here. She might even have found a life with us."

Lupe righted the wooden chair. "You think I am brutal?" The fire cooled in his ebony eyes. "Maybe you are right. I will tell you this. There will be another *coneja*." His voice softened. "But this time we will try harder to convince her of the righteousness of our cause."

Was this really Los Dejados' leader speaking? Marta wondered. In none of their face-to-face confrontations had she ever heard him admit she might be right...about anything.

☙ ☙ ☙

The Chief Inspector's phone demanded his attention the moment he entered police headquarters at nine on Monday morning. He quickened his pace, catching it on the fifth ring.

"Madrigal here!" He spat the words in a single, irritable burst.

"Sorry to hit you with this first thing in the morning, Jefe." It was Jorge Marín, one of two junior detectives in his three-man homicide department. "Got the body of a young woman out here in Colonia Escalón."

"What makes you think I'm interested in the latest report on your sex life, Marín?"

Madrigal enjoyed playing the role of gruff senior inspector with his team, although at thirty-three he was only a few years their elder. He liked his detectives and valued their judgment and professionalism.

"That's not it, sir."

Madrigal sensed Jorge's embarrassment and chuckled, Got you that time.

"This one is dead," Marín said.

"You should have been more gentle with her," Madrigal chided, continuing his game. After all, it was Monday morning. Mondays were usually slow. Santa Catalina was still enough of a Catholic city that the population was pretty good about refraining from murder on the Lord's Day. Friday and Saturday were another thing altogether. The cantinas were full. Parties celebrating everything from weddings and baptisms to Tía Juanita's ninetieth birthday gave the normally placid Santo Sangríans a reason to drink. When wine flowed freely in a crowd of more than a dozen people, it fueled tempers, rekindled smoldering jealousies, and threw gasoline on unresolved grudges fused to explode at the slightest spark.

By Monday, the Coroner's assistants had carted the bodies off to the central morgue. Madrigal's work consisted mainly of assigning investigative tasks to himself and his small staff. The playful banter was his way of saying to his city, I'm not ready to collect your dead bodies yet. Give me a chance to sit down at my desk, have a cup of coffee, scan the morning paper. Maybe by late morning I will be ready to go into your back alleys and view what is left of your stupid party arguments. But not yet.

Detective Marín found his professional tone again. "I think you should come out here, sir." He gave Madrigal the location.

In the congested morning traffic, it took the Inspector fifteen minutes to reach the scene.

"Who found the body?" he asked.

"A couple of kids."

"Were they involved?"

"Not likely."

Madrigal surveyed the crowd of onlookers that had gathered. Experience had taught him not to expect anyone at the scene to come forward with usable information. "Got a camera?"

"Yes, sir. I took photos of the body and the surrounding area."

"Take some of the crowd too. Just in case the one responsible is hanging around to admire his work."

Madrigal envied the sophisticated urban police forces in the States with their crime photographers and criminalists, medical examiners, and homicide task forces, all of whom brought their expertise to the solution of a single crime. In his three-man department, the team did everything but the autopsies. He was convinced sometimes that he and his men knew more about that piece than the medical rejects who worked in the refrigerated catacombs of the building next door.

"One more thing, Jefe." Marin lowered his voice. "I found a letter pinned to her clothing. I doubt we have a social killing this time."

Madrigal bent over the body, careful not to touch the paper. "Reads like a political manifesto. Where is Trujillo?"

"Off today, remember?"

"Well, he's on again. Get him out here. Now!" In the conscientious, hard-working Rodrigo Trujillo, Madrigal had the kind of policeman not always easy to find. Because of that, Madrigal had decided not to make an issue of what Trujillo thought was his closeted homosexuality as long as the detective's "problem" remained out of the public eye. The Chief Inspector preferred the U.S. military's policy of "Don't ask, don't tell."

Chapter 5

The rescue helicopter's aft cabin resembled the business end of a ground ambulance. "Let's go, folks," the pilot's voice squawked. "The Bonanza's ELT got us in here, but we gotta get ourselves out."

"What do you think?" Dr. Randi Morse asked.

Her counterpart, Fred Partridge, braced himself for the takeoff. "She'll make it, unless she's decided it's not worth the effort."

"ETA at Kern is twenty-five to thirty minutes," the pilot announced. "Tell our passenger to hold on, and we'll get her a warm bed for the night."

Visibility outside had closed in after a brief clearing allowed the pilot to follow the Emergency Locator Transmitter's signal to the crash scene. They had made it with only about an hour to spare before the site became inaccessible and their patient froze to death.

"Starting to snow again." Fred grunted. "Snow's for skiin', not flyin'."

With clearance from the Sheriff's Department and county coroner, Randi and Fred had supervised the removal and bagging of the two bodies they had discovered in the icy wreckage. They now applied their skills to stabilizing the only surviving victim. At the trauma center, a team waited to take over treatment.

"Notify KernTraum we've got a twenty-something female in pretty bad shape," Fred instructed the co-pilot. "Will update prior to touchdown."

"Roger that, sir."

"Vital signs?" Fred asked.

"Stable. No problems yet." Randi hated to lose a patient on the way to the hospital after the person had survived long enough for life-saving assistance to arrive.

"Hope she stays that way." She adjusted an oxygen mask over the young woman's battered and swollen face.

Fred peeled away the blanket, unzipped the girl's down jacket, and exposed her chest. "Abrasions over much of the upper body. Extensive bruising at the sternum, possibly broken, and I'd guess at least one, possibly several broken ribs. Broken nose. Lots of small cuts. Nothing so deep or long that it'll leave permanent scars. Far as I can tell, her injuries are of the mendable variety." He made vertical cuts along the pant legs. "Hmm, I was afraid of that," he muttered. "Right knee looks like raw meatloaf."

"Not surprised," Randi said. "It was mangled in the wreckage. She must've been like that a long time."

"Hope this young woman isn't a track star or something, 'cause she won't be running any races for a long time."

"If ever," Randi added.

"Any ID?"

She opened the wallet she had removed from the victim's fanny pack. "Analisa Marconi. Twenty-four. Almost 25"

"Any indication of allergies?"

"Don't see any."

"Organ instructions?"

"Pink card says they're all ours, but I think she might not be ready to pass them around just yet."

"Thank goodness. Once they get her fixed up they're going to find one helluva pretty face under all these cuts and bruises."

Randi aimed a sideways grin at her partner. "DMV photo says you're right. When a woman looks good in one of these, she's got to be a stunner."

Just as the copter touched down on the pad outside the ER at Kern, Analisa opened her eyes, which darted from side to side, full of confused questions and sheer terror.

"You're going to be fine, honey," Randi assured her. "We're pretty good at what we do. Now, you do your part."

❧ ❧ ❧

When Analisa awoke following the first surgery after her rescue—the one to repair her shattered right knee—she tried to pray for her parents and for herself. All she dredged from her inner self was wild anger aimed at the God she had always considered her friend. The deaths of John and Claire Marconi had left a void of infinite breadth and depth.

Without the parents she adored, no anchor secured Analisa to this world. The remains of her life—starting a new career, friends in the Bay Area, scattered relatives, Dave—were insufficient to replace them. The Marconis had plucked her from a life of deprivation. They were her models and inspiration. They stood beside her as guiding beacons through the squalls of her growing up years. Ready now to cast off her lines and sail into the post-grad-uate-school world of international business, she counted on them for counsel and loving support.

Lying beside their bodies in the wreckage, their two decades of shared life seemed but a few ticks of the clock, seconds on a racing stopwatch. They had traveled the world together, beginning in her native Santo Sangre and ending on an unforgiving mountainside in Southern California. Analisa refused to accept that her parents had made their final and most important journey without her.

John and Claire had always believed that adopting her was more than a random selection, no matter how acci-dental the process made it seem. They considered the coming together of their family the working out of a mas-ter plan. She recalled her dad's speech at the annual North American Conference on Adoption last summer.

"I'm sure you have your own personal religious and philosophical convictions. Call it karma, fate, or as I do, Divine Providence, our families were meant to be. I don't pretend to understand it, but I believe with all my heart that we were chosen from the beginning of time to be united with our children." His gray eyes filled with rarely shed tears. In the audience, Analisa and her mother clasped hands to give him strength.

Clearing the lump in his throat, he went on. "I...I can't tell you why it happened that...my daughter Analisa...was conceived in another woman's womb, the result of another man's pleasure. I've wished so often it had been Claire and me. But that's how the plan was destined to unfold.

"When our daughter was a little girl, we made up our own scenario of how it all came about. We'd say to her, 'When it was time for you to be born, God told you to go to Anaheim, California, to the Marconis' house. On the way, you took a wrong turn and ended up in Santo Sangre. We waited and waited, but you never showed up. It took us a long time to find you!'"

Tension-relieving laughter rippled through the audience. The sound of noses being blown followed in its wake. "My adoption story, like yours and every other family's, has a flip side. These past twenty years, my daughter's birth mother has never been far from my thoughts. How I wish she was here to see her child today—healthy, bright, intelligent, soon to be finishing graduate school—and as far as her Dad's concerned—the most beautiful girl in the world."

Analisa's blood flowed hot and prickly beneath her skin as people sitting around her smiled their agreement. "Every night I pray for that woman and thank her for the priceless gift she's given us." John gazed beyond the walls of the meeting room, beyond the borders of the United States, across the sea to a small island nation in the Southern Caribbean. "Martina Aguilada, wherever you are today...we love you." He cleared his throat again. "Thank you, dear lady, for the great gift you have given us." With that, Analisa's dad left the podium to a standing ovation from appreciative, moist-eyed listeners.

That was the unpretentious spirituality Analisa had learned from her father. Now, she lay in pain in the sterile atmosphere of Kern Medical Center, unable to make the slightest sense of her new reality. Although her injuries would eventually heal, she refused to participate in the process. This added severe strain to her already weakened immune system. Her knee became infected, requiring a second surgery. For the next few weeks, the medical staff monitored her closely for signs of pneumonia and further infection.

Gradually, her face returned to its former shape. The image she viewed in the mirror looked less and less like a pound of rotting meat. Each day, her breathing became less painful, indicating the mending of broken ribs. None of this lifted her spirits. Aunts, uncles, and cousins from both sides of the family paid occasional visits. She didn't expect more. Bakersfield was a long way from any of their scattered homes. Besides, Analisa rejected their support. From the day of her adoption, she had never "fit" with the Ellises and Marconis. They were polite in her presence, but she never felt they considered her one of their own. Once, she overheard her Uncle Joe tell his brother, "Why didn't you get an American child?"

Seething, her dad replied, "We got the child we wanted." The brothers almost came to blows over her.

Without her parents, Analisa's link with her relatives grew weaker still, as did her connection with life itself.

Chapter 6

Wednesday was David Gallego's regular—and only—day off. Each week after saying six-thirty Mass, he changed into civvies and jumped into his Volkswagen Jetta. His drive took him north through the worst of the L.A. rush-hour traffic and over the four thousand-foot Cajon Pass on I-5, not far from where the Marconis' plane went down.

Pulling into the Kern Medical Center parking lot, he'd mutter on cue, "I hate these places." Dave especially detested that bucket-of-blood ER at Anaheim General, where he served as on-call chaplain. To spend his day off around doctors and nurses, breathing the sterile odors of a medical facility, took all the courage—and love—he could muster.

Arriving mid-morning on Analisa's floor, Dave knew exactly what to expect. Each visit copied last week's and the one before that. Most of the day, he sat in silence, his chair pulled close to her bed, holding her hand. When she felt like it, he'd read from the newspaper or from a novel he brought with him.

After she had picked indifferently at a few bites of dinner, he'd kiss her on the cheek and say goodbye, knowing the iron door would close for another week on her self-imprisoned spirit.

Late one Wednesday, he'd had enough of her self pity. "Your life is like one of those old 78 rpm records. When the needle hits a crack, the record repeats itself in a continuous loop. In your case, the record's cracked on one question."

"Why didn't I die, too?"

"You got it." Patiently, one more time, for the hundred-and-first, -second, -third, -fiftieth time, he explained, "You're not finished here. God has something more for you to do with your life. Ask that question a thousand times, the answer's always going to be the same. So stop! I don't want to hear it again."

Analisa turned her head away, hiding her tears in the pillow.

"I'm sorry." Unconcealed agitation cast a shadow on Dave's apology. "It drives me nuts to see you like this."

"Then why do you keep coming?" she asked the opposite wall.

He forced himself to calm down. "Damn good question." He reached across her body and touched her chin, which angled to a rounded point at the bottom of an almost perfectly symmetrical face. Slowly, she turned to him. It tortured Dave to see how pain and loss had dulled those eyes that normally sparkled with intelligence, passion, and wit. Absent from her features were the dimples that stirred him when laughter called them from their hiding places.

"Let's see," he began. "Why do I come all the way from Anaheim to Bakersfield every Wednesday to visit a vegetable who should be fighting to get her body and mind back in shape to face the rest of her life?"

She stiffened. "Why do you come?"

"Can you believe I care what happens to you?" he said, his frustration rising. "Does it make any difference at all to you that someone in this world you're still living in cares about you enough to drag you back to life, even if you come kicking and screaming?"

Analisa brought Dave's hand to her moist cheek, then pressed her colorless lips into his palm. He rarely had the opportunity to touch any part of a woman's body other than her hands. He loved the feel of her face which, even in her diminished state, demanded attention. The fire in his chest cooled to a quiet glow. He hoped she'd let the energy he brought to her bedside revive the fading magnetic field that kept her body and soul united.

"Does it disturb you when I kiss you?" she said.

He smiled, feeling self-conscious. "It's part of my ministry to a friend in need of human warmth. And boy am I ever full of human warmth! Some days, too full."

The door of Room 314 opened and an aide brought in a tray with Analisa's supper. Dave withdrew his hand. "Here you are, honey. Got some nice hot soup for you tonight. The kind you like." The aide swung the arm of the rolling utility table over the bed and pressed a button on the console to raise her patient into a semi-sitting position. "Enjoy." She cast a backward glance at Dave on her way out. "See you next week, Father?"

"Definitely."

❁ ❁ ❁

The almost-three-hour drive home was the worst part of Dave's day. He had pumped Analisa full of enough affirmations and funny stories to last until his next visit. Every bit of energy he transmitted to her further depleted a limited reserve within himself. He had one day each week during which to renew his inner resources. Instead, he returned exhausted from the effort it took to drag his reluctant friend through another day of life.

I don't know how much longer I can keep this up, he admitted as he turned onto I-5 and headed south. To stay awake, he chewed on celery sticks he kept in a plastic sandwich bag in the glove compartment. He had learned this trick from a seminary classmate, Bill Enderhouse. "It's great!" Bill raved, like a celebrity endorser on a late-night infomercial. "No calories and it makes lots of noise. Did you ever hear of anyone falling asleep at the wheel chewing celery?"

Crazy as it sounded, it worked. Now, Dave needed some magic trick to help him carry on his demanding ministry during the coming week and to gear up for next Wednesday's Bakersfield marathon.

Chapter 7

February gave way to March the week Lydia Vitale died. It took several days for the story to make it onto the back pages of *La Prensa*. The account did not include the fact that the dead woman had been born a Santo Sangrían national. Nor did the report mention the letter Lupe Santana had so carefully worded. Marta Lopez knew this omission upset him more than the death of his precious *coneja*.

Lupe and Marta shared a one-bedroom apartment located in the overcrowded Barrio Rincón, a neighborhood the tour buses skipped. This was the city's most distant point from the sea, far from the Plaza de la Libertad and all the first-class hotels and casinos. And far from the cross-town alley where Marta and Antonio Gamez had dumped the Vitale woman's body.

Rincón was home to the invisible people whom the wealthy barely acknowledged as human, but without whose labor—and inherited poverty—they could not maintain their leisurely life styles. High unemployment kept clusters of young men hanging around street corners all day like flies on a rotting mango. They waited in hope for a pickup truck to stop and a construction foreman to point his finger at them and shout the magic words, "I need three strong backs for the day. You, you, and...you." Those lucky enough to have permanent jobs worked for low pay as maids, shop clerks, busboys, pool tenders, and custodians in the glitzy hotels.

"Are you sure you left the letter on her?" Lupe demanded. His outbursts against his fellow Dejadistas had increased in frequency and bitterness since La Coneja's death.

Marta choked back her rising temper. "Yes, I'm sure. I did it myself." She glared at Antonio Gamez, who sat in a corner, content to let her and Lupe battle it out. "Antonio was afraid to touch her even."

"You secured it, so it would not blow away?"

"Leave me alone!" she insisted. "I did my job like I always do. You should have gone with us if you were so worried about it. This is all your fault anyway."

"My fault?"

The midwife caring for La Coneja had notified Marta that the woman's third pregnancy was in trouble. "I warned you she needed medical attention. Did you listen?" She turned abruptly and went to the stove, muttering under her breath, "Typical male!"

"I didn't think the problem was serious enough to risk involving an outsider. Besides, she might have tried to reveal her identity. Then what?"

Marta bristled at Lupe's stubbornness. "She was too scared to open her mouth."

Lupe slammed his fist on the table. "The police are deliberately keeping the letter from the press."

Marta stirred the pot of *frijoles* with a wooden spoon. "We are all more tense than usual."

With the argument on the wane, Antonio ventured into the discussion. "The government is afraid. If rich foreigners start getting killed on our streets, tourism might dry up. I hear it happened in Miami."

"If the jobs go away, we only hurt ourselves," Marta said. Her employment as a seamstress in the dress shop at La Florida bought food for her child when Lupe was out of work, which was most of the time.

"They can ignore us once," Lupe said. "Next time, they will take us seriously."

Antonio tossed the newspaper on the floor. "The foreign press won't ignore us. Reporters are a persistent lot. When they smell a story, they dig for it like dogs for a bone."

"How do we know the story has not gotten out?" Marta said. Lupe seemed to have drifted away from the conversation. She stood behind his chair and worked her fingers into his muscular shoulders. Often this was enough to calm her lover's rage. "What are you thinking about, ?"

"Our next little mother rabbit."

For Marta's part, her personal rage had been satisfied. La Coneja's first child and now the woman's death, constituted sufficient reparation for Mariana's adoption. She was prepared to let go of her long-held bitterness at being left behind. If only Lupe and the other Dejadistas had it in them to do the same. Saying so was a risk, but she'd had enough of kidnapping, child-stealing, and a level of abuse that approached outright torture.

She rested her hands at the base of Lupe's neck, shook off a fleeting urge to strangle him, and continued rubbing the tension from his taut muscles. "I was hoping—"

"What were you hoping?"

"That Los Dejados would be satisfied with what we have achieved." She let the idea float free as a trial balloon. "We redeemed two babies for our country. That's something to be proud of."

"Some prize!" he mocked.

"One of those babies is now our son." She stanched tears she needed to hide from him.

"There will be another *coneja!*" Lupe proclaimed his decision with the finality of a Supreme Court judge.

Antonio had remained a mostly silent observer of this struggle for the soul of Los Dejados. "I agree with Lupe. If these women set foot on Santo Sangrían soil, let them pay for their earlier good fortune by giving babies back to their country."

Marta hated Antonio for choosing sides against her. Obviously, he wanted to be on the winning side and had decided she'd lose this contest of wills.

In bed that night, the force of Lupe's passion alternately delighted and frightened Marta. She understood the injustices that fed her partner's rage. His thrusts drove her wild with pleasure. They also filled her with terror that his final explosion might rip through her internal organs and inflict a mortal wound to her heart. She had never been afraid of him before. This time she wondered if she'd live to see the sun rise.

"Bitch *coneja!*" he grunted with a final jolt that sent his sperm darting upstream in what Marta expected to be yet another futile search for a compatible partner. Then he fell on her panting like an exhausted puppy.

For nearly an hour, she lay beneath him, grateful to have survived...and outraged that her lover might have longed for the departed Lydia Vitale at the height of their sexual tango.

Chapter 8

When Dave arrived for his weekly visit on the second Wednesday of March, Dr. Mark Gordon, Analisa's psychiatrist, was waiting for him.

"Can we talk a minute, Father?" He led Dave to a small waiting room near the nurse's station.

"What is it?" He studied the doctor's face and body language for clues as they settled into uncomfortable plastic chairs. "Has something happened to Analisa?"

"Nothing is new. That's the problem. She isn't giving us a thing. Her injuries have healed to the point where her physical therapists think it's time to start some serious rehab on that knee of hers. So far, she's just gone through the motions." The doctor flicked a piece of lint from his unbuttoned lab coat. "There's no physical reason for her not to recover fully. Yet, she says she doesn't care if she lives or dies, walks or spends the rest of her life in a wheelchair with a crippled leg. It's all mental from here on out."

Dave rubbed his tired eyes. A two A.M. sick call had interrupted his sleep. Saying Mass that morning had been an almost out-of-body experience. Since Analisa's accident, he had pushed himself beyond his physical limits to make these weekly trips to her bedside. Meanwhile, his priest buddies were giving him a bad time for not joining them anymore for golf, dinner, and a movie, their normal day-off routine.

"I'm frustrated, too, Doctor. It's not like her," he said. "I've known her since she was in high school. She's always been the one who lifts everyone else's spirits. But you've got to realize what she's lost."

Although Dr. Gordon's facial expression remained impassive, a wave of irritation dart across his unguarded eyes. Apparently, he was unaccustomed to being told, "You've got to realize," by anyone.

"I do understand, Father." This time, the doctor inject-
ed a nip of reproach into the title. "But she's still alive.
That's what is important."

"She's lost a lot more than her parents," Dave said,
pressing his point. "Analisa's adopted. In her mind, what's
happened is just one more in a series of abandonments
she's suffered since she was a little girl. She didn't expect
it to happen again, or at least not this soon, or as shock-
ingly as this. You know what I mean. It's all coming back
now, the fear, the insecurity. She feels completely alone.
It isn't true, of course, but that's how she feels. Give her a
little slack. She has to find a reason to go on. Living has
to make sense to her again. It'll come. I guarantee it."

Nice little speech. Dave wondered if he had gleaned
the lines from some old black-and-white movie and stored
them away in his memory under Dramatic Hospital Scene.

"I'm glad to hear that," Dr. Gordon replied. "I wanted
to talk to you because you're the only one she seems to
care about. If she'll listen to anyone, it's you." He looked
Dave straight in the eyes. "It's none of my business what
your relationship with this young woman is, Father. You
may be her priest or her lover, or both, but you'd better do
something to jump-start her life or you're going to lose
her."

The message made Dave's ears burn. What business is
it of yours? he thought. But Dr. Gordon was right about
Analisa. He might also be right about their relationship.
Without rebuttal, Dave rose and trudged down the hall to
her room.

❦ ❦ ❦

Analisa brightened noticeably when Dave entered. She sat
in a wheelchair, her right leg extended parallel to the floor.
A padded blue fabric brace with Velcro bindings made it
possible for her to walk short distances unaided, while pro-

tecting the healing knee joint from sudden movement in the wrong direction.

"Morning, Pal," Dave said.

She watched him shove away his fatigue and replace it with his patented keep-the-patient-smiling demeanor. "God, it's good of you to come all this way every week."

Dave stopped and glanced around the room. He stuck his head out into the hallway, then opened the restroom door to see if anyone was inside. "Oh, you meant me? You said, 'God,' and—"

Analisa laughed out loud.

"That's the first genuine laugh I've gotten out of you since you've been here." He leaned over and kissed her on the forehead.

She welcomed the press of his warm lips. Aching for more demonstrative affection, she contented herself with a priestly peck. "Feels good to laugh. I've missed it."

"It hasn't been for lack of effort on my part. For the past month, I've told you every joke I know and made up new ones when my repertoire ran out." Ignoring hospital rules, Dave sat on the edge of her bed.

Analisa's oversized cotton robe made her feel like a child wearing her mother's clothes. She had brushed her hair and spent extra time making herself look halfway human in anticipation of his arrival. The nurses and aides, observing the extra care, had treated her to some good-natured ribbing about "Father Daaaave" coming to see her again today. She straightened herself in the wheelchair. "You look exhausted. I'm worried about you."

"You're worried about me? That's a little backward, isn't it? You've got everyone outside this room worried as all get-out about you. Instead of being concerned for me, you'd better start thinking about what you're doing to yourself."

"I can see what these trips are doing to you," she said, deflecting his admonition. "Maybe you should stay away."

"I thought you liked having me visit."

"God, yes!"

Dave turned again to see if they were still alone.

"Stop that!" Analisa rested her hand on his arm and idly traced the fine muscle structure of his forearm beneath the wool sleeve of his jade green sweater. "Seeing you every week is the only thing that keeps me sane. You were with me at the crash site. You've been at my side ever since. Not just on Wednesdays."

Dave's eyes widened. "Whoa! Rewind that tape. What do you mean, I was at the crash site?"

A shy smile widened Analisa's mouth. "It sounds nuts, I know, but it's true. Just before I lost consciousness, you came walking toward the plane—what was left of it. You told me to go to sleep, that I'd live." Tears formed at the corners of her eyes, hung there a moment, then slid down her cheeks. "The last words I remember saying were . . . 'I love you.' And you said—"

"'I know.'"

"You do remember!" Analisa felt more animated than she had been since her rescue. Her grip tightened on his arm. "I wasn't hallucinating."

"I didn't say I was there. It's what I would have said if I'd been with you that day. If, somehow, my spirit got there without my body, then I'm glad you had the comfort of my company. I mean, with your mom and dad...and your injuries and everything. It must've been awful."

The mirror reflected her contentment. "I knew you were both real."

"Both?"

Her voice lowered. "You weren't alone. Another man was with you."

"Did he introduce himself?"

"No."

"What did he look like?"

Analisa took a deep breath. This had to sound insane. That was why she hadn't mentioned it to him before. "I wasn't in the best of shape. He was dark. About your height. He had this...heavenly smile. In my fog, I remember thinking, 'He's gorgeous.'"

Dave smiled. "Must have been your guardian angel looking over my shoulder."

"Maybe...if my angel's Hispanic."

"There must be at least a few Hispanic angels up there."

They bantered about the possibility of races and genders in the afterlife before deciding to let the mystery rest unsolved.

Analisa closed her eyes, calling upon memory and logic to grapple with her questions. "I hope it'll all make sense some day."

Dave cleared his throat. "So you want me to stop coming."

"No, but I feel selfish monopolizing your days off. Besides, I'm sick of being a sicko. I'm ready to say good-bye to this place."

"Okay, but you've got to promise me something."

"Anything."

He moved off the bed and stood in front of her. Resting his hands on the arms of her wheelchair, he bent over so their eyes met on the same plane, their noses inches apart. "You've got to walk out of this place on your own two legs. I want to see you back in Anaheim by...how about the Fourth of July?"

"I can do it." Her voice was resolute. She sat up straight. "I will do it. It's time anyway. You keep telling me there's a reason for me to be alive. I'd better find out what it is."

"Then it's a deal?"

"Almost," Analisa smiled. "Think you could get away from your priest friends once a month?"

"I don't know. They're pretty pissed at me. They're accusing me of having more than a pastoral interest in you."

Analisa longed to know if his friends had it right, but she intercepted the question in mid-flight. Asking violated the rules of friendship she and Dave had meticulously constructed, without ever talking about them.

"I'll come," he promised.

"In that case, it's hot dogs and Gardenburgers at my place on the Fourth."

❦ ❦ ❦

On his way out of the orthopedic ward that evening, Dave passed the station where Dr. Gordon leaned against a desk, reviewing patients' charts with two nurses. He gave the trio a thumbs up sign and called over his shoulder as the elevator doors opened, "You're going to see the real Analisa Marconi from now on."

A slashing rain followed Dave to the Interstate, the beginnings of a frigid late-winter storm that had moved down the San Joaquin Valley, reaching Bakersfield before dark. It followed him south toward Orange County. The swish of the windshield wipers had a hypnotizing effect as he sped homeward on the slippery highway. With his driving skills on automatic pilot, he let his mind roam freely over the events of the day.

Dr. Gordon's inferences about his relationship with Analisa gnawed at him. He hated being transparent. The priesthood provided a hiding place for his personal needs and problems. He liked that. He served as counselor and confessor. Others came to him for solutions to their problems. Analisa's psychiatrist had blown his cover.

He pushed Dr. Gordon's image aside and returned to Analisa. Her decision to take charge of her life again elated him. Although he had missed having her up the street during her college and postgraduate years, he supported her decision to go away to school. She needed to separate from her parents and emerge as her own person.

It had worked. Despite a nagging sense of personal disappointment, he had encouraged her to take the job offer in San Francisco, rather than return to Southern California. Her life was just taking off when— Dave was unclear about many things these days, but one thing was certain. He had never looked forward to a Fourth of July as much as the one to come.

What does that mean? his stern inner parent demanded. How should I know? Dave refused to call this voice his conscience. There was a difference. Gentle insistence of the Spirit characterized one; strident doom-saying, the other. Exposure by the flesh-and-blood Dr. Gordon was enough for one day. He was in no mood to argue with his internal Dr. Gordon.

Not good enough! the voice admonished. Admit it. You've been in love with that girl since she was fourteen. It's time you decided what to do about it. As much as Dave resented this intrusion, he had never succeeded in silencing this voice for long. He reached for the button to turn the radio on.

No radio! I want a straight answer.

Go to hell! He shifted his rear end in the driver's seat, feeling guilty about the vulgar outburst. Okay, he relented. How do I love Analisa Marconi? Let me count the ways. I loved her like everyone else loved her when she was a really great high school kid...I've loved her as a counselor loves his client, as a confessor loves his regular penitents...Now that she's an adult, I love her as a valued, trusted friend... And I love her—

He turned into the schoolyard behind the rectory and reached up to press the automatic door opener clipped to the passenger-side sun visor.

"Sorry," he said as the car rolled down the ramp leading into the combination church basement-garage. "We'll
have to finish this conversation another time." He parked
in the space marked "Fr. Dave" and shut off the engine.

Chapter 9

On the Saturday before the Fourth of July, Analisa sat with her knees touching the front of Suzi Ward's desk. Suzi, a former classmate at Marycrest, was now a rising star at Globetrotter Travel on Harbor Boulevard, not far from the Marconi family home on Whilhelmina Street. Analisa's stomach churned, and her hands felt like ice packs.

"Welcome home," Suzi said, tucking a stray handful of straight blond hair behind her right ear where it almost certainly wouldn't stay. "After you called, I did some checking on our ASR— Sorry. That's the AirSeaRail schedule program."

Analisa nodded. She remembered that Suzi had wanted to be a flight attendant until a summer job at Globetrotter turned into a full-time career.

"There's a nonstop out of LAX at eleven P.M. on Saturday the eighth." Suzi studied the airline data on her color monitor. "Arrives Miami 9 July at seven-thirty A.M. their time. I can put you on an SSA flight to Santa Catalina at nine-thirty. That'll get you to—"

The litany of airline schedules triggered flashbacks of Analisa's last flight with her parents. Suddenly, her skin felt clammy. The floor disappeared beneath her feet. "I— I can't," she managed as the office revolved in a slow, dizzy spin. She gripped the arms of the chair as if it was falling from the sky. "Forgive me."

"You okay?" Without waiting for a reply, Suzi hurried to the water cooler a few feet from her desk.

Analisa took the paper cup and sipped its contents. "Thanks. I thought I'd made more progress than I have."

"You want to forget the whole thing?"

"No." Analisa stiffened her rubbery limbs and sat upright again. "I have to get to Santo Sangre. I'll just take my time getting there."

"It'll cost more."

"It doesn't matter." Her parents' considerable estate of
life insurance and retirement plans had secured Analisa's
financial future.

❦ ❦ ❦

A warm breeze surfed ashore from the Pacific Ocean, taking the edge off what had been a blistering Fourth. Few
beachgoers remained from the crowd that had sought relief
at Seal Beach earlier in the day.

Analisa broke her sprint and threw her head back to
gulp a breath of air. Prismed drops of perspiration fell from
her chin into the soft, clean granules beneath her feet. The
warm sand welcomed her home like a long-missed friend.

Exulting in being fit enough to jog again on the open
beach, she toweled her face with the lower portion of the
faded tank top she wore over a blue sports bra. It felt great
to sweat when and because she wanted to. For too many
hours over the past four months she had perspired on
schedule for a sadistic physical therapist who pushed her
to do "five more leg curls!" or spend "just ten more minutes" on the treadmill.

Analisa rolled down her white elastic knee brace and
inspected the area around the long scar on the inside of her
right kneecap. "No pain," she announced when Dave
caught up with her.

He fell to his knees gasping for air. Unable to speak, he
grinned broadly and nodded up and down several times.

Analisa plopped down beside him, near enough to feel
the warmth of his perspiring body. "Is that all you can
say?"

"Right...now...yes."

"You're out of shape."

"I shouldn't have had that second hamburger."

"I offered you vegetarian patties."

"Barbecued oatmeal? Yuck! By the way, have I told you how proud I am of you? You promised to make it home by the Fourth, and you did."

"Beat the deadline by several days," she boasted as they exchanged high fives.

Dave circled her wrists with his thumbs and index fingers and leaned his forehead against hers. "It's so great to have you back." He released her and sat on the sand, stretching his legs out in front of himself. Silent minutes passed before Analisa emitted a long, deep sigh. "What's that all about?" he said.

"Nothing...everything."

"Try starting with 'everything.' I can't believe you have 'nothing' on your mind."

Analisa sifted a handful of gritty sand through her fingers, opened her palm and studied the grains that clung to her skin. She had conceived a plan through many restless nights in the hospital and nurtured it during countless rehab sessions. She had even discussed it with Dr. Gordon. Only since her return to Anaheim, to the ghostly rooms of her empty home, had it blossomed into a full-grown starting point for the next portion of her life. Now, on her dresser lay the travel tickets purchased at Globetrotter. She wanted to—needed to—share the plan with Dave.

"I really miss Mom and Dad." She gazed out at the ever-changing, ever-constant sea. The waves of the rising tide attacked the shore, capturing with each new thrust a few more inches of beachhead.

"Analisa, hello! It's me, Dave." He massaged the twisted linear muscle that ran up the length of her neck and into the base of her skull. "You can tell me anything."

"I need a family." Encouraged by having finally spoken the words aloud, she turned to Dave and repeated them in a stronger, more resolute voice. "I was just moving out into the big wide world. Master's degree. My own place.

About to start my first real job in the world—I don't count
summers at Disneyland. Now, I feel like...an orphan.
God! I am an orphan." She wiped her face with a towel.
Only with enormous effort did she hold back a sob. "I'm
grown up and ready to take on any challenge. Yet, there's
this four-year-old inside me who feels like she's right back
where she started twenty years ago."

Dave's eyes moistened. He drew Analisa's head to his
chest and tenderly tucked it under his chin. "Let it out."
His voice and touch were gentle, caring.

"I feel so alone."

"You have lots of family. Aren't there Marconis and
Ellises all over the place?" He laid his hands alongside her
cheeks and tilted her head to look into her eyes. "And you
have me. I'm your family."

Analisa returned his gaze and held it, searching his soul
for a meaning beyond his words. In that place of truth she
found no promise of permanent partnership, no shift of
commitment from Church to her. Without clearer words
than these, she had to believe he meant only what he said,
that they shared a unique and mutually satisfying friendship.

"You're partially right about my relatives. But they
have their own problems. I can't just plug myself into their
lives like a lamp in a wall socket." Analisa tried to look
away, but Dave only smiled and held her face more firmly
so she had to engage him.

"Go on."

"My presence reminds them of their own loss, their suf-
fering. All our conversations are about me. 'How are you
feeling, dear?' 'How's your rehab going?' 'It's so wonderful to see you.' They never talk about Mom and Dad. It's
all so...surreal, but well-meaning."

"Look, Analisa. Everyone who loved your parents was
injured when your plane went down. Be patient with us.
You've been occupied with the struggle to put your body

and your life back together. We're undergoing rehab too, but there's no physical survival work to occupy our time. All we have is our hurt. We need time to heal just like you do."

They walked along the water's edge, letting the cool sudsy foam tease their feet. "You have your parish community," Dave offered. "They're family, too."

"I don't mean to be disrespectful or ungrateful, but it's quite a stretch to call the folks I worship with my family." When he started to interrupt, she placed a silencing finger on his lips.

The two friends stopped when they reached the sea wall that separates Seal Beach from the outlet of the San Gabriel River.

"Shall we turn around or are you into rock climbing tonight?" he said.

"Let's rest a minute."

The lower tip of the sun, having just touched the horizon, provided the stunning vision of fire and water enacting their nightly duel for supremacy—a battle the ocean always won. In awe of the scene played out by forces infinitely more potent and enduring than herself, Analisa let her mind drift out like a ship in search of sunken treasures from the past.

John and Claire Marconi had kept alive her sense of rootedness in her native Santo Sangrían culture. In the process of giving her all the opportunities American citizenship made available, they had never tried to "gringoize" her, as they called it. Nor had they ever pretended her skin was as white as theirs. They helped her understand and cherish her identity as a Latina of Hispanic-Indian origin. She knew who she was, where she had come from, and how much fate had blessed her.

Even as a small child, she had taken her parents at their word when they said she'd be theirs "por siempre y por siempre." Unfortunately, "forever" was barely more than twenty years.

"How much more time can you give me?" Analisa asked, rousing Dave from his own meditation.

"Mi tiempo es su tiempo," he said with a typically impish grin. "There's no place I'd rather be than—" The rest of his thought remained just that, leaving her to guess at the unspoken conclusion to his sentence.

The ocean faded to black as sun and moon changed watch over the beach. The onset of evening lowered the temperature considerably, sending Dave and Analisa to the parking lot to retrieve their sweats. They decided to stay in the car which had preserved the warmth of the day like a pleasant memory.

Of Dave's three suggested family surrogates, Analisa had dismissed two—relatives and parish. It was time to deal with the third. "And you," she began, looking into his dark, clear eyes—almost perfect mirrors of her own. Doing so stirred something physical inside her that she struggled to keep at bay. "How can you be my family?" It was more a statement than a question, a jumbled mixture of love, sadness, and fading hope. "You don't get one of your own. Remember?"

"I've always felt we were about as close as two people can be."

"Oh, Dave, I'm so damn needy right now. It embarrasses me. Yesterday, when I went to Mass at St. Boniface, I looked around at all the families. I had the strongest urge to walk up to them and say, 'I'm an orphan. Won't you please adopt me? I need a mommy and a daddy.'"

Tears flowed freely now but failed to choke off the flow of words she had to share with Dave. "You're the only one who never says, 'I know exactly how you feel.'"

He slipped his arm around her shoulder. "I want to understand. Help me."

Encouraged by his support, Analisa addressed the realities of their relationship. "To be my family in the way I
need it right now, you'd have to spend a lot more time with
me than you're able or willing to." A film of tears blurred
her vision. "Nothing short of marriage would do the job.
And that's stupid and unrealistic."

Dave gave her shoulder a gentle squeeze. "It's crossed
my mind, you know."

"Okay, maybe it's not stupid. I'll settle for unrealistic.
And, no, I wasn't aware it had crossed your mind. What
does that mean?"

"When I let myself fantasize about doing something different with my life, you're always there. You're part of that
other me. That's what it means."

They had strayed into uncharted territory, following the
path of a friendship that had grown stronger every year.
Analisa explored Dave's facial expression, his body language, for evidence of a missing link that would take them
beyond the realm of fantasy.

"You're not a pimply fourteen-year-old any more," he
said. "You're a different person than you were when I
arrived at St. Boniface as a greenhorn, know-it-all newly
ordained."

"I was never pimply," she mumbled through a wet tissue fished from her fanny pack.

"Okay. I take back the 'pimply' part. You've grown up.
Boy, have you grown up!"

"We both have."

Dave's face wore a serious, almost frightened expression. "We've never talked about being a . . . 'couple'
before."

"Pandora's box," she whispered.

"Is there someone else?" The question revealed a man
groping uncertainly in the darkness.

"Nothing serious."

It was true. She had dated a fellow St. Mary's student during her junior and senior years. It seemed for a while that it might go somewhere. The relationship ended after an Easter break visit to his family in Oregon. Analisa found herself confronted by German-American parents with strong ties to their European heritage and even stronger feelings about their son dating an Hispanic-Indian adoptee. By graduation day, the relationship had careened off a cliff and crashed with an explosion of unkind words and hurt feelings.

Talking to Dave like this had introduced a major distraction into the plan she was about to lay before him. The only thing that kept her on track was her sense of its absolute rightness. She had to play out her decision, see what came of it, and take her chances with the future. Gathering resolve and courage, she formulated her next thought. "There's something I have to do before I can think of marrying anyone."

"What's that?" Dave's face scrunched up revealing all the scattered pieces of the unsolved male-female puzzle.

"I've got to find my birth mother." Oh, how good it felt to release those words from their solitary prison!

Dave wasn't a frowny kind of guy, but the horizontal furrows that appeared on his forehead seemed cast in plaster. "You're serious?"

"Totally." An unaccustomed sense of calm bolstered her resolve. "The idea came to me during those God-awful weeks of rehab."

"You always said it wasn't important."

"I started counting the abandonments in my life, beginning with the day Martina carted me off to Señora Dorada. One. Then, that good lady sent me off to the sisters at the orphanage. Two. Just as I was getting used to the nuns, Mom and Dad arrived and snatched me away across an ocean and a continent to a place where no one spoke my language, sang my songs, or ate my kind of food. Three. I remember thinking, 'These people smell like a flower stall in the marketplace.' They promised I'd never be abandoned again. Four. They were wrong."

Dave leaned closer and took her hand. "No one can promise forever."

"Not even you." A leaden sadness settled on her spirit. "I'm sorry. You didn't deserve that."

"People can only make promises, take vows. 'Forever' is in God's hands."

She pulled the seat belt across her chest and latched it with a loud snap. "Please, take me home."

Dave straightened in his seat, started the car, and exited the parking lot. They spoke little during the twenty-minute drive to Anaheim. He pulled into the driveway of Analisa's unlit single-story Whilhelmina Street home in one of those stately, but unpretentious, neighborhoods of old Anaheim, just north of St. Boniface. Although close to Disneyland, it was far enough away that the nightly fireworks display brightened the sky only a little.

He turned off the engine. "I've always liked this house."

"Mom and Dad bought it with the intention of filling it with kids. I always wondered why they adopted only one child. All my dad ever told me was, 'You're everything we ever wanted.'"

"Isn't that what every little girl wants to hear?"

"It worked for me. But now I think if I had brothers and sisters, I'd feel different. Maybe I'd feel more connected to—" She touched Dave's arm. "—everything. I'd be fixing up my apartment and thinking of ways to impress my new bosses at Markham International. Instead, I'm planning a blind search for the birth mother I never had any interest in before."

"When are you going?"

"Sunday."

"So soon?" he said, stung by the suddenness and finality of her announcement.

"I was afraid you'd talk me out of it. My resolve might not stand up to commonsense arguments."

He clutched the steering wheel. "How will you find her?"

"I don't know yet."

"What if she's passed away?"

"At least, I'll know. I'll come home." With a dull spiritual ache threatening to erode her determination, she added, "I have nowhere else to go."

"If she's alive, why not bring her back with you."

"Maybe." She'd had the same conversation with herself repeatedly during the past few weeks. "All my options are open. It's very freeing."

Just as he leaned across the seat to kiss her on the cheek, she turned her face toward him. Their lips met in a soft surprise. There was a taste of sea salt on his mouth, a remnant of their evening at the beach.

Every cell in Analisa's body cried out for him. Part of her wanted to drag him to her upstairs bedroom for the night. The fading part of her that still maintained some measure of control prevented her from doing something that foolish. But Dave wasn't just anyone. He was her best friend, the only man in her world she truly loved.

Rather than withdraw from his kiss, she rested the side of her head against the back of the seat and stroked his cheek, scratchy from sand particles and a day's growth of beard. She loved the press of his lips against hers, his masculine outdoor scent, the feeling of being suspended in time and space. When Dave slipped his tongue inside her mouth, she welcomed him.

Then, a new sensation radiated through her body in the darkness. His hand had found its way inside her sweatshirt, under her bra, and to her breast. The gentle, circular

motion that followed foretold wonderful possibilities. She
wanted him, but the thought he might say yes terrified her.

If only I knew his consent would be full...and forever.
He had given her no reason to think so.

Reality took hold as the first alarms sounded in her
head. "We can't," she whispered. It wasn't a rebuke, and
she had delayed calling this moment of ecstasy to an end
as long as she dared.

"I know." His hand drifted back to the steering wheel,
and he stared out the driver-side window. "I know."

Analisa adjusted her bra and reconstructed the customary wall of propriety that normally governed their relationship. "I don't want to shut you out. I'm afraid to invite
voices that might keep me from going ahead."

"Promise you'll call me if you need someone with you.
I'll be on the next plane out of here."

"Thanks, but what could possibly happen?"

"I don't know. Just promise."

His generosity touched her. "Okay. I promise."

🌺 🌺 🌺

On Analisa's bedroom walls hung her St. Mary's team photos and a Sacramento Monarchs poster. A leather basketball sat idle atop a bookshelf. In the wastebasket, a silent
electronic crowd waited to cheer the next wad of paper she
tossed through the miniature hoop.

She rolled restlessly in bed for several hours in an
unsuccessful effort to end what had been a special but disturbing evening. The imprint of Dave's lips still caressed
hers. She remembered the feel of his tongue probing
inside her mouth. Her breast tingled at the memory of his
hand playing idly about her nipple. Sharing with Dave her
decision to search for her birth mother had triggered their
crossing this new threshold of intimacy.

He's concerned about my safety... He's feeling protec-
tive... The kiss was an accident. She had never been so
stirred physically and emotionally. She told herself they
had lingered in the kiss out of surprise and the excitement
of unexpected discovery. Breaking it off when I did was
the right thing.

�â¼ 🌼 🌼

Dave was already awake when his alarm went off at six-
thirty. He showered and shaved, and still had some time
to spend in meditation before eight o'clock Mass. The
pummeling spray of water had failed to relieve the burden
he carried for his indiscretion with Analisa.

In church, he dropped heavily onto the padded kneeler
of a back-corner pew and closed his eyes. The aroma of
beeswax and the faint remains of incense left over from
yesterday's funeral Mass invited his senses into reluctant
tranquillity. The smell of flickering votive candles triggered recall of a dream he'd had during the early morning
hours. He believed dreams were messengers, helping him
make sense of his sometimes muddled life.

I was at a youth detention camp, Dave recalled, one
like Karle Center in the East Anaheim hills. His weekly visits to the Orange County boys' juvenile facility were difficult but always a highlight of his week. Except this camp
was near the beach. It was night, the ocean air chilly.

Dave leaned into the wooden pew and let his body disappear from awareness as his soul replayed without static
the messages of the night.

🌼 🌼 🌼

Kids are sitting on the damp sand around a driftwood fire.
I'm with them. A counselor stands up and says, "Okay,
everybody. Listen up. We're going to do some sharing.

The only rule is that the person who's sharing about his life has to wear this mask while talking." He holds up a full-faced, glossy ceramic mask. Despite its blood-red color, the mask's expression is neutral. "Let's keep quiet and listen with respect. You first, Father." And, he hands me the mask.

My stomach is tight. I put the mask in front of my face, clueless about what to share. I tell myself, be careful. I want to say something genuine, but I also want my private thoughts kept...private.

"Let's see. There's nothing particular I want to share, so this'll be pretty quick." A ripple of laughter around the circle. Then, something peculiar happens. I feel the mask molding itself to my face. I can't see it but I know its image and expression have become my own. It's as if the mask has grown arms and is reaching inside me to pull out all the feelings I'm determined to conceal.

"I'm filled with anguish from the tips of my toes to the top of my head," I say. I try to shut my mouth to keep from revealing more, but the river of words is breaking through the levees of my soul. "I'd cry an ocean of tears if I ever let the first one fall."

Now, I'm really embarrassed. How can I let these kids know the burdens I carry? I'm here to help them with their problems, not add mine to the load they already bear.

Everyone's staring at me...at the red mask. It must be broadcasting my pain.

A kid on the opposite side of the circle gets up and comes forward. He sits in front of me and takes my hands in his own. Looking out toward the water, where the waves roll in green phosphorescent loops onto the beach, he says, "That's a big ocean out there, Padre. Big enough to hold all your tears if you let 'em go."

Over the sound of the waves and whipping breeze, I hear someone sobbing uncontrollably. My heart goes out to him. It sounds like his body's going to explode. I look around the circle. I want to find the boy who is hurting and go to him. Then, I realize. The sounds are from my own body.

"What's the source of your sadness, Father?" one of counselors asks.

"Loneliness. It's killing me." Then, tears...trickling, at first, down the cheeks of the mask. They become a steady flow carving a canyon in the sand on their way to join the oncoming waves.

"See, Padre?" It's the boy who's holding my hands. "The ocean's wide enough and deep enough to hold your tears. You don't have to keep 'em inside any more."

❧ ❧ ❧

It was time for Mass.

Dave wiped his eyes with his handkerchief. The dream's implications disturbed him.

"Loneliness is part of life," he reminded himself. Examples of married parishioners who had shared with him their feelings of isolation stepped forward to support his philosophy. He always had an encouraging word, a suggestion to find relief by joining with others in some parish- or community-related activities. "In the meantime," he typically counseled, "see if you can find God in your loneliness."

The advice made an unpalatable breakfast on this morning. Dave looked down the nave of the Romanesque church and raised his eyes to the bigger-than-life-size cru- cifix hanging on the sanctuary wall facing him.

"What are you saying about my future, Lord?"
Silence.

The Spirit who had been so active during the hours of sleep seemed now to sleep herself, dreaming God's own dreams.

❦ ❦ ❦

The ringing of the cordless phone beside her bed awakened Analisa. It was 10:08 A.M. Being a morning person, energetic and creative in the day's early hours, she almost never slept this late.

With her body nested dreamily beneath the covers, her eyes rebelled against the day. Reluctant, she fumbled with the handset and managed to disengage it from its cradle.

"Analisa? It's Dave." Concern shadowed his voice. "Did I wake you?"

Her mouth felt stuffed with cotton balls. "Guess I slept later than usual."

"Sorry."

"It's okay." She rubbed her eyes open.

"I had to know how you are." He paused. "I mean, after last night."

"I'm fine." The memory of how they'd bumped mouths—by accident—and of his tongue pressuring hers brought a mellow pleasure that radiated throughout her body. "Really."

"I was worried. I mean— You know. I thought you might be...upset."

"I'm a big girl now. Like you said, not a pimply sophomore any more."

"You'd have a right to be upset." Dave paused. "I— I went too far."

"I'm angry, but not at you, Dave. I'm angry at the Church for not letting you live a normal life."

Silence on the other end of the line.

Analisa took a deep breath, wondering at the reversal of roles that had put her in the counselor's chair. It was Dave whose foundation had slipped. "Look, I owe so much to you. Maybe even my life. I still need you a lot. Please, don't go all little boy on me now."

"I won't," he vowed. "Remember. Call me if you need anything while you're there."

"Okay, but you probably won't hear from me for a while."

"I don't like the sound of that."

"Dave, don't read anything ominous into it. All I'm saying is I've got to do this. And I have to do it alone."

Chapter 10

Taking her time getting to Santo Sangre meant a full week of travel instead of twelve hours' flying time, including the Miami layover. Analisa boarded Amtrak's Sunset Limited at L. A.'s Union Station the following Sunday morning.

Before the crash, she had preferred company and conversation to solitude. From the time the train pulled out to the time she reached her South Florida destination, she spent her days and nights reading and thinking...mostly thinking. An endless string of possible scenarios occupied her thoughts.

What if she didn't find her birth mother?

What if she did?

What if she hated Santo Sangre? She didn't remember anything about it. She had never lived in an emerging country, except as a preschooler...and remembered little of what it was like.

What if she fell in love with the place?

What if I'm not strong enough yet to go traipsing around the countryside by myself? What if I come down with some horrible disease? She imagined herself lying sick and alone in a strange place with no one to look after her.

What if I die? She hadn't made a will yet. Thank God my parents had them. Who would be her beneficiary? Her parish? St. Mary's College? Dave?

And so it went from early morning when she awakened until close to midnight, when the repetitive clicking of the rails beneath her finally eased her into shallow sleep.

She wished she had planned for all the contingencies that might arise from the life-quest on which she had embarked. She recalled Dave's insistence that she call him if anything went wrong while she was away. As the miles between herself and Southern California increased, her bravado seemed more and more naive.

What could possibly happen?

Anything!

Analisa sighed as the red-white-and-blue-striped train started across the four-mile bridge spanning the Mississippi. She put her face to the window to watch the river disappear from view behind her. Crossing this great geological landmark felt like a significant event. For a Californian, it was something similar to sailors crossing the equator for the first time. Watching Ol' Man River distracted her from a question that had fought its way to the surface of her consciousness.

"What about Dave?"

She already missed him. More than she ever believed possible. She had chosen to exclude him from this part of her life. Doing so confirmed her independence, a sign that her parents' deaths constituted only a temporary derailment—Poor choice of words, girl.—on her forward journey.

"Am I in love with him?" She said it aloud, letting the steel-against-steel sound of wheels on rails absorb her words.

There it was, naked, demanding attention, insisting on an answer stripped of euphemisms and double meanings. The jigsaw pieces of her life scattered across her mind like a giant puzzle waiting for her to link them together.

Her feelings about Dave both excited and frightened her. "There's no future in it. He'll never leave the priesthood. I'd never ask him to."

With very little imagination, she painted a picture of her life loving Dave-the-priest. I'd get the leftovers, a few minutes here and there stolen from his daily ministry. She imagined them sneaking off to a secret rendezvous, but not so often that they'd arouse the suspicion of his priest friends.

I refuse to live like that. I have to think beyond Dave.

She considered selling the Anaheim house. Before the crash, she had already made the break. She enjoyed living in the San Francisco Bay Area, where she attended college. An exciting new job still awaited her. Maybe I'll buy one of those great old Berkeley homes or something newer in Contra Costa County.

There had to be a better role for her than that of a woman tragically in love with the perfect but unattainable man. If she wanted a family, she needed to be patient and trust that someone existed in this world in whose heart she would occupy the highest place.

In the end, she resolved to take her love for Dave, hold it up to the light, give thanks, and cherish it. Then she'd tuck it away in a special corner of her heart and go on with her life.

❀ ❀ ❀

The Caribbean Star wasn't a cruise ship, but it was big and it floated. Best of all, it was taking Analisa to Santo Sangre.

After spending three days and nights crossing the southern tier of states "from sea to shining sea" she had managed to book passage on a freighter carrying something or other to her native country. To boost profits and provide broader companionship for the captain and officers, the freight carrier accommodated a limited number of passengers, including a chaplain.

The voyage into the Southern Caribbean contained its own set of blessings, not the least of which was the sea itself. Being the youngest of the twenty or so passengers, there was little need to engage in long conversations. The older folks had different interests and left her pretty much to herself.

The ship's gentle rhythm combined with sun and sea to exercise restorative powers. She hadn't really prayed since her accident, having lost touch with that once-comforting intimacy of inner dialog. Tentatively at first, she repaired the downed lines of communication, conversing with God in a natural, informal way. In the process, she found some solace for her grief and loneliness.

Analisa spent hours on the passengers' promenade, leaning against the varnished wooden rail that shone like a gold bar when the sun hit it. She gazed at the sea, alternately looking northwest toward her past and southeast toward her future. She knew what lay behind in California, Dave and an impossible love. She had no idea what lay ahead.

The unknown drew her forward like a magnet. A small part of her begged her to dive overboard and swim back to Florida.

Chapter II

Arturo Cristobal awakened in the pre-dawn hours, his mind still fuzzy, his vision unfocused. Unsure of whose bed he shared, he felt for the bare back of the woman lying next to him. Turning her head slightly, he studied her profile in the semi-darkness. Gabriela Amaro, a patron of Santo Sangre's Opera Santa Catalina.

Last night he had sung the title role of Rigoletto, the hunchbacked court jester who inadvertently murdered his own beloved daughter. The performance left him feeling more melancholy than usual. On nights like this, he hated going straight from the Bellas Artes opera house to his empty beachfront mansion.

After begging off Gabriela's prior invitations, he accepted her offer of midnight dessert and a cool drink. Since she was more than ten years older than his own thirty, he saw no harm in detouring for a while before going home.

As he lay next to her naked body in the darkness, he was still unsure how they had transitioned from sitting under the umbrella-canopied table on her ninth-floor balcony to a hungry tumble in her spacious and too readily available bed.

No matter.

Sex with Gabriela had been just that. Temporary comfort in a lovely widow's arms. Physical release. And now, as she slept with a look of peaceful contentment on her face, he regretted having started something he had no desire to continue.

Slipping out of bed, his leg touched something damp. A spent condom. He felt cowardly, leaving her in the middle of the night, not even waking her to say goodbye. He dressed and tiptoed to her writing table. Finding a pen and note pad, he scribbled. "Thank you for..." For what? The *paté* and French bread? The drink? For offering herself to him? For not asking him to leave immediately afterward?

Slowly, quietly, he tore the sheet from the pad, crumpled it up and stuck it in his pocket. He wrote a simple "Thank you" and signed it, knowing he had to deal with Gabriela's feelings and expectations sooner than he wanted to, in the all-revealing light of day.

As he started his car, he composed his little speech. "I am grateful for your...kindness and hospitality...but I think it best if we did not see each other again."

❧ ❧ ❧

On her last night at sea, Analisa wondered how she would feel standing on the soil of her birth after twenty years—a lifetime. She recalled video clips of the Pope descending the stairway from his private jet, stepping onto a crimson carpet, kissing the ground in symbolic homage to the hospitable land. Or, she thought with a shudder, was he just thankful his plane hadn't gone down?

By the time the Santo Sangrían shoreline came into view as a hazy, purplish bump on the shifting morning horizon, she felt strong enough to accept whatever came of her mission, be it success or failure.

No one rolled out a red carpet when she descended the Caribbean Star's gangplank. No band played. No expectant crowd of local family and friends greeted her. Not a soul cared that a Santo Sangrían-American had arrived to search for human links to connect her past and future.

The sites and sounds of the ancient port surrounded Analisa as she made her way through the passenger terminal and out to the street. The shoulder bag she clung to like a life preserver contained her adoption papers, passport and traveler's checks. Minutes later, a taxi delivered her to the stately Hotel Gran Palacio.

The talkative bellhop who escorted her to her ocean view room dropped her suitcases near the closet door and stood at attention. Analisa pressed a generous tip into his palm.

"Gracias," he said, pretending not to notice the amount. He left the room with a satisfied grin and an offer to come to her assistance "any time at all."

Analisa opened the sliding door that led to the balcony. *What the hell am I doing here? I don't know anyone. My only friend's the friggin' bellhop!*

It had all seemed so right when she was in the theoretical, decision-making process. Formulating her plan during the final weeks of spring had energized her, spurred her rehabilitation, and motivated her to heal more quickly.

It had never seemed important before to make contact with Martina Aguilada or anyone else to whom Analisa might be related. It was something she planned to do at some point in her life, sort of the foreign adoptee's *ad limina* visit, but she had never attached any urgency to it. Now, it occupied her entire agenda.

If her birth mother was alive and had other children, she might feel...I don't know what to expect. I just have to do it. When it happens, I'll feel what I feel.

Suddenly, her emotions did an about-face. She longed to book passage on the next ship out of Santa Catalina and not stop until she reached the safe haven of her home on Whilhelmina.

I'm not going back! Not until I've seen this thing through.

She slipped into a pair of jeans and a light crescent-necked pullover. Her resolution spawned even deeper loneliness as she left her room to have dinner alone and explore the nearby Plaza de La Libertad, alone.

To distract herself from her empty feeling, she turned her thoughts to tomorrow's appointment with Don Ricardo Valenzuela, her parents' adoption attorney.

"Here I come, Martina," she said aloud. "Let's hope we're both ready for this."

Chapter 12

Analisa handed the taxi driver a card on which she had written the address, Avenida San Miguel, Paralela al Mar, No. 1953.

"Please hurry. I'm late for an appointment," she instructed in her best Spanish. By adding a sense of urgency, she hoped to guarantee an on-time arrival for her ten o'clock meeting with Attorney Don Ricardo Valenzuela.

The interior of the taxi was in better shape than its faded orange exterior. The bumpers and fenders showed the effects of many battles for the cab's share of the streets and parking spaces of the nation's capital. As soon as the old vehicle moved away from the curb in front of the Gran Palacio, fumes rose through the floorboards. Analisa rolled down both rear windows to let whatever air was circulating on this still, humid morning wash through the back seat.

The weather called for shorts and tank top, inappropriate attire for a formal visit to a law office and later to the American Embassy. Instead, she wore a conservative navy-blue skirt, a white shirt-blouse and complementary blue vest with white pinstripes. In her left hand, she clutched a slim cordovan leather briefcase that held her original adoption papers, the most important of which was the final adoption decree issued over twenty years ago by the Court of Minor Children.

The rotund driver said nothing, but kept his attention on the rear-view mirror more than on the road. Clearly, he wasn't watching for tailgaters. Whenever he caught her eye, his toothless smile invited conversation.

Analisa took the bait. "I was born here."

He grinned. "You know, Señorita, I thought there is somethin' especial 'bout you."

To her surprise, Analisa understood much of her driver's guttural street dialect. "I left when I was a little girl." Normally, she didn't tell strangers about her adoption. In her own mind, she was the child of John and Claire Marconi. Only since their deaths had the distinction between birth child and adoptee become significant. "It's my first time back."

"¿Verdad? No kidding?" the driver said. "Then, you must see everything, no?"

"No. Well, yes, maybe." In all the preparations for her return to Santo Sangre, she never considered taking time to vacation. Sightseeing held a low priority. If she failed in her mission to find her birth mother, she might see what the island had to offer in the way of tourist attractions before returning to California and the life she had put on hold.

"You jus' tell the main guy at the desk at Gran Palacio, you want Ernesto show you 'roun'. He know me real good."

"Thank you. I will."

At five after ten, Ernesto delivered Analisa to the closest facsimile Santa Catalina had to a high-rise office building. It was here, with Don Ricardo that she'd begin retracing the steps that led to her adoption. Depending on how cooperative the lawyer was, her search could be easy or difficult.

Don Ricardo greeted Analisa at the door to his private tenth-floor office. "Please come in, Señorita Marconi."

"Thank you." Analisa recognized him immediately from the photo she had extracted from her adoption album. "I'm grateful to you for taking the time to see me." The intervening years had grayed the hair that was already thinning when the photo was taken. He had put on some weight and his shoulders seemed more stooped. The intelligent eyes were the same, as was the overall aspect of sincerity her parents had always remarked about.

The "suite" Don Ricardo occupied was sparsely fur-
nished but contained the essential electronic equipment
for conducting an international business—a tired-looking
386 computer, a fax machine, and a telephone. A spec-
tacular view of the harbor and the turquoise sea distracted
visitors who might be critical of the dingy bare-bones interior.

"Let me look at you." Don Ricardo stepped back to
view her from beyond arm's length. "What a lovely young
woman you have become! Please sit down. I will never
forget the day the Sisters brought you to my office. You
looked like a lost little girl that day, let me tell you. I said
to Sister Anastasia— You know she passed away last year?"

Analisa shook her head.

"Lord have mercy on her, which I'm sure He will. If
anyone deserved mercy, that saintly woman did. I told her,
'This little one needs a mommy and a daddy to thrive.'"

"That's exactly what you said in the postcard you sent
to Mom and Dad," Analisa said, recalling the words she
had memorized as a little girl. "It's still in my album."

"You still have it?" A proud smile brightened his serious demeanor.

"I've read it many times. It's one of my prized possessions."

"Well, I went straight to my file, and the next family on
my list was the Marconis. You sat in that chair—at least,
one very much like it—when I telephoned them with the
news that I had the perfect child for them. I can see I was
not mistaken. I rarely am in these matters, you know."

Analisa had memorized her referral story. As a child,
she had thrilled to its repeated telling. It was special—and
sad—hearing it now from the lips of the only living partic-
ipant.

"Would you like to hear my parents' side of that story?"

"By all means."

"They waited months for that call. They thought something had gone wrong. They told me they were sure they'd be the first couple in the history of their agency not to get a child."

Don Ricardo shook his head. "Nonsense. They were ideal candidates."

"That's what their social worker said. When the phone finally rang and it was you, they were ecstatic. Dad said it took a lot to make him cry, but becoming a father for the first time did it royally." Analisa didn't tell him what her parents shared with her during her senior year in high school—the conclusion of her, and their—referral story. They celebrated Don Ricardo's good news with the most passionate lovemaking of their marriage. As her mom put it, "We needed to feel we'd given you the gift of life that day."

Analisa clung to the memory, but the urgency of her mission forced her to return to the business at hand. She ached for her parents more now than she had at any time since their deaths. *You're here with me, Mom and Dad. I feel you in this room. How I'd love to see and touch you.*

Don Ricardo took a seat behind his desk in front of a bank of windows. "My 'children' rarely come back to visit me. Occasionally, I hear that one or another has been to Santo Sangre, but they do not come to see me. I served my purpose, I suppose. As far as they are concerned, the link is broken." He leaned forward with his forearms on the scratched wooden desk, fingers loosely twined. "I suspect your coming to me is more than just old times revisited."

"My parents are dead."

"Poor child!" His jaw became slack. Taking a handkerchief from his back pocket, he dabbed it to his eyes.

"We were in a plane crash."

Don Ricardo rose to his feet. "'We?' *¡Dios mío!* You were with them?"

"The only survivor." Analisa wasn't fishing for sympathy. She'd had enough of that to last the rest of her life.
"Don Ricardo, I need your help."

His eyebrows arched. "Of course, but what?"

"I've come to find my birth mother. You're the only
connection I have to her."

He returned to his seat with a weary sigh. "I see."
Analisa doubted that he did, at least not clearly.

"I'm an only child. I lost all the family I had when our
plane went down. Before getting on with my life, I want to
reconnect with my original family...or try to." She took a
deep breath. "Finding my birth mother is the starting
point."

The attorney shifted in his chair, then sat back, thinking.
The gulf between them had deepened. Analisa feared he
was formulating a way to dissuade her.

Don Ricardo reached across the desk and took her
hands in his. "May I ask a very personal question?"

"Of course."

His tone became fatherly. "Who is it you are really
searching for?"

The question caught Analisa off guard. Her stomach
cramped and it became difficult to breathe. The answer,
previously hidden from her conscious self, leapt unexpectedly to her tongue. "I have to find the little girl who once
sat in that chair over there," she whispered. Managing a
weak smile, she added, "Or 'one much like it.'"

There it was. The bottom line. Her presence in Santo
Sangre wasn't about Martina Aguilada, although finding
her was the key. To be whole again, Analisa needed to
rediscover Isabella. At least, to reconstruct her sense of
who she was inside, at a level deeper than her American
language, upbringing, and education.

A sob rose from her abdomen. It rocked her frame on
the way to her throat. Tears tumbled into the blue depths
of her skirt. The sudden explosion of emotion embarrassed

and terrified her. With great effort, she steadied her breathing. "I'm sorry. Forgive me."

"Nothing to forgive."

Gradually, Analisa corralled her scattered feelings. As she held Don Ricardo's troubled gaze, panic blurred her thought processes. She felt him slipping away from her. The attorney walked slowly to the window and studied the street traffic below. A vertical line of perspiration outlined his spine through his white business shirt.

"I am philosophically opposed to adopted children coming back to find their birth mothers," he began. Analisa had the feeling she was about to hear a well-rehearsed lecture. Since she needed his cooperation, she decided not to interrupt. "The experience can be devastating...on both sides. We take children out of poverty, perhaps even save some lives by sending them to families in Europe or the States. Those children grow up, as you have, so...differently. You've seen and done things young people your age in Santo Sangre only dream of. Are you the same little girl a desperate mother relinquished and good Sister Anastasia brought to my office? No. You are someone completely different. Is that not part of your current dilemma?"

Analisa nodded. "I suppose."

Don Ricardo paced wall to wall in the narrow space behind his desk. "Martina Aguilada did not turn you over to Señora Dorada because she did not have money to send you to the university to study medicine or law." He spoke like a Sociology professor lecturing his students on the realities of life in a developing country. "She had exhausted the meager supply of hope she had of feeding and clothing all her children. It grieved her to hear her babies crying in the night from hunger and despair."

"I understand, Don Ricardo. Believe me, I do."

His eyes burned with conviction. "There is no way to predict how she will react when she sees you. She may

feel happy and proud. God knows, I would be proud to
have a daughter like you. On the other hand, your return
might destroy whatever fantasies she has invented over the
years in order to live with her decision."

Analisa's jaw tightened. "That's the last thing I want."

"Imagine the turmoil among her other children when
you arrive. You are a poster girl, as they say, for the price
they have paid for not being adopted." He gestured at her
clothing. "The day you walk into the dirt-floor shacks they
call their homes...what it cost them to stay behind will hit
like a hammer blow." He paused to let his words sink in.
"Will they welcome you as their American sister? Or will
you stir up long-dormant bitterness and resentment? Will
they love you? Or hate you all the more?"

Analisa's cheeks flushed. "I see what you mean." She
hadn't considered the impact of her return on any siblings
she might find. Seeing families happily reunited on television shows had fostered apparently unrealistic fantasies.
"But I have the means to help them."

"Become their social welfare system?" he snapped.

The rebuke stung. "That's not what I meant."

Don Ricardo sat down behind his desk in the ancient
swivel chair with its unpolished wooden arms and fraying,
padded seat. "The poor do not believe in Santa Claus.
Reality will not let them."

Analisa wondered. Did he hold the women who supplied babies for adoption in too high regard to see them
hurt even more? Or did his concern for the Martina
Aguiladas of Santo Sangre cease once he had arranged the
adoptions and collected his big fees from the foreign parents?

She decided to cut through his professional scruples.
With the late morning sun rapidly heating the office, she
needed an answer before moving on to her next appointment at the U.S. Embassy.

"Don Ricardo, I may not have considered all the angles you've exposed. I'm grateful to you for opening my eyes to them. You've helped me see what I'm doing through Martina's and others' eyes, not just my own." She decided to put her chips on the table, all or nothing. "I'm determined to move forward. Will you help me...?" She stifled the "or not?" thinking it best not to lob him an easy negative. Please don't let him refuse.

He shrugged and moved toward the twin filing cabinets that stood against the wall to her right. "That lost little girl Sister Anastasia brought to me so long ago has sprouted wings and flown back through my window like a homing pigeon. For a time, she found a secure nest far away. Now she is lost again, an orphan once more." Don Ricardo's rigid face softened. The tension drained from the muscles around his mouth, and a smile cracked his solemn face. "Since your case is so unusual, I will make an exception."

Analisa circled the desk and threw her arms around the veteran attorney's neck. "Thank you, Don Ricardo." She kissed him solidly on both cheeks. "Thank you!"

He struggled to recover his composure. "I—I am still not sure this is the best thing for Martina and her family."

"I promise to be sensitive and respectful."

Don Ricardo nodded as she spoke. "I believe you will keep that promise. What do you need me to do?"

The return of hope animated Analisa. Her words poured out in a stream of enthusiasm. "Tell me what you know about Martina. Is she alive? Where might I find her? Give me a shortcut. Help me not to waste a lot of time."

For the next half-hour, Analisa absorbed everything Don Ricardo told her about Martina Aguilada and where he thought the returning adoptee might find her birth mother.

Chapter 13

The first thing Analisa noticed about the American Embassy was its massive seven-foot concrete wall topped by unwelcoming, razor-sharp barbed wire. Ernesto caught her surprised look in the mirror and quickly shifted into tour-guide mode.

"They built the wall in the seventies. Comandante Fuego and his rebel army ran wild in the mountains. Lots of demonstrations. You know, in the streets. The Embassy became—how do they say it these days?—the flash point. Should have seen it, *Señorita!*" He seemed pleased with himself for knowing a modern term like flash point. "They don' need the walls no more, you know, but Santa Catalina's not Berlin. We don' like to tear things down. We let 'em get old. Besides, who knows? You Norteamericanos might need the wall again sometime."

When he pulled up to the main gate, Analisa handed him the fare and a tip that included some extra *cruzeros* for being friendly.

"Don' forget. My name is Ernesto. Tell the Jefe at the hotel when you want me. I take good care of you."

"Okay." But it wasn't a promise.

Analisa stifled a gasp when she saw the line of people snaking from the main gate down the street and out of sight around the corner. She'd never get inside on time for her appointment. Seeing no Americans in line, she realized she might possess the magic key to unlock the gate of this forbidding compound—a U.S. passport and an appointment with Vice Consul Eric Small. But, she chided herself, who are you that you can walk past all these good people? What makes you any different from them?

A wave of guilt swept through her. Had she become so Americanized that she no longer identified with the men and women who stood in this sweltering heat, waiting for...what? A visa to visit relatives in the States? A permit to work in America? An interview for a job cleaning toilets inside the Embassy?

Is my birth mother in this line? My brothers and sisters? Analisa searched faces in the crowd, looking for an image similar to the one she had just seen in the mirror of her compact during the taxi ride downtown. They stared at her in turn. Do they see a rich American? Or can they tell I'm really one of them, that I was born to the life they're living?

Don Ricardo's words rushed back to her. "You are a completely different person. Is that not part of your dilemma?"

There wasn't a new dress or pair of trousers in the crowd. The sun-dried and cracked faces had to be much younger than they looked. Her own skin was without blemish, the beneficiary of American hygiene and unlimited access to health and beauty care products. None of these women looked as if they had ever worn makeup or had their hair styled. An urge to cry out for Ernesto gripped her. Come back! Take me away from this place. She searched the street for a sign of his taxi, but he had long since gone off chasing his next fare, hoping to snare another high-tipping tourist. I can't run now. I've come too far.

A Santo Sangrían national in the uniform of a local security services company stood forbiddingly behind the multibarred, iron turnstile. Not more than nineteen or twenty, she guessed. With an automatic rifle slung across his chest, it clearly wasn't his job to represent the ideals embodied in the Statue of Liberty. "I have an appointment with Vice Consul Small."

"Passport."

Analisa fished in her briefcase and produced the royal blue document, aware that the people in line behind her coveted such a desired treasure. Reaching through the bars, she handed the guard her passport which he carefully examined. His eyes inspected Analisa just as thorough-

ly. Apparently, satisfied with both, he moved to a partly
sheltered booth a few feet away where he picked up a
phone and dialed.

Less than a minute later, he returned and motioned for
her to step inside the revolving iron gate. "Pase." She
heard a buzzing sound and the turnstile rotated easily at
her touch. Feels like I've entered the Holy of Holies, she
thought. The guard, whose demeanor still lacked even a
hint of human feeling, handed back her passport and
pointed to a door at the end of a concrete walkway.

There wasn't much to see inside the compound. A few
low white buildings. Some patches of lawn. Poorly
attended flower beds. She knew there had to be major
activity going on within this place, but the only person in
sight was the armed guard who had let her in.

Analisa entered the building through the metal door to
which the guard had directed her. Inside, another Santo
Sangrían national, this one a woman of upper-class breed-
ing, worked behind a glass window that had a dense, bul-
letproof look. A round mesh screen in the middle of the
barrier allowed voice communication. When the worker
didn't look up from the stack of papers she was sorting,
Analisa tapped on the window. The interruption irritated
the woman.

"Analisa Marconi. I have an appointment with Vice
Consul Small."

"Take a seat." The woman abandoned her post—and
the documents that had previously absorbed her attention.

Analisa looked around the uninviting waiting area with
its way-off-white linoleum floors. A line of molded blue
plastic chairs, bolted to the floor, lined the far wall. "As if
anyone could steal a chair and get through the gate alive,"
she muttered. A picture of the president hung on the far
wall. Probably bolted, too. By now, her jittery nerves
made it impossible for her to sit down.

A moment later the woman returned to her place on the other side of the window and resumed her sorting without a word to Analisa or even a glance in her direction. Analisa approached the window again, but as if reading her mind the employee pointed to the chairs. "Wait there."

Ten minutes passed before a door that led to the inner sanctum opened. "Ms. Marconi? Vice Consul Small. Sorry to keep you waiting." Eric Small contradicted Analisa's image of the mole-like bureaucrat, hunched over a desk, shuffling papers from morning until long after normal quitting time. He looked more the part of an Embassy guard in civilian clothing, perhaps even CIA.

Over six feet tall, muscular and tanned, he wore gray slacks, no jacket, a white button-down shirt with narrow vertical stripes of muted maroon. A boring blue tie hung from a poorly executed knot at his throat. His sandy-colored hair had a reddish-gold cast and a mind of its own. Analisa imagined him standing in front of a mirror after a shower, attempting unsuccessfully to comb it into some kind of orderly pattern.

Although he looked thirty, she guessed in light of his number-two ranking among the consular staff that he must be closer to forty.

"Please come in." The vice consul led her past the desks of Embassy employees and into a medium-sized, nondescript office. Two photos hung on the wall, one of the president—autographed—in a much nicer frame than the one she had seen in the waiting area. The other, in a matching frame, bore the nameplate of Ambassador Alexander Windsor. Neither appeared to be fastened to the wall.

Small gestured Analisa into a chair in front of his desk but surprised her by not taking his place behind the mahogany giant. Instead, he plopped into the chair opposite hers. She started to cross her legs but changed her mind when his eyes followed the motion with interest.

"What can I do for you, Ms. Marconi?"

Analisa took a deep breath. "I was born in Santo Sangre and adopted by an American couple. My parents died last winter."

"I'm sorry."

She removed her naturalization certificate from her portfolio and handed it to the vice consul, who glanced at it briefly and passed it back to her. His eyes registered genuine sympathy.

"This is my first trip back. I've come to find...well, I've come in hope of finding my birth mother and any family I might have here. My purpose in seeing you this morning is to check in with the Embassy." She smiled for the first time. "Since I'm here alone, I want you to know who I am and that I'll be roaming the countryside for a while. My father always said, when you travel to a developing country for whatever reason, it's always a good idea to check in at the Embassy. Let someone know you're around."

A cloud darkened the vice consul's previously pleasant facial expression. "I see. Excuse me a moment." He rose and left the room.

What had she said to trigger such a sudden exit? Did I really expect anyone here to care if I was in the country?

Small returned in less than a minute. He handed Analisa a sheet of Embassy stationery with the words TRAVEL ADVISORY lettered in bold print across the top. "This was circulated stateside in the spring." His voice was grave. "I wish you'd been advised of its existence."

Analisa read the first lines of text. "Female U.S. citizens born in Santo Sangre and adopted by American parents are advised not to enter the country..." She handed the paper back to him. "Why?"

"Several months ago, there was an...incident. An Italian national, a young woman, an adoptee like yourself, was found dead. She'd been missing for a long time...kidnapped. Apparently, she died in childbirth."

Small's explanation puzzled Analisa. She pointed to the advisory in his hand. "Then why this?"

"Although she wasn't murdered, the police found a note attached to her body. It contained a lot of militant anti-adoption rhetoric."

Startled and angry, Analisa objected. "You said yourself she was an Italian citizen. What does that have to do with me?"

"The local authorities consider any female adult adoptee who returns to Santo Sangre to be in danger. I had no choice but to issue the Advisory. Unfortunately, the system isn't perfect. You slipped through the cracks."

The first signs of panic buzzed in her head. Stay calm! He's doing his job. He doesn't want it on his conscience if anything happens. "I hope you're not telling me I have to leave the country."

The vice consul studied her eyes. She returned his gaze to show she wasn't afraid and wouldn't easily be deterred.

"At this point, I can't make you do that. It's my duty to advise you of what we know."

She forced a smile. "I appreciate your concern."

A female voice announced through the desk intercom, "Señor Cristobal is here, Mr. Small."

"Thanks, Nancy."

Analisa interpreted this as a signal that her audience was over.

"Arturo Cristobal's the number one baritone with Opera Santa Catalina. Something of a local hero."

"I'm not an opera buff, but I do appreciate a good voice."

"Then, I hope you get to take in a performance while you're in town. If what I read in the local papers is anything close to the truth, he's rapidly becoming an international star. I hear he's signed to do Tosca at the Met in the coming season."

When Small stood up, Analisa rose and started for the door. "Thank you for your time...and the warning."

The vice consul took a business card from a miniature oak rack on his desk. "To my knowledge, you're the first U.S. adoptee to return since Lydia Vitale's death. I'd like you to keep in touch with me during your stay." He turned the card over and wrote something before handing it to her. "My home number...in case you can't reach me here. If you move out of your hotel, I'd like to know. If you plan to travel into the interior, don't leave without telling me. And don't travel alone." A friendly grin broke the solemn mood. "Got it?"

"Yes," Analisa said. Outwardly, she played the "It's all nonsense" tune. Inside, the gravity of Eric Small's demeanor and the stark facts presented in the travel advisory had shaken her. Knowing no one else in Santo Sangre, she welcomed having a contact. That it happened to be the second in command of the consular staff, had to be a plus. *You were right, Dad.*

At the door to the waiting area, they met the man Small had described as Santo Sangre's living legend. "Arturo Cristobal," the vice consul said, "I'd like you to meet Analisa Marconi from the States."

"A pleasure to meet you, Señorita Marconi," he said in good but heavily accented English. He took Analisa's hand and covered it. His grip felt warm, the gesture sincere and welcoming.

"I'm pleased to meet you too." She had expected a graying, older man with a bushy beard and glasses. Instead, Vice Consul Small had introduced her to the most strikingly handsome man she had ever seen. Thick black hair crowned a head whose very shape and angle spoke intelligence and pride. Intense, dark eyes nested under dense, finely arched eyebrows. His aquiline nose hinted at transplanted Italian ancestry.

Cristobal's body looked athletic and comfortable in a tan blazer, white cotton pants, and forest green golf shirt. The color of his skin reminded her of a blend of the finest Indian teas.

She had met celebrities before and hadn't turned into a gushing teeny-bopper, but she felt lightheaded when her hand disappeared into his. Something eerily familiar hid behind his smile. Had she seen him on TV or in a magazine? She'd had moments of déjà vu before, but nothing like this. A powerful physical response rose from her toes to her brain, far more disturbing in its effect than any of those fleeting experiences.

"Ms. Marconi is a native Santo Sangrían. She's just arrived on our shores for the first time since leaving as a child." The vice consul engaged Analisa's eyes. "She may not be with us long, however."

Analisa's temper flared from the pit of her stomach all the way to her throat where she aborted its fury. She had no intention of leaving Santo Sangre anytime soon.

"How unfortunate," Cristobal said. "I had allowed myself a glimmer of hope that we might get to know each other. Perhaps over dinner some evening."

She had to show the vice consul he hadn't put the brakes on her life. "Yes...some evening."

"I would like to take you on a tour of my city after dark. Since time seems to be of the essence, may I skip the formalities and ask if you are available—" Cristobal consulted a small date book he had removed from the pocket of his blazer. "Tomorrow?"

She cast a defiant glance at Small. "Tomorrow's fine. I'm at the Gran Palacio."

Cristobal bowed slightly. "I will look forward to it. Eight o'clock?"

"Great."

Seeming pleased that she had said yes, he returned the calendar to his pocket. "Until tomorrow evening, then. I will call you from the lobby."

Thousands of miles from anyone she called a friend, Analisa felt strangely connected to this man from another country, another world. His invitation served two ends. It offered companionship before she immersed herself in the search for her birth mother. More important, it provided an opportunity to discover why she felt such a strong link to someone with whom she had little in common other than the land of their births.

Before leaving, Analisa shook hands with Eric Small. "I will find my family," she told him.

Chapter 14

That same evening, Chief Inspector Armando Madrigal sat alone in the crowded Cantina Tres Gallinas. He poured half of the contents of a dark local brew into his glass, careful not to let the creamy white head overflow onto the table. He disliked messes, in his personal life or in his work. Then, what in God's name are you doing in the homicide division? He had asked himself that question a hundred times. The answer always came back, Cleaning up people's messes.

It was already past eight o'clock. Madrigal shifted impatiently in his chair. Late. He had the same tolerance for tardiness that he had for messes. As snitches went, Henrique Mendoza wasn't typical. The son of a mid-level bureaucrat, he entertained his own aspirations for a career in civil service. Henrique had come forward with a far-fetched but potentially explosive story. Assigned to assist with the new inter-Ministry database project, he had become suspicious.

"Something funny is going on down in that basement," the boy told him the first time he called at the end of June.

"Well, I am happy you find your job at the Ministry amusing," Madrigal had replied, annoyed at Mendoza for interrupting his work.

Henrique outlined his assignment and the types of information that were funneling into the computer room from every major Ministry in the government. "My boss, Pedro Arroyo, is hiding something. I'm sure of it."

"Sounds like your project deals with sensitive information. It's his job to protect it." Madrigal's responsibilities did not include investigating the activities of an obscure computer programmer in the basement of some government building. What went on in the top floor offices was often more reprehensible than anything low-level employ-

ees got involved in. "Besides, this is the homicide division."

"I apologize, Inspector. I guess I have the wrong
department."

Madrigal knew little about computers but enough to
understand that access to information bestowed a kind of
power. In the hands of the wrong person or group, information created as much danger as any weapon of mass
destruction. Still, his first instinct told him to refer the matter to the Attorney General's office. Then, on a hunch, he
decided to deal with the boy himself, at least until I find out
more about his concerns and motives.

"Tell you what, Henrique. Suppose you keep an eye on
things down there and give me a call once in a while. I
don't want to hear about your squirmy feelings. I deal in
facts."

"Yes, sir."

The Chief Inspector dipped into a discretionary fund
and came up with a small stipend to ensure the young
man's cooperation in reporting anything out of the ordinary.

Earlier today, Mendoza was on the phone again. "Can
we get together? Arroyo might have some not-so-patriotic
uses for the reports he is generating from the database."

"We can talk on the phone."

"No, I must see you in person."

Madrigal set up the evening meeting.

There had been a time when the Inspector didn't care if
he worked twenty-four hours a day. He loved his job. It
gave him more pleasure than anything or anyone else in
his life. Those were the old days. Laura Sanchez changed
all that last spring. The magazine, *Prensa Libre*, had
assigned the energetic investigative journalist to interview
him. The story related to a notorious case in which a high
public official died under suspicious circumstances in one
of Santa Catalina's glitzy casino-hotels.

Laura was the most beautiful woman Madrigal had ever seen. During the interview, he told her things about his childhood, his feelings about his solitary life, secrets he had previously guarded from public view. Mid-sentence, he stopped abruptly and pushed his chair away from her knees, which almost touched his own. "I don't know why I am telling you all this personal stuff. This is off the record, isn't it? It is totally irrelevant." With interest, he watched Laura place her pen and notebook in her lap where they sank into the folds of her floral-print skirt.

"Irrelevant to my readers, not to me," she said, holding his gaze longer than a stranger normally would or should.

From that day, the journalist and policeman were as inseparable as their demanding jobs allowed. Two months later they married in a quiet ceremony in the Dolorosa Church in the middle-class Colonia Obregón. Laura Sanchez de Madrigal awaited him now, excitedly pregnant with their first child. For the first time in his adult life, he looked forward to going home at night. He'd see that his meeting with Mendoza was short.

Henrique entered the cantina trying too hard to look nonchalant. The kid has a lot to learn about undercover work, Madrigal thought. At least, the young man had sufficient smarts not to proceed directly to his table. That earned him an eight-point-zero on the Chief Inspector's score card. Instead, the eighteen-year-old took his time ordering a beer at the crowded bar. It took him ten minutes to work his way into the chair opposite the policeman.

"You're late," Madrigal said.

"My boss wouldn't let me out. I had to make an excuse to get away when I did. You are my sick uncle."

"Lies are dangerous. Too easy to get caught."

"You would have been sitting here until ten, if I hadn't lied."

"No," Madrigal snapped. He imagined Laura's slender, welcoming arms circling his neck, her warm lips pressed to his. "What have you got?"

"Maybe nothing, but I thought you should know. My boss lets me do the grunt work, but no one sees the reports he generates. Just him. I suppose he passes information up to the directors the way he's supposed to." Henrique glanced over his shoulder toward the bar.

Madrigal was impatient. "Go on."

"When I first became suspicious of Arroyo, I thought he might be one of those hackers who break into bank records and steal money. Or maybe he's stealing secret political or military information and selling it. The guy is such a genius with computers."

Madrigal glanced at his watch. He wanted to get home.

"Yesterday, we finally caught up with the activity of the past week. The list of new arrivals in the country had just been sent down by Customs and Immigration. I typed in the last names and Pedro told me to clean up the lab while he produced the report. A few minutes later, he pulled a sheet off the printer, sat back, and grinned like a chimpanzee. Whatever it was, he seemed really pleased with himself." Henrique leaned closer. "I heard him say under his breath, 'A miracle! A really big one.'"

"Doesn't sound incriminating to me." Madrigal steered the narrative toward a rapid conclusion. "Did you read that report?"

Henrique drank from his glass and wiped a foamy mustache from his upper lip with the back of his hand. "I did. Pedro slipped the page inside a manila folder and stuck it in the top drawer of his desk. I guess he thought I wasn't paying attention because he left the drawer unlocked when he went to the bathroom. I walked over and opened the file for a quick look. What I saw puzzled me."

"Come on, Mendoza. Cut it short."

"There was only one name on the paper."

"Okay. Who?"

"Analisa Marconi."

"That's all?" He had expected to hear the name of some prominent Santo Sangrían who might be ripe for blackmail. "Never heard of her."

"An American. Just arrived in the country."

"Why is he so interested in *una turista gringa*?"

"I checked her Immigration records, which are now cross-linked with all the other Ministries' records. She was born here. Adopted by Americans. Then, I remembered reading about the death of that Italian woman. I thought that—"

Madrigal jumped up from his chair. "You thought right, Henrique." Taking two crumpled bills from his pocket, he slid a five cruzero note under his empty glass. "That's for the waiter." He pressed the second bill into his informant's palm and left.

Chapter 15

Vice Consul Eric Small had just entered his office the next morning when Nancy Emerson rapped her knuckles on the open door and stepped in. "Autograph time," she announced, plopping a stack of visa applications on his desk.

Nancy was a stickler for detail, which Eric appreciated. Handling the minutiae so well freed her boss to concentrate on larger issues related to his job. As he added his signature to each paper, she observed him carefully.

"Don't trust me to sign on the right line?" he said.

"Just making sure you don't miss any documents. Uncle Sam pay me to keep you from making mistakes."

One of his duties as vice consul was to monitor the adoption processes of U.S. citizens hoping to find children in Santo Sangre. Foreign adoptions had been on the front burner since the death of Lydia Vitale.

"Any adoption visas?" he asked.

"One. On the bottom."

Eric pulled the document and examined it. "Two-year-old. Paperwork complete?"

"The attorney brought the mother in for her final appointment yesterday."

Consular regulations required that an adoption attorney bring a birth mother to the Embassy twice for a personal interview. The purpose, to obtain a sworn statement that she was unmarried and wasn't living with the father of her unborn or already existing child, or with any other person who might assume financial responsibility. INS insisted that mothers relinquish their children of their own free will.

"This one swore it was really her child. If you ask me, the kid doesn't look anything like her."

"Think she's lying?" Eric said, fully aware of the ramifications. If he determined the existence of fraud, he had to deny the visa. It didn't matter that the adoption had already cleared the Santo Sangrían Court of Minor Children or that, according to local laws—he glanced at the names on the document...Jack and Alice Maynard of Sheridan, Wyoming were now the legal parents of...he found the child's name—María Teresa Poblado.

"Tough call. I'm not supposed to say this, but—" Nancy glanced over her shoulder to see who might be lingering outside Eric's office, then leaned closer and lowered her voice. "The way I see it, you've got a kid over here who needs a loving home. You've got parents in the States dying to provide it. Life's messy. I say go for it."

"I'll pretend I didn't hear that." He studied a memo signed by the member of his staff who had conducted the interview. Under Comments he read the typed notation, "Witness seemed nervous. Details of story changed somewhat from first interview." Under the heading, Recommendation, was a handwritten, "Refer to VC for decision." Thanks a lot. Eric had the coward's option of passing the buck one step higher to Consul General Joe Schmidt. Unlike most CGs, Joe operated according to the principle of subsidiarity: pass problems up the line only when you can't resolve them in your own area of authority. "Let's get the kid out of this lousy country," Eric said, quickly signing the visa petition.

Nancy swooped up the papers. "I'll pretend I didn't hear that," she said and headed out the door.

❦ ❦ ❦

Analisa wasn't ready for the morning light filtering through the gauzy drape. Before she opened her eyes, the slightest movement of air tiptoed through the open window and touched her bare body like fingertips moving ever so lightly along the backs of her calves, up her thighs and buttocks and into the valley of her back. Half-dreaming, she murmured, "Don't stop...feels so good."

The night-long symphony of waves pounding on the beach in front of her hotel had a strange effect on her. Something about this out-of-the-way birthplace of hers was trying hard to reclaim her. She felt oddly at home.

Over breakfast, she memorized the few details Don Ricardo Valenzuela had provided about Martina Aguilada. "At the time of your adoption, she was living in the town of Santa Teresita in the upper highlands of the Chuchuán," he had said. "Getting there requires a long and pretty miserable bus ride, unless you can make some other arrangement."

She thought about hiring her new friend and personal taxi driver, Ernesto, to take her into the interior. What if he's really a serial ax murderer? she heard her mother say. I don't want to end up dead in the jungle. Where planning ended and daydreams began wasn't always clear. This cone-shaped patch of exposed volcano jutting out of the Southern Caribbean held answers to her most important questions. She was determined to conduct a systematic search, no matter how long it took. Whenever a doubt cast shadows on her confidence, she'd remind herself, "I lived through the crash that killed Mom and Dad. I can do this."

The only distraction from her planning was her evening date with Arturo Cristobal. She looked forward to having someone else to talk to besides Ernesto, Don Ricardo, and the hotel maid.

🌿 🌿 🌿

Nancy Emerson's voice spoke through the intercom. "Chief Inspector Madrigal's on line one, Mr. Small. Says it's urgent."

The local police didn't call the Embassy to see how things were going on Eric's side of the wall. Usually, it meant they had an American national cooling his heels in a cell at the Cárcel Central for drug possession, public drunkenness, or belligerence toward a police officer while being served a traffic citation. "Armando! How are you?"

"Fine. We need to talk, but not on the phone."

The Chief Inspector wasted no time making small talk. Eric respected him as a straightforward, honest cop, dedicated to his job—a string of virtues not common among public servants in Santo Sangre.

"Probably best I come to you," the Inspector said.

"No drunken sailors enjoying your hospitality?"

"I wish."

Eric replaced the black handset in its cradle and glanced at his watch. It'll take Armando about ten minutes to reach the Embassy. To make sure it didn't take another ten to reach his office, he called the guard station at the front gate and left orders to admit the Inspector immediately. Madrigal knew the drill, having been inside often enough to leave his weapon with the driver waiting outside in the police car.

❦ ❦ ❦

"How's Laura?" Eric asked after settling Armando Madrigal into the chair in front of his desk. The vice consul had been among the few Americans invited to the Madrigal-Sanchez nuptials.

"Laura's fine. She keeps telling me to invite you for dinner. So, consider yourself invited. How about this weekend?"

"Wouldn't it be better to wait until after the baby comes?" Eric said.

"I don't think so. Laura has this need to feel she is just as socially acceptable in her present condition as she was before. She admires Americans for treating pregnant women like competent human beings."

"Thanks for the invitation." Eric leaned forward. "Why the official visit?"

"I have no solid information yet, but something disturbing has come to my attention. You recall the circumstances surrounding the death of Lydia Vitale?

"There was a vague warning about possible danger to female adoptees." Eric opened a desk drawer and pulled a sheet of paper from a file folder and slid it across the desk to Armando. "I issued this Advisory. Washington's had it for several months."

"It seems not to have worked. Someone inside one of our ministries has taken an unusual interest in a U.S. national who just arrived in our fair country, a young woman in her twenties." Armando paused to take a breath. "An adoptee."

"Analisa Marconi."

The policeman affirmed the identification. "Have you taken up mind reading?"

"She was here yesterday," Eric said. "She's searching for her birth mother. You suspect the interest is more than bureaucratic?"

Armando's expression was grave, even for a policeman. "In light of what happened to the Vitale woman, I cannot ignore the possibility. I lack the resources to protect your citizens. I suggest you ship her home as soon as possible. The last thing I need is another foreigner showing up dead on our streets, especially an American."

"Not good for tourism."

"Let's just say it looks bad for everyone. Most of all, of course, for the victim."

"I'll take care of it." Eric extended his hand to his friend. "Thanks for coming to me early with this, Armando. I owe you one."

It was almost noon when Eric pressed the intercom button. "Nancy, get me a list of passenger ships leaving for

Miami this week. Then get hold of Analisa Marconi at the Gran Palacio."

❦ ❦ ❦

Analisa was wondering if Arturo Cristobal would turn out to be as charming as he seemed, when the telephone rang.

"Ms. Marconi?   Eric Small, U.S. Embassy."   They exchanged small talk before he got to the point. "It's come to my attention that your arrival in Santo Sangre has been noticed by the radical group that triggered the travel advisory I showed you." He refreshed her memory regarding the circumstances of Lydia Vitale's kidnapping and death. "I hate to do this, but I'm afraid you're going to have to leave the country sooner than you intended."

"You can't force me to leave!"

"As a matter of fact, I can." His authoritative tone convinced her he had power to do anything he wanted. "It's necessary. We can't risk something happening to you."

"How soon?"

"I remembered that you prefer not to fly, so I've checked the departing steamship schedules. If you don't mind going by freighter again, there's one leaving for Florida Friday morning. I've taken the liberty of booking passage in your name. I hope you understand."

She raked her fingers through her hair in frustration. "Isn't there someone I can appeal to?"

"You mean, higher up?"

She detected the faintest amusement in his voice. "You don't know how much it means to me to complete my business—to finish what I set out to do."

"I don't want to tout my importance, but you'd have to talk to the Ambassador or the Consul General or both."

"All right. How do I get an appointment?"

"You can't. It's my call. They don't overrule me on matters like this." His voice lowered. "I'm really sorry,

Ms. Marconi. Believe me. I wish I could make the whole
thing go away. We don't know who we're dealing with. I
think they're hapless lunatics, but they just might be a highly organized radical group. Either way, they've already
shown how dangerous they can be."

Analisa hadn't prepared for this scenario. An aborted
search for Martina Aguilada? Would she never find the
real Isabella, either?

"In the meantime, I'd advise you to stay as close to your
hotel as possible. At least, don't go out alone."

She thought of her date. "This evening I'll be with
Señor Cristobal."

"You'll be safe with him. People here take their icons
seriously. His fans would rise up and lynch them on the
spot."

Analisa's hand trembled as she put the phone down.
The vice consul believed his action served her best interests. Had he also provided an unexpected answer to her
prayers? It might not be her destiny to find Martina. And
Isabella might be waiting for her back in her apartment in
Berkeley and at her new job in San Francisco. In a matter
of minutes, weeks of decision making and careful planning
had unraveled. Don Ricardo had resisted helping her find
Martina before giving in. Vice Consul Small had been cool
to the idea, at best. Now this.

Later, in the shower, she prayed for guidance. There
was something about the innocence of standing naked
under a spray of hot water that made reflection easier.
Okay, Lord, what's going on? Did you lead me here only
to send me packing before I took a single step on my journey? Since God seemed to have put her on hold, she
poured a glob of shampoo in her palm and rubbed it into
her shoulder-length hair. I'm still here if you have any
advice. The lyrics of her favorite hymn sang inside her.
"Be not afraid...I go before you always." She hummed the

melody, then sang the words quietly. "If you walk amid the burning flames, you shall not be harmed."

"That's it!" Analisa had received her answer. Burning flames. She had lived through the plane crash. Ever since, she had felt the indestructibility that is often characteristic of people who survive incidents in which they should have died. Everything inside her defied the Embassy and the police. I'm staying right here. I'm finishing what I started!

Intellectually, she knew it was impossible to stay. Small had booked passage for Friday. She had to go. Just before turning the water off, she thought of Dave. What would he be doing now? Suddenly, she remembered where she had first seen Arturo Cristobal. "He was standing behind Dave at the crash site!" she said aloud. But how? Why? She understood why Dave's spirit had joined her. But Arturo Cristobal? A Santo Sangrían opera singer she didn't even know until yesterday?

She had one evening of her life to spend with him, after which she'd never see him again. She vowed to find out from the man himself how and why he had bilocated to a snow-packed California mountainside. And why he had flashed such a heavenly smile that she mistook him for her guardian angel.

Chapter 16

"Señorita Marconi, I'm in the lobby." Analisa's hand trembled as she held the receiver. There was a rise and fall to Arturo Cristobal's rich voice that gave his speech pattern a buoyant, musical quality. "Shall I come up?"

Analisa glanced around the room. Wet towel on the bed. Shorts and blouse crumpled in the only comfortable chair. "No! I'll be down. Give me five minutes."

"I will wait at the elevator."

Her memory of Arturo at the crash site gave new urgency to what had begun as a simple invitation for a social evening. She grabbed a light sweater from the closet near the door, insurance against an unlikely drop in temperature as the evening progressed.

"May I say that you look quite lovely?" he said when she approached him in the lobby.

"Depends on how honest you are."

"Very," he assured her.

"Then, thanks for the compliment."

They walked side by side through the busy lobby toward the main entrance.

"I'd say we're off to a good start." When Arturo smiled, as he did now, his mouth shifted slightly to the left giving his features a hint of impending mischief.

"I suppose." Did he mean their evening had started well, or did he have something longer-range in mind? If the latter, Analisa needed to make it clear there was no future for them beyond the stroke of midnight tonight.

Arturo reached for her hand, then hesitated, disguising the motion as a need to check his watch. "Time flies and there is so much to see. Shall I pick one of my favorite spots?"

Analisa wondered why she felt deprived of his touch. "Yes, I haven't seen much of your city yet. It's been mostly business...and making plans." She decided to withhold news of her early departure until later.

Arturo led her to the small parking lot in front of the Gran Palacio. "Which car is mine?" he asked, as if playing a game.

"Let me see. How about that white LeBaron convertible over there?"

Mischief turned to shock on Arturo's face. "You saw me drive in!"

"No. Honest. It was just a lucky guess."

"How do you do it?"

"Intuition." She felt very smart. "I see you as a...convertible kind of guy. This is the only one in the lot."

"Sorry. I do not own a LeBaron." He pointed to a late '90s BMW. "That one."

"You tricked me!" Their laughter harmonized. A wave of unexpected pleasure rippled through Analisa's body as Arturo held the car door open and watched her swing her bare legs and sandaled feet inside.

There was something warm and comfortable about this opera singer she found appealing, even beyond his Latin good looks. In high school and college, she'd never had a close relationship with an Hispanic male. There was Dave, of course, but every consideration of him demanded an asterisk and canonical footnote.

Arturo climbed in beside her, started the engine, and pulled out of the parking lot into the evening traffic. "What shall it be first, dinner or sightseeing?"

"I don't know a thing about Santa Catalina's restaurants. I didn't prepare for this trip like a tourist. I've had only one thing in mind, finding my birth mother."

"And if you don't?"

Analisa bit her lower lip. She refused to admit that a bunch of local nut cases had already tossed her plans in the garbage. "I'll go back to California, go to work...get on with my life."

"Alone?"

"Maybe. Who knows?"

"Is there someone waiting for you? In California?"

Was this the Latin male's way of making polite conversation? Or did Arturo sense they had little time to get to know each other and that he needed to accelerate the process?

"Not really. Well, someone's waiting who cares. But he's not waiting in the way I think you mean."

Confusion dominated his response. "Do you always speak in riddles?"

"Not always. Just when people I don't know very well ask personal questions."

"Then, I withdraw the question, as trial lawyers say."

Something about Arturo gave her confidence he would respect whatever she told him about herself. "My best friend is a priest in my parish. David Gallego. Father Gallego." When Arturo's eyes darkened, she broke the tension with a teasing smile. "Don't run too far with that thought."

"This...Father Gallego. He cares for you very much."

"Yes. Very much."

Arturo's polished-mahogany eyes were sincere, probing but not intrusive. "And you care for him."

"Yes. He's part of my reality."

Analisa wondered if Arturo was aware that his spirit had sped off to a mountainside on a miserable February afternoon, that he had appeared at the crash site with this same priest in whom he was now so interested. No matter. Arturo's presence with her at the moment Life and Death had fought over her knocked down the walls a man and woman normally hid behind during the early stages of their relationship. She sensed he felt it too. Knowing she might never see him again made it easier to speak her heart, to share her secrets with him. All but one.

Arturo, too, seemed stunned by their ability to leap-frog the customary first-date generalities. "Well." He cleared his throat. "Since you have so little time to be a tourist, I will do my best to make it worth your while."

She had stored an enormous amount of tension in her body since long before leaving Anaheim. In Arturo's inviting presence, she felt the strain evaporate through her pores. Feeling suddenly limp and de-energized, she let her body sink into the leather seat. "You're easy to talk to," she said. "Look, I'm not that hungry. Let's just drive around for a while?"

"Drive it is. Let's start with the casinos on the north shore. Then we can double back to the Plaza de la Libertad and the presidential palace. From there we can walk to my house." When Analisa objected, he quickly added, "The opera house, Teatro de las Bellas Artes."

"You live there?"

"No," he laughed. "Not literally. I have a little place on the beach beyond the last casino. What I mean is, I feel most alive and at home at the theater."

"Then, I insist you show it to me. The opera house, that is."

After a drive-by tour of the city's major night spots, Arturo parked the BMW at the east side of the plaza. No sooner had he exited the car than a gaggle of street kids surrounded him. They had recognized the vehicle and now vied for the privilege of guarding it. He took some bills from his pocket and distributed them to four boys, stationing one at each fender.

"I hire one to watch the car and the others to watch the kid who is watching the car."

"They all know you," Analisa said.

"They see me as one of their own. I suppose I am something of a role model to them."

Role model? she puzzled. Since when had street urchins started modeling themselves after opera singers?

As they walked toward the gingerbread Bellas Artes, Arturo explained. "Both of my parents had died by the time I was nine. My aunts and uncles were too poor to take care of me. One night I overheard them discussing a plan to take me to the orphanage. Being a pretty cocky little guy for my age, I decided to take my chances on my own rather than get lost in an institution. I slipped out of the house during the night and came down here to the plaza. I never looked back—and never went to any orphanage." His voice lowered, as if he was applying internal first aid to an old wound that had never completely healed. "No one even came looking for me."

"That's awful! How did you survive?"

"The next day, the realities of living on the street crashed through my bravado. I was hungry and without a *cruzero* in my pocket. I had to find a way to make a living. My only talent was singing. For some reason, God had given me a voice. I was a choirboy at Santa María de Soledad before I ran away."

Walking beside Arturo, now a major opera star, she tried to imagine him as a young boy. It was hard to connect this confident, poised professional with the terror he must have felt when left to scratch out a living on the streets.

"So, you sang for your supper?"

"Exactly!" He nodded two or three times in approval, as if she had solved a math problem in school. "During the day I went down to the docks and looked pathetic. One U.S. dollar a song. The cruise passengers were usually in a generous mood."

"Did you sing opera?"

"*¡Dios no!* Church hymns, folk songs, pop tunes. Anything I remembered or learned. I have a good memory. If I heard a song on the radio, I could sing it immediately afterward."

"Lyrics too?"

"Every word. My first introduction to English was the radio. I picked up enough to get by."

"Amazing."

"At night, I stood in front of the opera house before and after performances. And I sang. My cap was usually full of coins at the end of the day. It was pretty good money for a kid. It kept me alive, plus a few of the other boys who had a harder time making it on their own."

"Weren't you scared? In the States, terrible things happen to street kids."

"It is no different here. Drugs. Prostitution. Children sold for—I beg your pardon. I should not talk to a lady about such things."

"I'm an adult."

"I forget that Americans are more open about these things."

"Please don't stop. I want to hear your story."

"One evening, I noticed a beautiful woman in the most gorgeous evening gown I had ever seen. She stood there listening to me. Her friends tried to pull her away, but she refused to budge. At first I thought I was seeing a vision of my dead mother. Instead, she turned out to be my fairy godmother."

"Who was she?"

"The great diva, María Antonia Salazar, the first Santo Sangrían soprano to become an international star. When I finished my song, she took me aside and asked a single question. 'What is your greatest dream?' I guess she knew street kids dream a lot. Sometimes that is all we—they— have."

"And . . . ?" He had Analisa hooked.

"I told her I wanted to sing inside the opera house, not on the sidewalk out front. It was a brash, stupid thing to dream, but I must have said the magic words. She took me home with her that night. Cleaned me up. Gave me a room in her house, singing lessons, private tutoring."

"Right out of a Dickens novel."

A light shone in Arturo's eyes. "I never thought of it like that. Fortunately, when my voice changed it only got deeper and richer." He stopped walking and spread his arms wide apart. "And here I am. The finished product."

"What a great story!"

They arrived at the stage door of the venerable performing arts center. "The mayor once offered me a symbolic key to the city. I told him I preferred a real one, the key to the opera house."

Arturo unlocked the iron door and reached around the jamb to find the light switch. In a moment they were inside, climbing a wooden stairway that led to the great stage.

"There is one thing I must add to my story. I get feted and praised everywhere I go, but I never forget where I came from. That little boy singing on the sidewalk is still inside me. He has grown up, but everything he felt and experienced is still there. It will always be part of who I am."

A newly kindled flame burned inside Analisa. It was as if she had found another piece of the puzzle of her life and dropped it into place. But she wasn't sure why it fit. "I envy you."

"Why?"

"I've just come to realize that my American upbringing, wonderful as it was, stripped me loose from the little girl in the orphanage. I never thought much about her or—" She looked away to conceal the sudden shift in her emotions. "Or missed her, until yesterday. Now, I want more than anything to find her again, to discover who she really is."

"Is Analisa your real name?"

"Yes."

"I phrased the question badly. That is not what I meant."

"Analisa wasn't my birth name. I was born Isabella María Aguilada."

They stood in the semi-darkness of the wings. Arturo took her hand and placed it over his heart. "Like the young Arturo who is still inside me, Isabella has been with you all your life."

"But you remember him! I never knew her." She had hoped to build that bridge by meeting Martina. Now, she had to find another way to make contact with Isabella.

He laid a warm hand along her cheek. With a fingertip he deflected the path of a solitary tear. "It is I who envy you, Analisa. I skipped a lot in condensing my story. I left out all the negatives. When reporters interview me now, they romanticize my early life. 'From the streets to the stage!' The life of a homeless boy is not romantic. Or fun. If Señora Salazar had not rescued me, I might not be alive today. If alive, I might not be someone you cared to spend the evening with."

When they walked out onto the great stage, Analisa looked up at the stack of horseshoe tiers rimming the dimly lit theater. A nervous tremor coursed through her body. What must it feel like to stand on this stage and perform before a full house, knowing that every note that leaps from your vocal chords will be judged on the spot as deserving of bravos or boos?

Arturo drifted into silence. Analisa suspected he had fallen prey to one of his recurring childhood nightmares. "I certainly would not be here in this theater," he said, picking up his previous thought. "Worst of all, we would not be here together."

"Then, I owe a great debt to Señora Salazar."

Analisa no longer considered Arturo a stranger. Despite the brief time they had known each other, she had already added him to her circle of life. She knew they'd keep in touch as they moved on with their separate existences in distant parts of the world. "Have you ever been married?"

"No. When I began taking engagements abroad, I realized something. I have three options when it comes to marriage."

"Some people have none or think they don't have any." She watched his face for a sign of amusement but found none. Evidently, he was one of those honest men who respond to a question by giving more information than you asked for.

"One," he continued as if he hadn't heard her, "give up my international career and perform locally only. I am not ready to do that. As much as I love this theater, Opera Santa Catalina provides too small a stage for a singer with my ambition. I want to see how far my talent will take me." He took a deep breath. "A second option is to drag my wife around the world with me. A woman needs a home, children . . . stability."

"Not all women."

"The kind of woman I want for a wife would not crave my nomadic lifestyle. Finally, I suppose I could travel the world and leave my wife here for long stretches of time to manage the estate and raise our children. Not a healthy situation. I have seen what happens to male singers when they are away from their families for months at a time. Loneliness leads to alcohol...mistresses in every big city. It is no life for a married man. At least, not for me."

"So, there's never been anyone?"

"Well, I will just say no one has yet offered me an appealing fourth option."

Analisa threw her hands up. "Now I have two celibates in my life."

That remark produced an amused grin. "Not like your Father Gallego. I prefer . . . 'currently unattached.'"

"But looking?"

"Always. It will happen. Someday. I might be middle-aged by the time it does. By then, I may have different priorities."

Analisa wondered for a fleeting moment if she might have been the one to offer him that elusive fourth option. She'd never know.

Moving toward the darkened footlights, she sat cross-legged facing him. Her sandaled bare feet rested under her full skirt. "This place demands music. Sing something for me. Please."

Arturo seemed flustered. "I have no music with me, no accompanist."

"Please."

"What should I sing?"

"My mother had a CD of Andrea Bocelli singing an Italian song...something about never forgetting first love. The only words I remember are '*prim' amore*' something or other."

He began to hum a melody.

"That's the one! Can you sing it?"

"Of course. The lyrics tell us that, no matter what happens to us...how many lovers we might have, how many marriages even...we always remember—'can never forget' is the way the song phrases it—our first love, '*il prim' amore*.'"

Dave's image flashed into Analisa's imagination sending a rush of color to her cheeks. She focused on her toes, wiggling them to drive his presence away.

"See?" Arturo said. "I have not sung a single note, and you are already thinking of your first love."

"Will you please stop talking and sing the song?" she insisted. "I hope you don't make little speeches like that when you're performing."

He appeared hurt and apologetic. "I hit a sensitive nerve."

She nodded.

"Forgive me."

Another nod.

Arturo sang, softly. Then the sound, pure and true, rose in volume and took flight toward the upper balconies. His voice seemed to come from some inner creative spring, more spiritual than physical. Transfixed, Analisa raised her eyes. She saw a little boy in street rags, holding a tattered cap in his hands. Arturo sang directly to her eyes, using them as pathways to transmit each note and syllable to her hungry spirit.

When the song ended, he stood over her. Reaching down, he helped her to her feet. She breathed deeply to quiet the heaving in her chest. He took her in his arms and kissed her, gently at first, then with greater urgency. She liked the way their bodies complemented each other and felt no urgency to withdraw. Instead, she closed her eyes and pressed closer to his chest, certain that a full orchestra accompanied their duet. The heat she felt had to be from kliegs spotlighting their embrace. When she opened her eyes, no stage lights illuminated the area in which they stood. The pit lay silent. Their only audience, the empty velvet-padded seats.

Without breaking from her, Arturo pulled back to engage her eyes. "I will help you find your Isabella."

She had no doubt about the sincerity of his promise. Whatever it meant, they had to continue the search somewhere away from Santo Sangre.

They dined at El Papagallo, an open-air waterfront restaurant. Analisa was grateful for the distance their terrace table provided. The speed at which they were growing closer—along with a generous glass of imported Chilean wine—blurred the line between reality and fantasy.

Arturo drove slowly, taking the long way back to the Gran Palacio. She didn't mind. The late evening air was fresh and salty. A gentle breeze blended the ocean's fragrance with a potpourri of tropical scents emitted by the city center's parks and gardens. When they pulled up in front of the hotel, he turned the motor off.

"It's been—" she started, but the usual after-first-date clichés deserted her.

"That sounds too much like 'It's all over.' That is not what I want to hear."

She looked ahead at the passing late-night traffic. Only a handful of pedestrians were in view, most of them making their way back to their hotels after a night on the town. In the shadows, twenty feet from the main entrance, a couple stood locked in a passionate embrace. Seeing them sent a wave of envy through Analisa. Like Arturo, she didn't want the evening to end.

"It's not goodbye," she said to the passenger-side window. When she turned to look at him, he searched her face. Was he, like she, searching for a map to guide them on the road to an unknown destination? She dreaded returning to her solitary hotel room.

Seeming to sense her dilemma, Arturo said with renewed vigor, "I have an idea. Let me come up...for a while, I mean."

There was no suggestion in his words or actions that he meant anything more than to offer his company. Remembering what he had said earlier about avoiding long-term attachments, Analisa corralled her emotions. "I don't think that's such a good idea." Tell him you're leaving Santo Sangre! she admonished herself. Let him know there's no point pursuing this tropical summer romance.

He looked disappointed. "I want to see you again." It angered her that she had driven his smile away. Its absence revived the loneliness his presence had banished for most of the evening. "I have another idea," he said. "Tomorrow night I sing the role of John the Baptist in *Salome*. It is my last performance of the season. Then, I have some time off before I leave for a concert in Madrid."

He touched her bare arm, sending shivers up her neck on this warm evening. "It would make me very happy to have you in the audience."

"You're on."

He brightened. "You will come? Really?"

"I'd love to watch you perform—" Analisa blushed at her gaffe. "I mean, hear you sing." Informing him of her impending departure had to wait until after Wednesday's performance.

Arturo was waiting at the passenger side of the driveway when she opened the car door and stepped out.

"I had a wonderful evening," she said.

Arturo kissed her again, lightly this time. The touch of his mouth on her lips was warm and full of promise. "Your ticket will be at the Will Call window, along with a pass to come backstage afterwards. I will wait for you in my dressing room."

He gave her hand a parting squeeze and drove away.

Chapter 17

Marta Lopez and Lupe Santana, the couple in the shadows of the Gran Palacio's entrance, closely observed Analisa and Arturo's good-night kiss. Lupe pressed his body hard against his partner, arms locked behind her back. Her welcoming breasts swelled against his chest through the thin cloth of her hand-embroidered blouse. Despite the masculine surge Marta felt against her pelvis, no true passion charged their embrace. They had put real lovemaking on hold. Lupe's attention focused not on Marta but on the BMW idling at the hotel entrance and on its occupants.

Earlier in the evening, she and Lupe had lingered near a bar on the Calle Montenegro. The spot offered an unobstructed view of the hotel's polished brass-and-glass doors. From there, they got their first look at the one they had targeted as their next *coneja*. They observed with interest the Marconi woman's departure from her escort.

For several hours, Lupe and Marta had strolled the plaza. When tired, they sat at the edge of the giant blue-tiled fountain that dominated the park across from the hotel. Despite their movements and the seasonably heavy traffic, at no time was the hotel entrance outside their line of vision.

Lupe tightened his embrace, as if squeezing the breath out of her might somehow injure this Marconi person whose very presence on Santo Sangrían soil they considered both an outrage and an opportunity.

"They take our baby girls from us," he grunted under his breath as Analisa passed through the doors and into the lobby, "strip them of everything they have inherited—birthright, culture, language, morals—and turn them into rich little whore-bitches. They'd bleach their skin if they could."

"She is here only two days and already she has found a wealthy man," Marta spat with contempt. The contrast between herself and the American adoptee sent her fantasies into flight—a full squadron of "what ifs?"

What if she had been adopted?

Would her skin be as pure and unblemished as this one's?

Would her clothing have the same "Made in the USA" look?

She might be the one arriving back at the Gran Palacio in a late-model European car, after a tour of the town on the arm of a handsome man of means.

Would I be— She braked her imaginings and almost gasped aloud. The next *coneja*?

"Fine looking, isn't she?" Lupe said. "Healthy. Athletic figure."

"What about him?" Marta countered. "A good-night kiss and gone. A real man takes that one upstairs for the night."

"Let him save her for Los Dejados."

"She is too skinny." Marta already felt jealous at the thought of Lupe coupling with this quite exquisite younger woman whom she had to admit was a classic Santo Sangrían beauty in North American dress. "Those breasts will not produce much milk."

"Breasts we can borrow. This one will give us lots of babies."

Marta bristled. To her, every fertile woman in Santo Sangre posed a threat.

"Who is this guy anyway?" Lupe wondered aloud. "Maybe we should check him out before we grab her. Did you get the license plate?"

"Not necessary."

"You know the son of a bitch?"

"Everyone knows him, but you."

Lupe glared at her.

"You are not going to like this." It was unlike Marta to play guessing games with her volatile mate. She quickly supplied the information he was waiting for. "He is Arturo Cristobal, the opera singer."

Lupe banged the soft underside of his closed fist against the concrete wall. He took a deep dragon's breath and exhaled fire. "Shit! Goddamn shit!"

🌱 🌱 🌱

Analisa entered the darkness of her room. The red light on her telephone pulsed. Turning on the bedside lamp, she went to the sliding glass door that led to the balcony. On the off-chance that Arturo might still be in the parking lot, she leaned over the railing. The same couple she had noticed near the entrance to the building were now looking up at her. For an instant, the three of them made eye contact. She felt a vague threat in their gaze. Remembering the waiting message, she shook off the feeling and went inside.

The Spanish instructions on the phone said, "Red light: Call hotel operator." Something about the couple downstairs disturbed her. Were they looking at me or just in my direction?

"You have a message from a David Gallego," the hotel operator said. She gave the Anaheim number, which Analisa dialed immediately, calculating the difference as four hours earlier than Santo Sangrían time.

Dave answered. "Analisa! Good to hear your voice."

"Yours too." All her life Dave had been within easy reach. Now, he sounded far away, on another planet.

"You've been on my mind day and night," he said. "How're things going?"

"Fine." Pride prevented her from telling him everything had suddenly changed, that she was being run out of her own native country.

"Must be tough...being all alone, I mean."

Analisa hesitated. The taste of Arturo's kiss lingered on her lips. "I'm not exactly 'all alone.' I've made one friend."

"Oh?" Dave's voice fell a full octave, telling her he already suspected this new friend was a male. "Who?"

She had stepped into that peculiar, uncharted area of their relationship. Normally, a woman in her position had no reason to hedge when talking to her parish priest about a new male acquaintance.

"He's an opera singer. Something of a local hero, I'm told."

"An opera singer!" Dave's voice rose closer to its normal pitch. "Must be fat, bald, and fifty."

Analisa let him live with this hopeful vision. She skipped the details of her evening out and her preliminary feelings about this new person in her life. "I have a ticket to hear him sing tomorrow night, then I'll probably never see him again."

"Well, I'm glad you've got company."

Across the miles, she visualized the exact expression on Dave's face. Sincere, earnest, wanting to be loyal and noble while his own emotions whirred with turmoil. She had seen him like this before, trying hard not to inject his own feelings into her life and decisions. It was one of the things Analisa loved about him.

"I'll let you go. Good night, Analisa."

"See you, Dave."

She returned to the balcony and looked down to the nearly deserted street. The lovers had departed.

☙ ☙ ☙

There was no lovemaking between Marta and Lupe that night. Instead, her mate gathered Los Dejados' inner circle of five, all in their twenties and thirties. One by one, the sleepy-eyed group straggled into Marta and Lupe's two-room apartment. At three-thirty in the morning, the last of the core leaders, Pedro Arroyo, arrived.

"This better be important," he muttered. "My girlfriend is really upset that I left her in the middle of the night. She already thinks I'm married to my computer at the Ministry."

Antonio Gamez grunted. "Believe it or not, Señor, some things are more important than your sex life and your computer."

Lupe jumped in to douse the flames. "That machine whose workings I do not begin to understand has, by some miracle, produced a candidate to be our new *coneja*."

Affirmed by his leader, Pedro ignored Antonio's remark. "But why the early wake-up call, Jefe?"

"The Marconi woman," Lupe said. "We need to act fast or we might lose her."

"We cannot let her get away!" Pedro said. "She is perfect! You read the printout."

Lupe stood up and began pacing. "I did read it and you are right. Our source at the Gran Palacio has learned that she is unmarried, and the people who stole her from us are dead." He added sarcastically, "This time, there's no mommy and daddy waiting for the little bitch back home."

"We followed her tonight," Marta said. "She was with Arturo Cristobal."

"The opera singer?" First astonishment, then concern sounded in Antonio's words. "Doesn't that make her a greater risk? She may not have anyone waiting for her in the States, but a man of his stature could cause trouble for us here."

"Not if we take her today," Lupe said.

"He kissed her," Marta added with a mixture of caution and disgust.

"Good for him!" Pedro said. "Maybe he is a real Santo Sangrían, after all."

"I have devised a detailed plan on just how we will snatch this Analisa Marconi," Lupe said. "We will grab her at the hotel and get her into a car." He let the idea sink in. "From there, we will bring her to our secret location in the *barrio*. People here pay little attention to what their neighbors are up to. If they do see something, they keep their mouths shut."

Bottoms shifted as the Dejadista council processed Lupe's accelerated plan. "This time tomorrow night I will have her pregnant, and we can move her out of Santa Catalina."

Marta rolled her eyes. "You think it's all so simple." She hoped Lupe understood she meant both his plan and his chances of impregnating the woman the first time they had intercourse.

"Los Dejados sympathizers in the interior will house La Coneja until my child is born," Lupe continued. "To keep the locals from becoming curious about what happened to the newborn, we will keep moving La Coneja around the country, as we did the last time. You know the routine." He puffed out his chest and grinned. "I will get her pregnant...and keep her that way as often possible."

"Always you," Marta ventured.

"Wrong, as usual, Marta. I propose that, in the unlikely event the woman fails to conceive within three months, the privilege will fall to Pedro Arroyo, in recognition of his role in finding our second *coneja*."

"Okay!" Pedro was wide awake.

Marta saw that Pedro was already constructing his own house of fantasies. She also let herself believe this was a sign that Lupe might be more committed to their relationship than she had thought.

"All in favor?" Lupe said. The motion passed, with the loudest "Aye" coming from his understudy.

"God is with us!" Antonio exclaimed. "He has provided us with the perfect woman. That proves our cause is just."

Marta grunted. Only she seemed to doubt Antonio's theology.

Now fully involved, Pedro asked, "When do we take her?"

Lupe surveyed the group, assessing the council's mood and resolve. "Before noon."

Once again, the council approved his plan.

"Do we know enough about her business here and her schedule to pull it off?" Antonio wanted to know.

Lupe deferred to Pedro, who removed a page of notes from the file folder he guarded as if it contained the secret code for launching a nuclear attack.

"According to the Ministry's database," Pedro began, "she is here as a tourist. Apparently she has come back to see the place where she was born. It is not unusual for these types to nose around in archives for information about their real parents. Our contact at the hotel tells us she rises early and eats breakfast between eight and nine. In the hotel restaurant."

"Marta, you will be the floor maid. Antonio, stay in the corridor with the laundry cart." Lupe's words rattled like a burst of fire from an AK-47. "I will drive and wait at the service entrance. We must be quick and efficient."

Marta's adrenaline flowed. The rush of excitement she had felt when they grabbed the Vitale woman had astonished her. She had reacted like a wild animal getting her first taste of human blood and wanting more. Despite her misgivings about some aspects of Los Dejados' operation, her whole being was suddenly engaged in their new adventure.

"What about Cristobal?" Pedro asked. "Is he really a problem?"

"We do not think she is deeply involved with the guy," Marta began, before Lupe cut her off.

"Tonight was probably a casual social engagement."

"She sent him packing with just a good-night peck," Marta added. "How special can he be?"

"The cops have been nosing around Rincón trying to get information about our dead *coneja*," Lupe said. "There is nothing to worry about. The women who attended her are tight-lipped and know what will happen if they don't stay that way. No one outside this room knows who wrote the note they found on her." He paused for dramatic effect. "Are there any questions about the plan to snare our new *coneja*?"

There were none.

"Do you all understand your assignments?"

They did.

With their plan cemented, Marta decided it was time to bring up the other subject that was on her mind.

At the time she and Lupe met and fell in love, they shared a personal venom for adoptees. Both had been left behind to live the hard life of Santo Sangre's lower classes, while a more fortunate sibling had escaped to a life that offered education, money, and the opportunities that went with them. She supported him when he gathered others around them and when he formulated a concrete plan to repay themselves and their country for the theft of their brothers and sisters.

But now, Marta feared that Los Dejados might have gone beyond philosophy and principle. Beyond revenge. It might be too late to prevent the enslavement of Analisa Marconi, but at some point it all had to end. It must end, she resolved with a shudder. I will not spend the rest of my life in that hell-hole women's prison. She believed the stories of beatings and rapes told by former female inmates of the Cárcel Central. She even heard the warden tolerated such behavior as routine diversion for his guards. She said none of this directly to her fellow Dejadistas.

In coming to this moment, she'd had to examine her motives and look at her role in Los Dejados with a new vision, to think in a new way about her future with Lupe. While Lydia Vitale was alive, Marta had accommodated Lupe's divided passions. Now, their first *coneja* was dead, and they had found another to replace her. If this one died, how many more? How willing was she to share her man with them, even for the noble cause they served? Will he ever be mine alone? And how long before they made a fatal mistake and the whole movement came crashing down on their heads? Being the only woman on the inner council isolated her, leaving her no one with whom to share her confusion. Despite the ease with which they had dismissed her opinions in the past, the urge to press forward compelled her to speak.

"Each of you knows I support our cause with all my heart. I have done so from the start. I am just as eager for this new day to dawn as you are." It was a safe beginning. The moisture in her palms and the tightness in her throat revealed the risk she was taking. "We have all suffered injustice from a system that enables foreigners to swoop down on our country and take advantage of desperate mothers, robbing families of their sons and daughters, brothers and sisters. We have not only the right but the obligation to reclaim our lost children. And what better way than to detain the Stolen Ones and use them as vehicles for restitution?"

A ripple of approval rumbled through the room. "Now, I speak not as a member of the council of Los Dejados but as a woman . . . and a civilized human being."

Her listeners shifted in their seats. Marta knew these men tolerated her position within the core group only because of her status as Lupe's woman. Their support ran no deeper than that.

"What crime has this Marconi woman personally committed against us or our nation? She was just an innocent child when they took her away. I call upon Los Dejados to treat our new *coneja* with basic decency."

Marta paused to let her words bore into their minds and hearts. She had to find out what kind of human beings sat in this room, whatever the implications for herself.

"At some point, all these women had a choice of what to do with their lives," Pedro argued. "They could have come back."

Marta glared at him. "Fine. Let us suppose for a moment you are not Pedro Arroyo anymore. You are living in the United States as Peter...Smith. You have been to the university and now have a high-paying job as a computer programmer."

"Sounds good to me," he said with a smirk. The other men agreed.

"Then one day you say to yourself, 'What am I doing here in America with a job I love and all this money? My real mother and perhaps my brothers and sisters are in Santo Sangre living in some hovel, scratching out a living as day laborers in construction or harvesting coffee on the plantations. I am not really Peter Smith. I am Pedro Arroyo. I should go home and live with my own people.'" She made eye contact with each council member in turn. "Is that what you would do?"

The silent men stared into the corners of the room or studied the grooves in their fingernails.

Marta pumped up her courage. "What I am getting at is this. Let's win her over to our cause. Make her realize she is Santo Sangrían by birth and will be until death. In time, she may even realize we have done her a favor by reconnecting her with her precious roots." Since her listeners expressed no overt protests, Marta moved on to her final and most controversial point. "Allow her to keep her first child, at least."

"What?" Lupe was out of his chair. The others muttered disapproval.

"Give her something to live for!" she shouted over their grumbling. "Is it too much to ask? How does that violate our noble principles?"

Lupe looked around the room, collecting the expressions and reactions of the others. "We are a democratic organization. Everyone has a voice and a vote." His unexpectedly temperate response surprised her. "What do you think of Marta's proposal?"

"What is your opinion, Lupe?" Pedro wanted to know.

"Yes," Antonio echoed, "where do you stand?"

"Cowards!" Marta raged. "What do you know of democracy? Must you wait for your leader to make up his mind before you know your own?"

"She is right," Lupe said. "I want to know what you think." He fixed his eyes on Antonio and seemed determined not to release his gaze until the timid man had expressed an opinion.

"I confess I did not like what happened to our first *coneja*," Antonio said. "Dumping her in the street. I am not a savage. Now I live in fear the police will catch us and put us all in jail for murder."

"We did not kill her!" Pedro reminded him. "She died of natural causes."

"Shut up!" Lupe shouted. "I want to hear what Antonio has to say."

"Some democracy," Pedro mumbled.

"I agree with Marta," Antonio said. "If our cause is just, we should be able to win the Marconi woman over to our side."

Lupe catapulted from his chair. "If?"

"You took an oath," Pedro interjected.

"I will keep my word," Antonio said in his own defense.

"I see," Lupe said. "So, how do you vote?"

"With Marta."

"We have two votes for more lenient treatment of our *coneja*, none for keeping things the way they have been. Pedro?"

All eyes shifted to the computer expert.

"We all know that in the eyes of the law what we are doing, though morally right, is illegal." Pedro looked with contempt at Antonio and Marta. She doubted Pedro possessed any morals but kept the thought to herself.

"A single defection will destroy us," he concluded. "We cannot allow it."

"Then how do you vote?" Marta said, anticipating the answer.

"Against your proposal. I do not believe in inflicting punishment for no reason, but if we get soft we will lose our resolve and the high tide of our movement will trickle into the sand and disappear."

"A computer expert but a lousy poet," she said. She had expected to lose Pedro's support. He had never forgiven her for choosing Lupe as her mate instead of him.

"I vote with Pedro." Lupe avoided looking at Marta as he spoke, oblivious to the hurt and rage bubbling to the surface of her spirit like a molten lava flow. "We have two votes for changing our approach, two against."

One other person occupied the room, Eliseo Madrid. Round as he was tall, he had sat in silence like an overstuffed beanbag chair throughout his colleagues' discussion. Eliseo had always been the hardest one for Marta to read. She never knew what was going on inside that giant pumpkin head of his. His eyes, buried in their sockets, never seemed to open more than a slit even when he was awake. His facial muscles lay so deep beneath his fatty flesh that no movement rippled to the surface. She had no way of knowing if he was smiling or frowning.

"The deciding vote is yours, Eliseo," Lupe said. "Marta and Antonio want to change the way we treat our new *coneja*. They want us to win her over by better treatment and by letting her keep her firstborn. Pedro and I are against this change. We believe our conejas must pay the highest price for their past good fortune, that there is no room for compromise."

Getting information out of Eliseo was a process. He preferred to write his responses rather than talk. For this purpose, he kept a small spiral notebook in the breast pocket of his double-extra-large shirt. He took it out now and scribbled on a blue-lined page. Ripping the note out, he handed it to Lupe.

"Eliseo votes...no."

Chapter 18

Analisa sat at the glass-topped table on the balcony that jutted out from her room. From this perch, she viewed the full sweep of the beach and the gentle curve of the bay at whose midpoint lay the heart of Santa Catalina. She wore white linen trousers, pleated and comfortably roomy, and a hunter-green silk shirt. Her sandals waited to be found somewhere near or under the bed.

The entertainment section of the morning paper featured an interview with Arturo Cristobal and a shot of him as John the Baptist. Analisa studied the photo. A furry animal skin covered his torso, leaving one broad shoulder exposed. His left arm was extended, index finger pointing in accusation, undoubtedly at the wicked seductress, Salome. Although the beard and makeup masked his natural youthful appearance, there was no hiding the intense eyes, the noble, chiseled face. He looked appropriately saintly as the Messiah's firebrand precursor.

The prospect of being with him again excited her. She exhaled a soft whistle. "Heck of a hunk." As much as she tried to focus on her present dark realities, Arturo Cristobal had unleashed feelings inside her that were simultaneously exhilarating and disturbing. The man in the photograph seemed far different from the street-urchin-become-opera-star/local-hero she had kissed on the stage of the grand Teatro Bellas Artes.

The memory of that kiss had spent the night with her, along with the clean, masculine scent of his solid body. Tonight she'd return to the opera house under far different circumstances, her formal introduction to the world of opera and to the professional side of Arturo Cristobal.

Arturo lived in a world she knew nothing about and into which she saw no way of fitting. It was best to find out

early if all he wanted was to add her to his coterie of ador-
ing groupies.

Even as she formulated the thought, she knew something more special than that might develop between them,
given sufficient ripening time. That's the problem. Time is
our enemy. The realization brought more sadness than she
expected. How will I ever find out if there's an empty
place inside him I might fill? She wondered about that elusive fourth option he spoke of. Was there a place in her
own heart waiting only for him?

"What nonsense!" she said aloud. "I'm attending the
opera. That's all. Then, I'm leaving Santo Sangre. Period.
End of relationship." She wondered how many times in
her life she would experience near misses like this one. I
could be walking down the street one day and step into a
store just as my soul mate passes that very spot. Who
knows? If I don't duck into that store, we might literally
bump into each other, apologize, then look into each
other's eyes and see a perfect reflection of our other half.

But she hadn't come to Santo Sangre in search of a soul
mate. The object of her quest was Martina Aguilada.
Lately, she had added the even more important search for
the true Isabella María. Analisa believed the two were
linked. Being rushed out of the country thwarted both
endeavors. And why? Anger rose in her chest and tightened her jaw. Because of events I have no interest in and
over which I have no control.

"Servicio," a woman's voice called out after a knock on
the door.

"Can't she read the Do Not Disturb sign?" Analisa
grumbled.

A second, louder knock. "¡Servicio!"

Annoyed, Analisa dropped the newspaper on the glass
table and marched to the door, slipping into her sandals on
the way. The hotel employee, stack of towels in hand,

brushed by her with a broad smile and spitfire chatter about how many rooms she had to clean before noon.

Analisa followed her into the bathroom. "I put the sign out." She pointed toward the door knob. "I do not wish to be disturbed."

The woman seemed not to hear. Instead she pushed her way back into the bedroom. Then, with a sudden move she dropped the towels and locked an arm around Analisa's neck from behind. In the same motion she pressed a damp rag to Analisa's face. An acrid odor robbed the surrounding atmosphere of oxygen and burned Analisa's mucous membranes.

While Analisa's brain screamed a futile plea for help, the woman stuffed a dry wash cloth into her victim's mouth. Analisa gagged in an effort to reject it. Too shocked at first to respond to the attack, her instincts clicked into action. She flailed at her assailant. Although no taller than herself, the woman was larger boned and no slouch as a wrestler. Despite absorbing two solid elbows to the ribs, the attacker managed to keep the cloth in place over Analisa's face.

"Help me!" the woman shouted over her shoulder in Spanish.

In an instant there were two of them. A man buried both hands in Analisa's hair close to the scalp and yanked her head back.

If I don't stop fighting, he'll pull my hair out by the roots. Several times she heard him repeat the word *cone-ja*. She struggled one more time to get away but tripped and crashed against the bathtub. The side of her head cracked against the faucet, sending a shower of sparks flying inside her brain. The woman climbed on top of Analisa and kept pressing that damned cloth to her nostrils. She tried to hold her breath, but with each gasping reach for air she felt dizzier, as if suffocating, spiraling out of control into the depths of a bottomless well.

This can't be happening!

With the last light of awareness, Analisa felt herself being lifted into some kind of rolling basket. They covered her with what felt like a load of sheets and towels. Sticky, warm liquid dripped into her eyes, down her cheeks, and into her mouth.

God, I'm bleeding!

With her last conscious thought, she wondered, How can I let Arturo know I might not make it to the opera?

❦ ❦ ❦

Lupe Santana waited in the alley outside the hotel's service entrance. Like most other cars in the city, the idling old Chevy sedan spewed a cloud of noxious fumes that clung to the heavy air in the narrow, walled-in space. A Dejadista pharmacist's assistant had supplied the chloroform, but Lupe's luck had run out when he tried to borrow a van. It might look suspicious to be loading the contents of a single laundry basket into a passenger car.

This is Santo Sangre, he decided. Nothing's perfect here.

Slick with perspiration, his hands clutched the steering wheel. Cramps sent a call to defecate. Alternately, he watched the door marked Reservado Servicio from which Marta and Antonio planned to exit with their bagged prey and the alleyway exit to note any signs of interest in his presence. He didn't like the logistics—one way in, therefore only one way out.

He was eager to see his new *coneja* up close. His brief surveillance had told him Analisa Marconi was in excellent physical condition, the most important thing. That he found her quite beautiful and sexually appealing came as an added bonus. In fact, while he waited for Marta and Antonio to appear, his brain generated images that sent wake-up signals to his genitals.

I will see to it that La Coneja stays—as he once heard on American television—barefoot and pregnant. He liked the saying.

"What about Marta?" asked a voice from the other side of his brain—the small part that hadn't been silenced by anticipation of a lovely new bed mate. The voice urged him to consider the level of his commitment to his partner. He brushed aside the distraction. Marta knows what this is about. She has suffered like the rest of us.

Don't be so sure, the voice countered. Females are jealous of their men. Turn your new *coneja* over to Pedro right off. His work exposed her. He deserves her.

"La Coneja is mine!"

Sure that he had shouted the words, he checked in all directions. What little activity there was in the alleyway went on uninterrupted. Either he had imagined crying out, or no one had heard him.

A gray laundry basket poked its blunt nose between the double swinging service entrance doors, sending Lupe into a state of high alert. All fantasies and inner wranglings vanished like vapors. He surveyed the scene one more time. Still no undue attention to his presence or to the uniformed pair pushing the wobbly basket down the ramp into the alley.

Marta, a wild expression on her face, yanked open the back door of the sedan for Antonio. She sprinted to the other side and climbed in. Her accomplice dumped the bulky mound of sheets and towels into the back seat. He scrambled in, letting out a yelp as he scraped his shins on the door frame.

Lupe who had been nervously revving the engine didn't wait for the back door to close. He rammed the gas pedal to the floor, peeling rubber as the Chevy lurched down the alleyway toward the street. Antonio struggled in vain with the rear passenger-side door. Banging against a row of trash cans, it slammed closed on its own, smashing his wrist.

☘ ☘ ☘

Throughout his performance, Arturo Cristobal kept an eye on the box reserved for Analisa Marconi. It remained empty to the end. He had given better portrayals of the doomed New Testament prophet. When the final curtain fell, his forgiving fans chorused their bravos. Bowing graciously, he knew they mainly cheered his reputation.

You were too forward, he chided himself as he changed out of his costume and sat at the dressing table to remove his makeup. It hurt to be rejected like this, especially by Analisa Marconi. Can you fall in love with someone this suddenly, he had wondered during a mostly sleepless night following their date. Her sweet voice and manner had brought music to the dark, empty chambers of his soul. But mostly it was her don't-lie-to-me eyes that captivated him. I'll never lie to you, he promised her, lying alone in the dark, no matter what the nature of our relationship in the future.

He had let himself think that perhaps he had finally met the one he always knew was out there, waiting for him to find her. You rushed things. She never heard of you until the day before yesterday.

Why this transplanted Santo Sangrían had shed not only light but hope on that lonely place within he had no idea, but he had to find out. There was so little time to do so. If anything angered him, it was that. He had hoped to find the reason tonight.

His first thought was to go home and nurse his depression. His BMW had a different plan. At eleven-thirty, he found himself in the lobby of the Gran Palacio not knowing what to do next.

What if she does not wish to be disturbed? What if she
is...with someone? Are you willing to make a fool of yourself to find out?

The night concierge recognized him at once. "May I
assist you, Señor Cristobal?"

Arturo saw a way out of his dilemma. "Yes, please. I
invited Señorita Marconi—Room 542—to be my guest at
the opera this evening. She did not use her ticket." He
hesitated. "She may have had something else to do, but I
am concerned she might be ill. Have you seen her this
evening?"

"I know the young woman you speak of. To my knowledge she has not left the hotel all day."

"Would you be so good as to call her room? I would
like to assure myself that she is well."

"Certainly." With a certain flair, the concierge picked
up the house phone at his desk and dialed Analisa's room.
"I am sorry, Señor Cristobal. She does not answer." He
made this confession, as if he considered himself personally to blame for the fact that one of his guests had so incon-
siderately broken her appointment with Santo Sangre's
theatrical icon. "Perhaps I dialed incorrectly. Let me try
again... No. Still no answer. I am very sorry."

"Thank you." Arturo slipped the man a generous tip
and began a slow search of the lobby area, including the
gift shops, restaurant, and bar. Several times, he stopped
to sign autographs and chat with admirers, which he did
with his usual grace, while fighting to conceal his impa-
tience.

Twenty minutes later, he returned to the concierge's
station. Reading the man's name badge, he said, "Señor
Yñiguez...Rodrigo...Please ring Señorita Marconi's room
again?"

"Certainly."

When that attempt proved fruitless, Arturo leaned closer to the man and whispered, "I am more than a little con-

cerned that she does not answer. She might be very ill."
He slid another bill across the counter but didn't release it.
"I need you to accompany me to her room."

"Of course," the concierge said, giving the response
that thawed the frozen gratuity.

Arturo had every right to be annoyed at Analisa for
being so inconsiderate. But he wasn't. Something about
her had shed light on a too-long neglected area of his spirit. The streets had toughened him, making him wary of
people's sincerity and motives. The refinement of his professional training and social polish had merely sanded the
rough spots. Just below the surface lived a frightened,
rejected child. The boy's entrepreneurial instincts had
served the young adult Arturo well in dealing with greedy
talent agents and stingy impresarios. But at thirty, the thrill
of success no longer filled the emptiness of house or heart.

When the elevator door opened at the fifth floor,
Yñiguez deferred to Arturo, letting him exit first. He
remained a deferential half-step behind the singer as they
approached Room 542, pass key at the ready.

"The door is open!" Arturo's alarm and agitation multi-
plied with each passing second.

The concierge had a more optimistic reaction. "Then
she must be here." He slipped the key into his jacket pocket and called discreetly, "Señorita Marconi? Ms. Marconi,
are you here?"

Arturo pushed past him and entered the unlit room
which gave every appearance of anticipating the return of
its occupant. "Her purse is on the dressing table," he said.
Moving quickly onto the empty balcony, he looked left and
right at those adjoining it. The morning paper lay open on
the table, his photo staring back at him. "Nothing out
there," he said when he returned to the bedroom.

The concierge poked his head into the bathroom.
"Señor!" His voice quivered. "Look!"

The rod holding the shower curtain had fallen into the tub. The plastic sheet lay in a crumpled wad, half in the tub, half on the floor in front of the toilet. Traces of dried blood marred the shower tiles. Toiletries lay scattered in a chaotic mess on the wash basin counter and floor. Arturo's eye followed a long, vertical scratch on the bathroom door. The whole scene confirmed his worst fears. "¡Dios! Why?"

The concierge started to answer, but kept silent. Arturo's temples throbbed. He made an extra effort to get air all the way to the bottom of his lungs. I am not even supposed to be here! He had intended to accompany Analisa to the end-of-season party. They should be dancing and making plans to see each other again and...kissing, as they had on the first night.

Only twice before had he felt like this. The first time was during the Montenegro regime. The secret police had arrested a popular professor on the trumped-up charge of inciting his students to engage in antigovernment activity. Arturo joined a band of colleagues from the conservatory to march in solidarity with the university students to protest the unjust incarceration. It was to have been a peaceful, nonviolent protest. Suddenly, word spread that military police in full riot gear had blocked all entrances to the square. Someone yelled that the soldiers were about to fire upon the protesters. The crowd scattered in every direction, hiding behind bushes, jamming doorways, scrambling over walls and rooftops. The unity that had been impregnable only moments before dissolved into a "save yourself" flight to escape injury, possibly death.

The second time had been before his operatic debut in the role of the elder Germont in Verdi's La Traviata at the Teatro Bellas Artes.

Arturo steadied himself against the bathroom threshold and tried to clear his head. "Call the police," he ordered.

The concierge started for the bedside phone. "Not from here! We may have already contaminated evidence. We must not make it any worse."

Chapter 19

Arturo paced back and forth in the suite the hotel management had made available to him. His unfocused eyes wasted the view of beachfront and ocean that tourists paid plenty to enjoy. A knock jarred him from his nightmarish thoughts. "Come in!"

Chief Inspector Armando Madrigal entered. On his face, the burdens of responsibility and bad news. Arturo motioned him into a chair near the wet bar. "Well?"

"My men have conducted a thorough examination of the crime scene." Madrigal's tone was somber, respectful. "There is no evidence of forced entry. Nor does robbery seem to have been the motive."

Arturo's rage went beyond normal concern for another human being in danger. He needed to wallow in that rage, at least for now. Later, he'd have time to sort out why this atrocity had left him feeling so personally violated.

"You say you were with Señorita Marconi last evening?"

"Yes."

"Did you notice anyone paying unusual attention to you?"

"Not that I am aware of." Arturo's memory flashed to the couple in the shadows of the hotel entrance, but he dismissed them. "We toured the city. I showed her the opera house. We had dinner. I brought her back to the hotel."

"Where did you eat?"

"El Papagallo, on the pier."

The inspector recorded the name in his notebook. "Tell me what you know about Señorita Marconi."

"Very little, really. I met her the other day at the U.S. Embassy...She was born here. Adopted by an American couple. Her parents died in a plane crash last winter...I invited her to the opera tonight. When she failed to come,

I became concerned. I thought she might be ill. You know, the local water, or something like that. So I came to see if she was all right. I . . ." He had run out of words that made sense.

The Inspector closed his notebook. "I'd be grateful if you would make yourself available should we have any further questions."

"Of course." Arturo took a card from his wallet and wrote his private number on the front. "Call me any time."

Studying Arturo's face, Madrigal took the card.

"What is it, Inspector?"

"I don't know how to say this delicately."

"Then, just say it."

"Your interest in Señorita Marconi's disappearance seems quite . . ."

"Personal?"

"Yes."

Arturo flushed. "I have hardly had time to get to know her, Inspector. But, yes, I suppose I do have a personal interest in getting her back unharmed." With a shrug, he added, "Please do not ask me to explain it. I cannot."

Madrigal hesitated, digesting the response. "I'm going to tell you something. This is a delicate police matter. You must keep it in the strictest confidence. We have evidence that whoever did this specifically targeted Señorita Marconi for abduction."

The news sapped what was left of Arturo's strength. His knees buckled, and he dropped into a nearby chair. "Why? ... Who?"

"There is a group calling themselves Los Dejados. They oppose the adoption of Santo Sangrían children by foreigners, believing such adoption to be a form of kidnapping. They retaliate by snatching female adoptees who return to this country. Apparently, the idea is to force them to have children as some kind of restitution."

"That's insane!"

"No doubt. But they are already implicated in the death of one young woman...an Italian national."

"An adoptee?"

"Yes."

"They murdered her?"

"The actual cause of death was complications of childbirth. It makes little difference. We consider it a homicide. Having lost their first victim, they seem to have found another to replace her."

The thought of Analisa being held against her will and used as a sex slave and baby machine sickened Arturo as nothing had in his whole life. Without knowing how to begin, he vowed to use all his resources to find her and save her from this lifelong, living hell. Even if it meant banging on every door in the city. "How do they identify their victims?"

"Officially, I must say only that we are investigating this. Unofficially, you can read this to mean I am working closely with the American Embassy on this matter."

"May I go now?"

"By all means," Madrigal said. "Remember. What I told you is for your information only. Do you understand?"

"Yes. Thank you." Arturo left the room. Using the wall to steady himself, he made his way uncertainly down the ornately papered hallway toward the elevator.

❦ ❦ ❦

Dave Gallego sat across the mahogany dining room table from Father Tom Raymond. The remains of the traditional "fatted calf"—a prime rib roast—lay on the table between them.

The high school girl who staffed the rectory office in the evenings popped her head into the room. "Your appointment's here, Father Dave."

"Thanks, Sarah."

He began his evening schedule helping Steve Forrester and Natalie Hines firm up a December date and time for their wedding ceremony. At seven-thirty, he counseled— rather, listened to—Margaret Arnold. Unlike Steve and Natalie, Margaret wanted no more of marriage, at least not with the taciturn Ed Arnold.

"He's forty-two years old, Father, and all he cares about is his damn computer. I used to pray for power outages so he'd give me some attention. Now, he's taken care of that by plugging his system into a damn battery backup unit." She apologized for the vulgarity.

From Margaret, Dave moved on to the Ministry Center and a liturgy planning meeting. The members of the com-mittee wanted to know the theme of his weekend homily. He faked that one, tossing out some broad themes. At least he knew the gospel reading for the coming Sunday. Excusing himself after dodging that bullet, he moved on to the less-threatening Knights of Columbus, where discus-sion centered around work assignments for the upcoming pancake breakfast. After the meeting, one of the Knights cornered him seeking advice on how to deal with his incor-rigible sixteen-year-old son.

At ten-thirty, Dave dragged himself up the stairs to his room, which was actually three rooms, counting the bath-room. A twenty-five-inch television set and VCR occupied a corner opposite the sitting room sofa. The Spartan bed-room housed a double bed, dresser, nightstand, and anoth-er, smaller TV. Unlike a married man's living space, noth-ing about these celibate quarters revealed the influence of a female presence or taste.

After a long day spent battling for the hearts and souls of God's people, there was no one at home to wind down with. Tom was ensconced behind his own closed door down the hall. Canned laughter from some dumb sitcom forced its way through the hollow-core door and raced down the short hallway toward Dave's room. He hadn't yet figured out why parish priests preferred to be alone, watching their separate television sets, nursing their separate feelings of isolation. Why can't we admit we need each other's company during this weary time at the end of the day? he wondered as he brushed his teeth and invented new excuses for not flossing or using the rubber tip to massage his gums. We preach community, but deep down we believe the need for it is a weakness. He rinsed his mouth and watched the soapy water swirl down the drain. We tell ourselves we're tougher than the layman. Our patron saint's the bleepin' Lone Ranger!

He thought about Steve and Natalie, probably chatting happily about their future now that they had an actual date, time, and place for their marriage. He wondered if they'd end this day by going their separate ways. He doubted it. Steve had his own apartment, and Natalie had hesitated ever-so-slightly before giving her parents' address as her place of residence. That's okay. He envied them, as he had envied a lot of young couples he had married.

Channel 2's late news was just starting as Dave slipped into bed. He often read past midnight, but tonight he was on all-night emergency call. The odds were fifty-fifty he'd be summoned to one of the local hospitals. Is it my imagination, he wondered, or do Catholics get into more accidents than Protestants and Jews?

Dave considered hospital chaplaincy the unglamorous underbelly of parish ministry. This was especially true of the 3 A.M. visits to a blood-and-guts ER. The church expected him to apply the healing sacramental oil and pray for someone stupid enough to drink all evening, then make a pass at another guy's girlfriend.

The lead news story interrupted his distractions. He had missed the opening but locked in when he heard "Santo Sangre."

"The victim was apparently abducted from her hotel room in downtown Santa Catalina. Police in the tiny island republic will say only that they are following a lead but have no suspects at this time. A U.S. Embassy source, speaking on condition of anonymity, suggested the crime may have been committed by a local terrorist group opposed to the adoption of Santo Sangrían children by foreigners. Why this victim, who is unmarried, was targeted remains unclear at this hour."

"What's her name?" Dave shouted at the reporter.

"Once again, Analisa Marconi, a U.S. citizen from Anaheim, California, was the victim of an apparent kidnapping carried out earlier today in broad daylight at a luxury hotel in the capital of Santo Sangre. In other news, Chief Ron Wilson of the L.A.P.D. insisted today . . ."

Dave leaped out of bed, cursing at the glowing video messenger. He wanted to sprout wings and fly out the window. "Why didn't I push harder to go with her?" He fumbled on his nightstand for the scrap of paper on which he had scribbled Analisa's overseas number and grabbed the phone. The light on the number pad glowed a sickly green, mirroring his feelings exactly. He punched in the number.

"Hotel Gran Palacio," the operator answered. "How may I direct your call?"

"Señorita Marconi, please," he blurted. The irregular beat of his heart drained oxygen from his brain. "Room 542."

Silence on the other end. Then, a male voice. "I am sorry, Señorita Marconi...is no longer registered."

"No longer registered? What does that mean?"

"I can only refer you to the American Embassy for further information."

"You bet I'll call them!" Dave's vision blurred, and he felt his way back to the bed where he plotted how to rescue Analisa.

At 4 A.M., he was still awake. No point trying to reach the Embassy for another hour or so. The hospital hadn't called. For the first time, he actually wanted the phone to ring. He needed the distraction of work to keep his worst fears at bay.

The voice of the newscaster droned inside his head, "Analisa Marconi, a U.S. citizen...the victim of an apparent kidnapping . . ."

Chapter 20

Analisa's first waking sensation was nausea. A trace of putrid chemical hung about her nostrils like a terrifying nightmare. The drug, whatever it was, had scrambled her memory, leaving her disoriented. Wave after wave of dry heaves convulsed her body, as it fought to rid itself of the substance. Gradually, her insides stabilized. Her head cleared. She needed to reconstruct the events leading to her present state but focusing her thoughts proved difficult.

Blindfolded and naked, she was propped up on what seemed to be a hard, cot-sized shelf. That damn maid! Why have they done this to me? And why had they taped her wrists around her shins, so that her thighs pushed against her breasts?

With difficulty, she edged along the wall, feeling her way inch by inch with her elbows and toes. "Where are my clothes?" she asked the darkness. Wherever she was, the room had the smell of accumulated neglect. Her nostrils flared to snatch what little oxygen remained in her dusty prison space. A dull ache drummed from a spot behind her left ear. It traveled across her temple and pulsed a savage beat below her eye. Despite the stifling heat, a chill convulsed her body. Dim light made a futile effort to penetrate the blindfold.

What day is this? How long have I been here?

Reconstructing the events that had brought her to this place wasn't easy. She had started the day—Wednesday, if this was the same day—excited about going to the opera and spending one last evening with Arturo Cristobal.

Then, the attack!

Does anyone even know I'm missing?

Another wave of dry retching sent stabbing pains into her chest and abdomen.

Why did this happen?

A faint echo whispered, "Lydia Vitale." It was Vice
Consul Eric Small's voice. She forced her memory to
replay his exact words, Your presence in the country is
known to people who may be responsible for her death.
Why hadn't she taken his warning more seriously?

Arturo Cristobal! What must he think of me? She imagined him waiting at the theater. What would he have done
when she failed to show? What would I have done? That
was simple. I'm not into chasing after a guy who stands me
up.

She hoped Arturo was more forgiving than herself.
Perhaps he called the hotel to ask for her? Sure, like a
famous opera star is going to worry about someone who
had better things to do than hear him sing. With a free
ticket!

Still, something had sparked to life between them that
night on the stage of the Bellas Artes. She prayed that he
had at least been interested enough to make inquiries.

❊ ❊ ❊

Analisa had been awake for about an hour when she heard
footsteps outside the room. She stiffened at this first sign
she hadn't been abandoned and left to starve. She welcomed the sounds of life as much as they filled her with terror.

"Give her more time," a woman pleaded in Spanish.

It was the voice Analisa had heard in her hotel room.
The maid! Her first instinct was to unleash every obsceni-
ty she knew.

"Open the door and get in there," a man ordered.

"Open it yourself," the woman snarled.

Analisa had a morbid interest in the bitter exchange.
She hated being alone. At the same time, she preferred letting this woman absorb the man's wrath.

A key entered the lock with a metallic scrape. Analisa crushed her knees even tighter against her chest and turned her face to the wall.

"You are awake, Señorita Marconi," the woman said, obviously struggling to put the English sentence together. It was a young voice but not a friendly one. The woman approached, bringing with her the scent of cooking oil and garlic which pushed aside the mustiness that dominated the atmosphere. Analisa wanted so much to see her.

Footsteps shuffled farther away in the room, a man's feet, Analisa guessed. She resented having these strangers' eyes fill themselves with her nakedness. A chair moved. She pressed harder against the rough wood-planked wall, as a new wave of terror jolted her body.

"I regret your injury," the woman said. "I did not intend to hurt you. If you had not fought me . . ."

This has to be a dream, Analisa decided. If it is, nothing bad can happen to me. Soon she'd wake up in her hotel room, angry that she had fallen asleep and missed the opera.

The woman sat down beside her. "It is my duty to explain why you are here...and why you must stay with us."

Analisa offered no sign that she heard the woman or feared her in any way. She became a sculpture, without sight or voice, making no contact with her captors other than listening.

"You were stolen from us...an innocent child." The woman spoke in maternal tones, not scolding but as if revealing facts long hidden, information a grown child needed to hear and understand. "Perhaps without malice, your North American parents did...a terrible thing. They stripped you of your birthright. Robbed you of your rich culture, your language, even your name. In turn, they offered a life of opulent poverty.

"You have returned to us," she continued. "Now, you have an opportunity to give something back to your country, to make...restitution for what you have become."

Analisa's spirit emerged from the distant place to which it had fled. So, it's money they want. What were the terms of her ransom? Barely moving her lips, she whispered, "How much do you want for my release?" She hardly heard her voice and for a moment doubted she had actually spoken.

"No money!"

What little warmth Analisa had detected in the woman's voice had vanished.

"You will pay your debt...another way."

"How?"

"*Niños.* You will give us babies to repay Santo Sangre for the Stolen Ones."

"I don't under—" Suddenly, Analisa's fate became as clear as the cloudless morning had been. They had no interest in her money. They wanted her living flesh...and her babies. Like Lydia Vitale, she had received a life sentence without possibility of parole. They allowed her no defense, no opportunity to plead her case with persuasive arguments.

The woman must have sensed her captive's dawning comprehension. She spoke more rapidly, using the English words she knew, Spanish to fill in the blanks.

"You were born here. This is where God intended you to live. You will spend the rest of your life with us."

"Who are you?" Analisa asked with as much insistence as she dared.

Resuming her normal pace, the woman said, "For now you shall know us only as...Los Dejados."

Analisa repeated the words, trying to make sense of them.

"The Abandoned Ones." The woman spat the words. "Those who were left behind." Even in her terrorized state,

Analisa sensed the woman's bitterness and pain. "Fate plucked you from the life you were born to and gave you every advantage the world offered. Did you ever in your life of ease and comfort think about the brothers and sisters that same Fate passed over?"

Life of ease? Analisa thought. She had never considered her life easy. She had studied hard and worked her way through school to help her parents with the cost of a private college education. She had a job waiting for her and, despite her insurance nest egg, intended to continue working for many years to come. Yet, from her captors' point of view, the opportunity to grow up in America where they thought the streets were paved with gold must have seemed like the greatest of blessings and injustices.

"Listen to me, Señorita Marconi!" The woman's throat was tight, her voice strained. Analisa obeyed. "Have you ever thought about your true mother? Have you ever once cared what became of her and the other children she bore?" The heat of this wildfire raged across the parched terrain of deprivation, with too-vivid memories charring everything in their path. "They went to bed hungry, sick from picking their food off a spider-infested dirt floor, while you ate well, went to the best schools, wore fine clothes, got invited to parties. There were no parties for Los Dejados, no stylish clothing."

"You said yourself I'm not the guilty one."

"That no longer matters." She got up and stood beside Analisa. "First you will eat something. Then, your new life will begin."

When the man across the room cackled, Analisa's skin shriveled. Her jailers left the room, leaving her alone again. The two pairs of footsteps faded, replaced by sounds of tropical life. Flashes of lightning sent shards of brightness through her blindfold, followed by explosions of thunder that shook the pallet on which she huddled. Wind and rain pounded at the windows.

What irony, she thought. The elements are anxious to get in, when all I want is to escape.

The storm ended minutes later, almost as suddenly as it had begun. Interrupted by the rain, neighborhood birds resumed their bold chatter. Rivulets of perspiration idled their way between Analisa's breasts on their way to her navel.

The lightning had an energizing effect. It jolted her from her lethargy and stiffened her backbone to resist the violence that lay ahead. For the first time since her abduction, she felt something besides sheer terror. Anger washed through her like a cleansing shower, removing the grime of despair.

She had never allowed anyone to abuse her. I won't start now, no matter what they think they're going to do to me. She began by playing back what the woman had told her.

Fate plucked me from the life I was born to.

So? Isn't that what adoption's all about? Who knows why some kids are chosen and others aren't? Isn't that one of the great mysteries of life?

Did you ever think about us, your brothers and sisters who were passed over?

Sure. Often. Analisa knew how lucky she had been.

Had she ever thought about her birth mother?

Why the hell do you think I'm here now?

You will give us babies to repay your country for the Stolen Ones.

Analisa shook her head. I don't think so!

🌸 🌸 🌸

"Should I go to Santo Sangre to help find Analisa?" Dave wondered out loud over breakfast. His mind was already ninety percent made up.

Tom tossed his starched napkin onto the linen table-cloth. "I can't believe we're having this conversation."

Imitating Tom, Dave dropped his napkin on the table. "Me either."

"I know you and Analisa are friends. I didn't realize it went...deeper than that."

"Don't let your imagination run wild. It hasn't gone 'deeper than that.'" Dave hoped Tom believed his version of the truth. "It's just that...there's a new equation operating now."

"She's in trouble."

"A classic understatement."

"I'm sure the police and the Embassy will do everything they can. The best thing we can do is pray for her."

Dave twisted sideways in his chair. "Get real, Tom." He wasn't angry at his co-worker. No other priest had been more supportive. Not every parish welcomed a black priest with the warmth St. Boniface had. "Let's not turn this into a discussion about the efficacy of prayer. I've just about decided to go. I'll need some time off."

"You think you can add something to what they're doing at the local level?"

"I know her. They don't. I know how she thinks...what she must be going through. She's probably just a case number to them."

They heard footsteps on the stairway outside the dining room.

Tom nodded in the direction of the hallway. "Have you mentioned any of this to Janet?"

Dave shook his head. He had the greatest respect for Janet Ebersol, associate pastor and his equal on the staff of St. Boniface. Even as a teenager, Janet had felt the call to pastoral ministry. Being Roman Catholic, this left her with fewer options than her Protestant sisters with the same desire to serve God and church. Never at any time in her nearly fifty years had she given serious consideration to joining a community of women religious. "Wasn't my call-ing," was how she put it.

"Did I hear my name?" Janet called from the hallway. She stuck her head into the dining room and glanced at the tray of bacon on the table. "Looks good." She broke off half a slice with her fingers and put it in her mouth. "I'm not a great fan of bacon." She licked her thumb and index finger with the relish of an actor in a Farmer John com-mercial.

"So I see," Tom said. "Sit down a minute."

"No thanks. I have other plans. I was just coming down the stairs when I heard you ask Dave if he had men-tioned something-or-other to Janet."

Dave sighed deeply, unsure he wanted to extend the discussion. "We were talking about Analisa."

"Poor thing. Anything new?"

"I want to go over there," Dave said.

Tom seemed determined to involve Janet. "Stay a minute. I'd like Dave to get a woman's perspective on this."

Dave didn't think Dave needed a woman's perspective. He trusted his own instincts and feelings. Since he also trusted Janet's, he relented. "You know Analisa and I have been friends since she was in high school."

"No need for a detailed history," she said.

"That's what I like about you," Tom said. "You're a get-to-the-bottom-line kind of person."

She frowned. "I hope that's a compliment."

"Well," Dave continued. "I'm thinking of going to Santo Sangre. Maybe I can be of some help to the police. No one there knows her."

Janet moved one of the high-backed chairs and sat down. For what seemed like an eternity, she studied Dave's eyes, his face, his fidgeting hands. Oddly, he felt warmed by her gaze. It was good to have a woman as a peer in the ministry. Good for the parish and, at times like this, good for the priests whose maleness gave them access to a sacrament and title unavailable to equally or better-qualified women like Janet.

"I've never said anything before," she began. "Figured it was none of my business. I know there's a special relationship between you and Analisa, one that may defy traditional definitions, explanations, and what the old-timers liked to call 'clerical propriety.'" She smiled. "I never felt there was anything but a genuine love and respect between you."

Dave sagged in his chair. "Am I that transparent?" The hard wooden chair back kept him from falling over.

"Only to me," Janet said.

"Good."

"And to every other woman in the parish."

"Oh God!" He cleared his throat. "Okay. Now what about Santo Sangre? Tell me what you think."

"My opinion? As a woman?" Janet's soft gray eyes were kind, nonjudgmental. "Normally, I'd say leave her alone. She's a big girl, a woman, as I guess you've noticed. But this isn't a normal situation. After all the Marconis meant to this parish, I'd be disappointed if someone didn't go. I vote for you."

She glanced at her watch and started for the door. Turning to Tom with an innocent shrug, she said, "You did ask my opinion."

Tom looked defeated. "Yes, I certainly did."

"Thanks, Janet." Dave felt humbled but genuinely grateful.

"Let's hope Analisa returns to us," Janet said. "It'll be interesting to see just who comes back, the Analisa we knew or someone very different, a woman we haven't seen before."

Janet had zeroed in on Dave's worst fear—Analisa returning so changed or damaged by her experience that they had lost the common ground on which they had stood all these years. The last thing he wanted was for her to become, like many other people he had been close to, one more dot on the timeline of his life.

Chapter 21

It was nearly dawn by the time Arturo Cristobal returned to his estate in the Colonia de la Paz on the North Coast Highway. As usual, he was alone in the five-bedroom house.

After preparing dinner each day except Sunday, his cook/housekeeper, Emilia Jimenez, returned to her family across town in a taxi hired and paid for by her employer. In the morning, another taxi waited at her door to drive her to the estate. Because she respected his privacy more than any of her predecessors, Arturo paid her well, even when his extended absences permitted her to spend most of her time with her husband and six children.

Arturo plugged in the coffee pot Emilia had left ready for him. He opened the refrigerator but saw nothing remotely tempting. Mug in hand, he moved to his bedroom and opened the drapes. A few feet beyond the sliding door, a large rectangular lap pool caught the colors of the rising sun. It sent an invitation to seek solace from his worries in its warm waters.

"I will report Señorita Marconi's abduction to the U.S. Embassy immediately," Chief Inspector Madrigal had assured him. "They will notify her family in California."

"Her parents are dead. She has no one. That's why she came here. To trace what might be left of her birth family."

It wasn't true, Arturo recalled, that Analisa had no one. There was a Father Gallego. He should be notified. Not by me, though. This sudden attack of jealousy rocked Arturo. It was a feeling he had never experienced before. Not over a woman. Occasionally, he had felt twinges of jealousy when another baritone plucked a prize role from his grasp. He had never cared enough about a woman to experience the sort of misguided loathing he now felt toward a priest of the church who had a prior claim on Analisa's affections.

He stripped off his clothes and grabbed a robe and towel from the bathroom. Perhaps swimming laps would neutralize his rampaging anxiety. He set his athletic body on automatic pilot, alternating twenty-five-yard laps with a "three-B" medley of breaststroke, backstroke, and butterfly. At the end, he added a fast-paced freestyle lap for good measure.

His demons survived the exorcism. Arturo climbed out of the water and slipped into the absorbent white robe on which the royal purple initials, AC, were embroidered in script over the left breast.

Two seemingly disconnected events had converged to throw him into his current state. In recent months, he had grown dissatisfied with his once-coveted bachelorhood. A vague longing to share his life, his success, and this too-large, too-empty house, had worked its way into his consciousness.

None of the women he had known, some quite beautiful and talented, had held his interest longer than it took to have dinner at César's or sit through a concert at the Bellas Artes. He counted on the fingers of one hand, including his thumb, the women with whom he had slept.

How then had Analisa Marconi found the key to the hidden chamber in which he stored his unshared love? He had been eager to spend last evening with her to prove he had correctly read the messages of his heart.

The depth of his misery and fear for her caused him to wander aimlessly from room to room. No use going to bed. Instead, he sat down at the glistening grand piano in his glass-walled conservatory. The morning sun that filled the circular room with light lacked strength to penetrate the darkness that had settled upon him. He prepared himself to live without sun or light until Analisa was free and safe again.

Without having made a decision to play or sing, the
words, *Il prim' amore non si scorda mai*, filled the room.
The first-love lyrics served as the medium through which
he transferred his emotions into the keys and thence into
the fresh morning air.

Song was Arturo's form of meditation. Many times he
had heard the old choir master at Santa María de Soledad
say, "St. Gregory himself told us, 'He who sings prays
twice.'" Arturo wasn't sure to this day what it meant, but
something told him it was all right to believe it.

As he sang, he prayed his song to go forth and find its
way to Analisa, providing comfort and strength if alive, or
serving as his heartfelt, bitter eulogy if she was not. "One
never forgets his first love." With these words, the song
concluded. If God is ever good enough to let me get hold
of those evil bastard cowards, he swore, I'll kill them with
my own bare hands.

With this unholy vow, silence fell upon the Cristobal
estate.

❦ ❦ ❦

Through the windshield of their unmarked Corolla, Chief
Inspector Madrigal and Detective Rodrigo Trujillo watched
Pedro Arroyo park his bicycle behind a bench on the south
side of the Ministry of Customs and Immigration. It was
just after nine in the morning, the day after Analisa
Marconi's disappearance.

The technician removed a chain from his jacket pocket,
and wove it through the spokes of the back wheel and
around one of the bench's wrought-iron legs. He sealed
their union with a combination lock, making bike and
bench look like a couple of old veterans settling in for a
few hours of mostly fictitious war stories.

"So that's what a computer whiz looks like," Madrigal
said.

Trujillo grunted. "For a smart guy, he looks pretty stupid, if you ask me."

Arroyo was slightly built and short, even by Santo Sangrían standards. He wore wire-rimmed glasses and seemed to have just gotten out of bed.

"Let's go!"

Driver and passenger doors swung open like the wings of a seagull taking flight. Both men raced toward Arroyo who had just descended the steps to his basement office and inserted his key in the lock.

Trujillo reached down and grabbed the back of the technician's light windbreaker, giving it a sharp twist. Arroyo's body contorted as he stumbled off-balance and fell against the stone wall of the ministry building. Instinctively, he struggled to free himself from his attacker's grasp—a futile maneuver. The detective managed to keep his footing and tightened his grip on the young man's clothing.

"Pedro Arroyo, I am Chief Inspector Madrigal of the Santa Catalina Police. I have a warrant for your arrest on suspicion of complicity in the abduction of an American national." He opened the leather folder that held his photo ID and gold-plated badge. Dangling his authority an inch from the suspect's nose, he added a brusque, "Come with us."

"You crazy? I'm a computer technician, a civil servant." He pleaded as if one if not the other of these titles had to be sufficient to prove his innocence. "Ow!" he yelped as Trujillo handcuffed his wrists. "I'll be late for work."

Madrigal tossed a smirk at his partner. "Very late, I'd say." He pushed the terrified man into the back seat of the police car. As they sped away, his prisoner glanced longingly at his chained-up bicycle, then slumped into the seat.

"Looks safe to me," the Inspector said. "You did such a good job securing it, I suspect it will still be there if you ever get out of prison."

❦ ❦ ❦

By noon, the skies over Santa Catalina had clouded. A light veil of mist fell, increasing the humidity. Arturo's innards rebelled against the impotence of inactivity. He retrieved a business card from the jacket he had worn two nights before. He had scribbled Father David Gallego's name on it, along with "St. Boniface—Anaheim." Why he had written it, he wasn't sure. Now, he was glad.

He punched overseas information on his telephone keypad and leaned back into a white leather sofa that faced the grand piano. Beyond the beach, the ocean's mood had darkened in beat with his own.

An operator informed him there was no listing for a David Gallego in Anaheim.

"Of course, he must have a private number," he muttered. He then asked for and got the church's number.

"St. Boniface," a woman answered.

"Father Gallego, please." A moment later he heard, "Father Dave speaking," the response downbeat, without warmth.

"Father, my name is Arturo Cristobal. I am calling from Santo Sangre."

"Yes?" The priest's voice seemed wary, expectant.

"I am a friend of Analisa Marconi." Arturo hoped this might reassure him.

"I wasn't aware she had any friends in Santo Sangre."

Arturo felt no need to apologize for calling himself Analisa's friend. "She mentioned your name. I'm afraid I have some unfortunate news. Señorita Marconi has been—"

"I already heard. It was on the news last night. The report was sketchy. What more can you tell me?"

"Not much. She was abducted from her hotel room sometime yesterday."

"Please, Señor Cristobal," Father Gallego pleaded, "tell me what you know."

The noticeable thaw at the other end encouraged Arturo to share more. "I am the one who discovered she was missing. There seems to have been a struggle in the bathroom of her hotel room. We found some blood, but I do not think she was seriously injured. At least, not at the time of her abduction. I assure you the police are doing their best to find and rescue her."

"I'm flying down. In fact, I was just packing to leave. I'll be on he last flight from Miami to Santa Catalina." Father Gallego had responded more like an intimate family member than a parish priest. "May I call you when I get there? I don't know anyone. It will be pretty late when I arrive."

"I would be honored to have you as my guest, unless you prefer to stay at the cathedral or a local parish."

"I'd rather stay with you, if you're sure it's all right."

Arturo gave Father Gallego his telephone number and wrote down the details of the priest's flight arrangements. "I'll meet you at the airport."

Arturo's next call was to Chief Inspector Madrigal.

"You'll be happy to know we have in custody a suspected accomplice," the Inspector said. "He claims to know nothing, but he's involved—right up to his trim little mustache."

"Let me come down there and wring the truth out of him!" Arturo's knuckles whitened from choking the molded plastic handset.

His sudden rage amused Madrigal. "Good thing I'm the policeman and you the singer."

The Inspector's stifled laughter deflated Arturo. He loosened his grip on the innocent receiver. "A priest is coming from the States. He appears to be a close friend of Señorita Marconi. He will be staying with me."

"A priest?"

"I was surprised, too." Arturo didn't want to fuel the conversation, out of respect for Analisa.

"Let me know when he arrives. I may want to talk to him."

Chapter 22

Some time after Analisa's jailers left her in the stale-smelling prison, the door opened again. The woman. She placed a small tray on the bunk. "You must eat," she said, cutting Analisa's wrist bonds. "Remove the blindfold."

Analisa reached behind her head to untie the knot, a simple action that made her arms ache. With hands and eyes liberated, she sought the face of her kidnapper. At the same time, her hands moved toward the aroma emanating from the steaming plate of beans. She expected to see the features of a hardened criminal. Instead, a classic *mestizo* Indian returned her gaze, face almost perfectly round; intense, with inset eyes that looked capable—given other circumstances and opportunities—of reflecting all the love in the world. In them, Analisa read ambivalence, envy, and a boiling mass of nameless emotions.

In addition to the steaming bowl of beans, Analisa found a hunk of brown bread and a glass of water in a green plastic tumbler. She didn't know how long it had been since she had eaten. Her stomach gave no clue because her brain had ceased sending the usual signals telling her when to eat or drink, when to urinate, or when it was time to sleep. Seeing the water made her aware her throat was a desert. She reached for the glass and stopped. Automatic alarms sounded the foreign traveler's caveat.

The woman read Analisa's dilemma and gave a half-smile. "You drink." She mimed the action. "*Agua* okay. From bottle."

Analisa hesitated, then decided she didn't care if the water was from a crystal mountain spring or the nearest toilet. Greedily, she put the tumbler to her lips and forced herself to sip rather than gulp. "*Gracias.*" Clutching the container to her body the way she did her purse in a crowd, she said, "Who are you? *¿Quién es?*"

The question surprised her jailer. "We are Los—"

Analisa cut her off. "No. I want to know who"—she pointed—"you are? What is your name? *¿Su nombre?*"

The woman glanced toward the open door, and Analisa realized she wasn't the only frightened female in the room.

"My name is Marta."

Analisa repeated the name with what little authority was left in her voice, "Marta, I want my clothes."

"Después."

"After what?"

"He will come soon. After that," was all Marta volunteered.

"What is his name?"

"No. Not allowed."

"You're afraid of him too, aren't you? *¿Tienes miedo también, Marta?*" By using the woman's name often, Analisa hoped to connect with her, woman to woman.

Another glance toward the door. "*Sí.* A little. Sometimes. Not always."

Analisa sensed her life was in the hands of this woman and the man who had sat in silence during her earlier visit.

"If you won't tell me his name, tell me something about him. Por favor, Marta." She patted the mat. "Please sit. Talk to me for a moment."

Marta edged toward the pallet as if assessing the danger from both sides. "I cannot be away long. He will come...looking."

"Just for a moment...please."

"A good man," Marta began. "Suffered much. He was oldest child. Mother never married. Had several men. Children by all. Too many babies. No money. The men were lazy. Drunkards. Lu—" She caught herself, paused, then continued. "They beat him. At ten years old, they sent him to find work, but too small. Very little earnings. To provide, his mother offered the two youngest babies to a lawyer. Girls. He gave food. Some money. Told her, 'I will find rich Norteamericanos.' My friend hates his mother for giving away his sisters. He hates his sisters for leaving him behind to live in Santa Catalina's streets of hell."

Marta turned her head away, hiding tears that threatened to overflow the banks of her large almond eyes. Analisa thought of Arturo, bright, talented, forced onto the streets as a child to make his own way. She reached out to touch Marta's hand and noticed she wore no wedding band. Analisa had assumed her jailers were husband and wife. "Is that your story too?"

"I too was left behind."

"Los Dejados."

"Sí." Marta wiped her cheeks against the shoulder of her plain, coarse blouse.

"And now you've found a way to get revenge."

"You call it revenge. We do not consider it so."

"In your eyes, I too was a victim."

"Victim!" Marta raged at the comparison. "I have no education. I work part-time in a shop for low wages. The rest of the week I scrub floors for rich women too lazy to clean their own houses. They pay me a few *cruzeros* to do their dirty work. I cannot buy the clothes you wear. My hair will never look like yours."

Analisa retreated from that line of argument. She needed to befriend Marta. Her captors would never accept the idea that this adoptee from streets-of-gold California was a victim in the same way they were.

"You're right, Marta. I'm sorry. I was the lucky one."

Marta picked up the bowl of reddish-black beans. She urged Analisa to eat, which she did, reluctantly at first, then more greedily until the bowl was empty. Marta took the dish. She started to pick up the tray, but stopped and laid a callused palm against Analisa's cheek. Her once-resolute eyes swam in shallow pools of doubt and fear. Although Marta's lips barely moved and no sound escaped her finely shaped mouth, Analisa was sure she had formed the word, "Hermanas."

"Sisters? You and me?" She wondered what Marta meant. To prolong their conversation, she asked, "Is he your husband?"

Marta lowered her eyes.

"Your lover, then?" Analisa searched for the answer in Marta's expression, but she had turned her head away a second time.

"I suppose," she whispered.

"You love him?"

Marta gazed into Analisa's eyes. "He is my hero."

"Does your hero love you?"

The hint of a proud smile parted Marta's lips. "In his way. *Sí.*"

Analisa had a good idea of what awaited her. Surely, Marta, too, knew the routine. It was impossible to reconcile the contradiction between Marta's love for her man and what she tolerated in the name of revenge.

"How do you feel when your lover sleeps with another woman?"

Marta pulled the strings tight around the sack of her spilling dignity and pride. "Neither lust nor love brings him to your bed. It is for Santo Sangre alone."

"For love of country you'll stand by and let him rape me?"

"No rape!" Marta insisted.

"Do you expect me to give myself to him willingly?"

"He knows. The other *cone*— She was never willing."

"What did you call her?"

"Nothing."

"'Ko-nay' something." Analisa shrank back with the realization of how Los Dejados viewed her role in their scheme of restitution. "You were going to say, '*coneja.*' Is that what I am? Your lover's little 'mother rabbit'?"

"Shut up!" Marta immediately glanced toward the partially open door.

When she tried to get away, Analisa grabbed her wrist and welded her fingers to it. "How do you know I can have children?   Have you researched my medical records? What if I don't produce? Will you kill me and eat me for dinner?"

"You will not be harmed."

Analisa didn't believe it. She pointed to her naked body and showed Marta the gash on her head. "What do you call this? A day at the beach?" She relaxed her grip. It felt good to take the offensive, although it was clear that jousting with Marta wasn't a worthy warm-up for what lay ahead.

In other circumstances, Analisa could have liked Marta, perhaps even been her friend. Right now, she was angry and frustrated that this woman had let herself be so deluded. Marta gathered the tray and moved toward the door.

"I want my clothes!" Analisa demanded.

"Soon." The door closed. The key turned in the lock.

❊ ❊ ❊

Later, when the man entered the room, hysteria signals raced through Analisa's nervous system. She fought to stay calm, focused. Los Dejados had stolen her body. Her mind belonged to her. To come out of this situation alive and intact, I have to stay in control. Control. Her only weapon in this battle for integrity and survival. You've talked your way out of jams before, girl. Well, this one's the mother of all jams.

The man closed the door behind him. The click of the lock was like a judge's gavel pronouncing sentence. Without turning the light on, he moved toward her in the semi-darkness. Stopping at the table, he struck a match and lit the stub of a smoke-blackened candle.

Analisa kept her head down but turned toward him just enough to notice he was barefoot and wore a pair of faded cut-off blue jeans. Nothing else. Mentally, she covered her own nakedness. She pretended he was blind, unable to see the breasts only partially concealed behind a double shield of folded arms and tucked-in knees...that he hadn't noticed the tufts of exposed dark hair camouflaging her vaginal area.

Hoping to distract him as long as possible, she said, "I'd like to know who you are."

He sat down at the end of her pallet, inches from her toes. A pervasive odor of onions and garlic from a recent meal offended her nostrils. With a pen knife he withdrew from his pocket, he cut away the tape from her ankles. Although free, she maintained her drawn-in, defensive posture. "My name is not important." He seasoned his Spanish with an occasional attempt at English. Analisa recoiled at the sound of his surprisingly high-pitched voice, but there was no hint of imminent threat in his refusal to identify himself. He pointed to his chest, then to her. "You are one of us now."

"I will never be one of you!" With nowhere to go, she clung to the wall.

He touched her foot. "In time."

"Never," she repeated in Spanish.

He brightened, almost smiled, apparently pleased at her attempt to use her native tongue. "My...friend...she told you why you are here." His hand moved across her ankle and advanced lightly up her calf.

This gentle approach didn't fool Analisa. He had trespassed on private property without permission and with malicious intent. Think! she commanded herself. Take charge before he does. But creative options were in short supply.

He eased his hand into the sharp-angled cavity behind her rigidly bent knee. Only his index finger ventured forward along the underside of her thigh.

Stall him. Find a way! She sensed she was not in danger of being beaten as long as she did nothing to provoke him into an irrational act. Presenting a calm exterior, keeping him distracted with ideological issues, might at least postpone the sexual assault she dreaded. It might also save her life. "Tell me more about Los Dejados."

"For long time, foreigners come to Santo Sangre...for babies. Among them, the people you call parents. They steal our children with help from money-grabbing attorneys who exploit the poor."

Analisa snuffed an instinct to defend her parents. She looked at him directly for the first time, conjuring a subhuman maniac whose touch, whose very presence so close to her naked body, she found repulsive. Instead, she discovered a battle-scarred landscape on which Nature had intended to cultivate a different kind of garden. Like Marta, Analisa's assailant was more wounded-child than monster, his development stunted by poverty and long-cultivated rage. She understood why Marta accommodated his excesses.

Tempering her outrage, she continued in a steady voice. "I was adopted as a child. You yourself admit it's the attorneys and foreigners who are responsible? Why punish the innocent?" She unlocked her fingers and pointed to herself. "Why punish me?"

"The attorneys cannot make babies for us. The foreigners are either barren or too old. You are young, healthy. It falls upon you and those like you to repay your country. You came to us. So we took you." His hand, which had been in a holding pattern along Analisa's lower thigh, advanced toward its target.

"What if I don't get pregnant?" She jammed her accordianed body deeper into the corner where the walls met and let the thought sink in. "What if I can never have children?"

He flashed a schoolboy smile. "Do not worry. You and me, we make babies okay. Lots." He said it as if having his children was all Analisa wanted from life, all she dreamed about.

She glanced toward the door. "What about your girlfriend?"

He followed her eyes as if expecting to see Marta standing in the shadows. "She understands." He spoke with the misguided confidence of a man who was sure he knew what every woman felt and wanted. "What I do is for our country, our people, our national pride."

Analisa granted his sincerity. As for the "no lust" malarkey, his hand already cupped the undefended gates of her genital passage. Enough said. Every cell in her body urged her to lash out at him, to flail with her fists, scratch his eyes out with her nails. Some unseen force paralyzed her limbs. Focus on Marta! "She loves you. She feels jealous and hurt." He pried her knees apart. In a panic she cried, "I thought you loved her!"

With one hand he unbuttoned his jeans. "I do. One day, she will be my wife." His fingers roughly probed her moist interior.

Analisa grimaced in pain. "If you love her, you won't do this!"

"She...approves."

Analisa wriggled from side to side to make it more difficult for him to climb on top of her. He was too strong. Soon he had her pinned beneath him. Sweat dripped on her from his bare chest. Groping at her breasts, he took a nipple in his foul-smelling mouth. Somehow, he had managed to work his shorts down around his knees. She felt the pressure of his full erection against her flesh.

The most terrifying part of this inhuman assault was her inability to prevent him from ejaculating once he penetrated her. Pummeling him with her fists, she wrapped her legs around his waist and squeezed with all her might. "No lust!"

He grabbed her shoulders and shook her so violently her neck whiplashed. "I am a man!"

Clearly, he had lost patience. Analisa feared a beating or worse if she continued. "Marta!"

Her assailant froze, his throbbing organ directed missile-like at its target. He pushed her roughly against the pallet. Wild, black eyes stared inches from her own. Their noses almost touched. "How do you know her name?"

Analisa turned away, but he grabbed her mouth and forced her to look at him.

"How do you know her name?"

Calling out had been useless. She regretted that both she and Marta would now feel his wrath. "She...told ...me," Analisa confessed through lips pressed so tightly against her teeth that blood from broken skin wet her tongue.

Every muscle in Analisa's body stiffened, then yielded to a series of undulating spasms. Her eyes rolled erratically in their sockets. Her head jerked from side to side. Saliva spilled from her mouth and rolled across her cheeks.

The man released his grip. He jumped off the pallet and stood gaping at her, his shorts around his ankles, penis retreating in horror. "¿Qué pasa?"

Her sweat-covered body contorted again, wildly spasming. Her pelvis arched nearly a foot off the mat before free-falling in the wake of another convulsion. Analisa heard her attacker crash into furniture and knock over a chair as he rushed to get out of the room.

The lock turned.

The door opened and slammed shut.

Chapter 23

Arturo Cristobal followed Father Gallego through the hard-wood double front doors and into his mansion's spacious marble foyer. Analisa's friend had arrived on the last flight of the day from Miami. After the necessary identification greetings and the practical retrieve-the-baggage-get-out-of-the-airport conversation, their after-dark drive up the coast had taken place mostly in silence.

Arturo led his guest to an upstairs bedroom that, like his own, looked out onto the swimming pool. Waves rolling onto the white sand beach beyond the house drummed a distant, mournful beat. Curtains moved lethargically in a half-hearted breeze that entered through open French doors.

"I hope you find the room comfortable, Father."

"It's great," the priest said without enthusiasm. "I wanted to come with her, you know."

The unsolicited comment surprised Arturo. "But you did not. Why?"

"She refused to let me. It was her personal quest. She insisted on doing it alone." Father Gallego's shoulders drooped. "I never thought she'd end up being the object of the hunt."

Arturo identified with the priest's depression and guilt. All day he had asked himself how he might have prevented Analisa's abduction. The answer was always the same, Nothing. Knowing his innocence didn't help. "You must be tired after your long flight."

"Yeah." Father Gallego removed his black suit coat and tossed it onto a nearby chair. Slipping the white plastic collar from its neck guides, he opened the top buttons of his short-sleeved shirt and sat on the edge of the bed. Arturo stepped into the hallway. "As much as we both wish to help her," he said. "There is nothing we can do tonight. Get some sleep."

"Thanks for meeting me at the airport."

Arturo nodded. "I will be downstairs for a while if you need anything."

He idled into the conservatory, sat at the piano, and with one finger tapped out a forlorn melody. Less than ten minutes later, he heard footsteps on the stairs. Father Gallego entered the room. He had changed into shorts and a golf shirt.

"I did not expect to see you until morning, Father."

"Tired but wired," he said with a mirthless grin. "How can I sleep when Analisa's out there—" He gestured in no particular direction. "—Somewhere? My eyes refuse to close."

"I feel the same way."

The two men moved onto the verandah.

Standing poolside, Arturo said, "Perhaps a swim to help you relax."

"No thanks. I'm not in the mood for anything I might enjoy."

Instead, Father Gallego paced the concrete deck. Arturo joined him and for several minutes they walked side by side in silence. There was something he wanted to ask the priest. It refused to come out. Finally, he found courage to formulate the question. "Father—"

"Call me Dave."

"I know priests have little experience in such things, but...do you believe in love at first sight?"

Dave physically recoiled at the question. "Why ask me?"

The chill in the priest's voice confused Arturo, but he pressed forward. "Because you know Analisa better than I do. Much better."

"You said yourself, I'm inexperienced. Maybe you should ask someone who knows more about these things."

Arturo stiffened. The priest's reaction was that of a rival for Analisa's affections, rather than a friend and advisor. "Look, Father— Dave."

Dave looked into the dense sky and said, "I'm sorry. I must be more wiped out than I thought. What about 'love at first sight'?"

With the electrical charge between them temporarily grounded, Arturo proceeded. He chose his words carefully, qualifying them when necessary to leave room for the possibility he had misread what he and Analisa had experienced. "I think that is what I felt when I met Analisa."

"And you think she felt the same way."

"I cannot be sure, but I think so. We experienced a... How can I describe what happened? A tender moment at the opera house."

Dave stopped pacing and looked at him. "The opera house?" He looked like a man who had been hit in the stomach and was doing his courageous best, unsuccessfully, to hide the effects of the blow.

"I wanted her to see where I work, so to speak. Something happened I never felt before with any other woman. That was Tuesday. Wednesday evening, I intended to confirm that she felt as I did."

"Or that you were mistaken."

Annoyed at having this alternative stated so flatly, Arturo hesitated, then acknowledged, "Yes, I suppose. That, too."

"Look, Arturo, Analisa's sensible, down-to-earth. She thinks before she acts. I can't see her falling in love on a first date."

"I see." Arturo wondered if Dave truly understood the workings of Analisa's heart or only thought he did.

"I've known her a long time. How long have you known her?"

Conscious of his disadvantage, Arturo said, "A few days." He grew quiet, regretting he had exposed his feel-

ings so openly to this stranger whose motives were still a
mystery. "I know what I felt. Only God knows what she
was feeling."

"And one other person. Analisa."

"And Analisa," Arturo conceded with a descending
inflection. He had let Dave cast doubt on something he
had been quite sure of. With the flame that burned in his
heart momentarily doused, Arturo stuffed his hands in his
pockets and walked with a leaden step. It aggravated him
that the priest's mood had brightened. At least, Dave
seemed to walk with a lighter step than before.

Dave was the first to break the silence. "When can I
meet with the police?"

Arturo welcomed the change of subject. "I will call
Chief Inspector Madrigal first thing in the morning."

🌺 🌺 🌺

Exhausted, Analisa lay still, not daring to open her eyes or
move until positive she was alone. In the silence and darkness, she let one hand search for a corner of the thin sheet
beneath her. She used the cloth to wipe spilled semen
from her navel, nearly retching in the process.

When her breathing returned to normal, she whispered,
"Thank you, Jerry Oldheiser!" in tribute to a college classmate. "It really works." Jerry had once feigned a seizure
to save himself from a brutal mugging in West Oakland.
The ruse had earned her a reprieve. For how long, she did-
n't know.

🌺 🌺 🌺

Marta had never seen Lupe so out of control of his emotions. She said nothing when he ran through the kitchen
on his way out of the house. He had thrown a shirt on but
hadn't stopped to button it. Nor had he put his sandals on.

Something terrible must have happened in the upstairs room, she told herself.

"She had a fit! Just when I—"

"Where are you going?"

"I don't know."

"Well I do." Whenever Lupe said he didn't know where he was going in that tone of voice, she usually found him in his favorite bar, drinking away the little money they had. She dreaded his return and was glad she had left her son with her sister since the morning of the kidnapping.

"Don't go near her until I come back with Pedro and Antonio!"

Marta shuddered with a sudden vision of her worst nightmare. Los Dejados's *coneja* crusade was about to explode in their faces. She wasn't afraid for herself. She had always known and accepted the risks. What she hadn't factored in was the effect it might have on her child. Who would care for him if the police arrested her and threw her in jail? My sister? She can barely feed her own children. As devoted to Lupe as Marta was, only one person merited her total and unconditional love, her son. She'd take him away to the interior and hide from both the police and Los Dejados.

Fool! What chance do you have to escape?

❦ ❦ ❦

The man who had attempted to rape Analisa as a service to his country did not return to her cell. Nor had she heard his voice in the building throughout the day, which she thought was Friday. Or was it Saturday? Her head ached and dark welts had risen on her arms where he had pinned her down. She had received no food or water. Nor had Marta come to empty the urine-filled chamber pot which Analisa removed to the farthest corner of the room.

Finally, sometime in the early evening, Marta unlocked the door and entered. "You are ill?"

"Not anymore." Analisa let herself relax a bit.

Marta picked up the chair the man had knocked over and sat down. "Has it happened before? The fit?"

Analisa felt a big but necessary lie in the making. "Once. I went out with a student at the university. It was our first date. At the end of the evening, he wanted me to—you know—have sex. I said no, but you know how men are."

Marta's eyes responded with understanding and identification with Analisa's story.

"We'd been to a party. He was a little drunk. When he tried to force himself on me— Well, it happened. Just like last night. That was the only time. Until now."

Marta's eyes narrowed. "You have never had sex with a man?"

Analisa looked away. "Never." That part was true.

"Then, you do not know if it would happen with a man you cared for very much."

"Maybe it would. Maybe not. I've been too frightened to do it again, with anyone." Analisa didn't have to pretend to look terrified. She felt far from safe. There was no telling what Los Dejados had in store for their flawed *coneja*.

Marta, too, looked anxious.

"Is he very angry?" Analisa said.

"He is a proud man. You have wounded his manhood. No one must know, especially the other men. They are ignorant of women's feelings and...problems."

Analisa guessed that Marta rejoiced that her man had not found in his new *coneja* an able sexual partner. At the same time, Marta had to be worried about the possible consequences for Analisa and herself. "He'll kill me, won't he?"

Silence. Then, "It does not look good."

"Help me escape."

"I do not dare!" Marta reacted as if her lover had already caught her in this proposed act of treason.

Analisa quickened the pace of her entreaty. "If you do, I'll tell the police you aided me."

"If I do, I will lose Los Dejados." Tears filled Marta's eyes. "And my child... I might as well be dead."

Analisa trembled. "Don't let him kill me, Marta. "

🌺 🌺 🌺

Marta left Analisa and returned to the kitchen. She had reached a crossroad in her life. For the next four hours, she battled two formidable opponents, fear and conscience.

"Frightened" did not adequately describe the bloodless feeling in her head. She had everything to lose by setting La Coneja free. With nothing to gain from helping Analisa Marconi, there seemed only one choice. Wait for the men to return and support whatever decision they made. But Marta had lost her taste for blood. Of all the Dejadista council members, she alone seemed to have heard the call of conscience. She alone believed their solution was as evil as the crimes it redressed.

Marta had never truly known Lydia Vitale, not as a person. Once she had identified and kidnapped her, Marta had no further contact with the woman. The chief reminder that La Coneja had been a real woman was the infant boy Lupe delivered into her arms less than a year later. As the child grew, looking less and less like them, his face became a mirror in which Marta daily beheld the image of his birth mother.

For a long time, Marta continued to believe it was right for their _coneja_ to produce children for Santo Sangre. It wasn't until she brought the Marconi woman to this house, not until they had spoken face to face, woman to woman, yes even sister to sister, that conscience had toppled the final barriers of resistance.

Marta went to the cupboard and poured herself a glass of wine. Moving to the rough wooden table, she set the glass down and plopped into a chair. What we are doing is wrong, she confessed, burying her face in her arms. God help me, it is wrong!

🎔 🎔 🎔

Analisa looked up to find Marta standing in the doorway. Her round cheeks were wet. Her swollen eyes frightened but resolute. "Tell me what to do."

Analisa's lungs released the breath she had held too long. "Bring my clothes. Unlock the doors." For the first time since her abduction, she experienced a flicker of hope. With Marta's cooperation and a lot of luck, she might get out of this situation alive and whole.

Marta left the room, returning within minutes. "I cannot find your shoes," she said in a slow monotone.

Analisa put on the wrinkled, blood-stained garments. "Forget the shoes." Being dressed for the first time since her abduction, even so grubbily, infused her with new energy.

Watching from a corner of the room, Marta seemed defeated, as if she was the prisoner, Analisa her jailer. Analisa wished her no harm, but she had only one desire, to get away from her prison and the clutches of Los Dejados. Marta had to deal with her own problem.

"Where are we?"

"¿Perdón?" The question startled Marta.

"I don't know where I am. I must get back to my hotel."

"Barrio Rincón. It is past midnight. No taxis." She shook her finger in warning. "Dangerous for a woman to be on the streets alone."

"Dangerous?" Analisa almost laughed. "If I stay here, your friends will kill me. I'll take my chances. Which way do I go?"

"Go right...to the boulevard. Then left. A long way. It takes you to the Plaza de la Libertad."

"Where can I find a phone?" Analisa put one hand to her mouth, the other to her ear. "¿Teléfono?"

"Tonight?" Marta's fright-level had dimmed her mental capacity.

"Yes, tonight!"

"Look for a bar." Again she warned, "It is dangerous at this hour."

Analisa hurried to the door. She stopped abruptly and turned. "Come with me."

A faint smile played briefly on Marta's lips. Her eyes flickered with life. "To America?"

The question touched Analisa deeply. Without intending to, she had exposed a place within Marta, filled with childhood dreams and fading fantasies of a better life.

"I...I meant, leave with me now."

Marta's eyes dulled again. Whatever brief foray into hope she had allowed herself died. "I must wait for Lupe."

"So that's his name!"

"He will need me."

Analisa marveled at Marta's loyalty to her undeserving man.

"I will distract him long enough for you to get away. That will atone in part for my sin."

Eager as Analisa was to quit her cell, she had to give Marta one more chance. "He isn't worth it. You know that."

Steel hardened Marta's gaze. "What do you know about the 'worth' of a Santo Sangrían life?" The words were bitter, full of loathing.

Analisa fled the room with Marta's reproach scorching her ears. She found the stairway and crept down, her bare feet making no sound on the steps. Had Marta and Lupe set a cruel trap for her? Was he lurking at the bottom of the stairs? She reached the front door without incident and stepped into the night, breathing the air of freedom. Without looking back, she ran toward the boulevard, ignoring the pain the cobbled street inflicted on her soles and ankles.

Analisa had covered barely fifty yards when a car pulled alongside her at the curb. A man jumped out of the front passenger door. He shouted her name and chased her down the unlit street. Her mind raced faster than her bruised feet propelled her. She was no match for her pursuer. A large hand grasped her shoulder from behind. With all the adrenaline draining out of her, she gave up. No use fighting. She was their prisoner again, their *coneja*. Her brief taste of freedom made this second capture worse than the first. Tears of despair streamed down her cheeks.

The man panted heavily. "Señorita Marconi?"

It wasn't Lupe. How did he know her name? She offered a tentative, barely audible, "Yes."

"I am Chief Inspector Madrigal...Santa Catalina Police...Department." He removed his ID from the breast pocket of his suit jacket. "You run pretty fast for a—"

Analisa was too grateful her ordeal was finally over to fret over a gender slight. She clung to the policeman and wept into his chest.

He patted her lightly on the shoulder. "You are safe now."

The driver of the police car entered the house she had just abandoned. "Anyone inside?" Madrigal asked Analisa, as he helped her back to the unmarked car.

"One. Marta. I don't know her last name or where the man went. She called him Lupe."

"His surname is Santana."

"He hasn't been around all day."

"We have been watching this place for several hours. Apparently, this fellow leads a group called—"

"Los Dejados."

"Exactly. We had a tip we might find him here."

The other policeman met them at front door. "Empty, Inspector."

"She can't be far."

"I don't want to press charges, not against her," Analisa told him. "In a way, she's a victim too."

"It is no longer your choice." Madrigal's tone was professional, but understanding, respectful.

A second police car lurched to a stop in front of the house. Marta slumped in the back seat like a deflated punching bag. She was crying but had the same defiant look Analisa had seen just before leaving.

"Caught her going over the back fence," the officer said.

"Good job, Marín. Close this place up and keep a watch on it, front and back. Santana might still show up."

By this time, uncontrollable tremors wracked Analisa's body. Madrigal wrapped his jacket around her shoulders and helped her into the car. "We must get you to the hospital."

Chapter 24

Analisa leaped from her hospital bed the moment Dave and Arturo entered the room. Ignoring the pain in her bruised feet and arms, she hugged Dave tightly for a long time before either of them spoke.

There were tears in his eyes when he said, "I came the minute I heard."

"I'm so glad to see you!"

Arturo had held back, deferring to the priest. Analisa saw him over Dave's shoulder and realized that complexity abounded in this affectionate trio.

Without letting go of Dave, she reached out to Arturo. "I couldn't get to the opera."

Arturo took the hand she offered and pressed it to his lips. "*Querida*, are you apologizing for being kidnapped?"

"Just for not being there."

"I was crazy with worry. I went to the hotel—"

"So, how are you doing?" Dave interrupted.

Grateful to be alive and free, Analisa considered her injuries insignificant. "The doctor released me to go home. I told him I didn't have a home."

"I do not wish to impose my will," Arturo said, "but may I invite you to move in with us? Dave and I will do our best to make you feel at home."

"Thank you. I guess I'll have to find another ship to take me to Miami."

"Ship?" the men chorused. "Miami?"

"I didn't have a chance to tell you... either of you. Vice Consul Small booked passage for me. I'm—or I was—leaving Santo Sangre today."

"But we are just—" Arturo blurted, letting the rest of his disappointment dangle in midair.

Dave's reaction was more upbeat. "I think that's for the best. What about Martina?"

"I guess it wasn't meant to be."

"When you're ready, we can fly to L.A.," Dave said.

Analisa frowned and shook her head.

"Oh, I forgot. We'll both take a ship to Florida and Amtrak it from there."

Analisa recognized the competitive push-pull operating between these two special men in her life. She felt like a tennis ball being batted from one side of the court to the other.

Since there was no certainty she was safe yet from Los Dejados's mad designs, Analisa welcomed the idea of not returning to a hotel room. On the other hand, having two men fawning over her, dictating her actions, held its own perils. A bachelor and a celibate. What did they know about her feelings or what she needed? But she hadn't selected these two men at random on a street corner.

One was her best friend.

The other? This new presence? No predicting the place he might yet occupy in her life.

Arturo's and Dave's proximity, their breathing the same air with her, strained the sides of their fragile triangle. Analisa felt responsible for sorting out these relationships, keeping them neat and unconfused. She wondered if, at her best, she had the physical and psychic energy to do it. In her present condition, it seemed impossible. Faced with her options, she relented. "You're on...both of you."

❦ ❦ ❦

Analisa's room in the Cristobal mansion looked eastward toward the sloping, upside-down cone of the Chuchuán volcano. The action-packed hours of her escape and rescue, the subsequent medical examinations, and Dave's unexpected appearance had left no time to assimilate her ordeal.

She stepped onto the balcony and looked upward toward the volcano's domed cap. Thinking about the liquid mass boiling at its base, she tried to generate a matching hatred for Los Dejados, for Marta, and especially for Lupe Santana who had violated her.

No one would blame me if I hated them. But she didn't. During the eternal hours of Analisa's captivity, Marta's impassioned words had penetrated her consciousness, changed her forever.

Why was I chosen?

Why were they left behind?

She had always believed that her adoption was a tiny part of a master plan for the universe. She wasn't sure anymore. Not since she had met the Unchosen face to face. What she once considered divine favor now seemed like an accident of fate. It took only the slightest alteration of the cosmic blueprint to imagine Marta in the role of recent graduate of St. Mary's, the one with unblemished skin and the subtle sheen of polished nails.

If hatred wasn't an option, other feelings vied for dominance. Among them, grief and rage.

Undefined sorrow made her feel heavy, as if living in slow motion.

Outrage free-floated inside her, banging against her rib cage like a tossed sledge hammer. It arose from two sources. Los Dejados had not only stripped away her clothing and robbed her of her freedom. Lupe Santana and company had also disrupted her mission to find Martina Aguilada.

With the sun warming the back of her neck and shoulders, she breathed in the fragrances of the tropics. And listened to the mountain.

Show me the next step.

❈ ❈ ❈

"Analisa?" Dave called from the open doorway.

"Out here."

In a moment he was beside her. "Chief Inspector Madrigal just called. Great news! They've rounded up the ring leaders."

"Lupe Santana, too?"

"Yes. The Inspector told Arturo, and I quote, 'We have cut the head off this misguided movement.' He expects fringe supporters and hangers-on to scatter and maintain a low profile. Madrigal wants us—wants you, that is—to come to the Central Jail in the morning to identify the suspects."

"Then, it's safe for me to stay in Santo Sangre!"

"I thought you'd want to get out of this place."

Analisa bristled. "This 'place' is my native land."

"So what? You're as American as I am. It's the only home you've ever known."

"That can change."

Dave threw up his hands. "I don't want to fight with you. Not here. Not now...not ever." When the charged air had regained its balance, he continued. "Come back with me."

Analisa heard this as a plea to find an abiding place for him in her life. She took him by the arm and walked him back into the bedroom. She was resolute, her body erect, if still unsteady. "I'm not ready to leave."

"Not ready?"

"If they let me stay, I'm going to find my birth mother."

"Then, I'll stay too. We'll look for her together."

Analisa played with this fantasy for the briefest moment. "I don't think people here are used to having good-looking priests escort unmarried women around the countryside. Not even for the noblest of reasons."

That silenced Dave for a moment. He glanced toward Arturo's room. "I'm losing you." The words emerged as a deep groan.

Analisa understood what he meant, that she might never be his, not fully, not the way he wanted. She grasped his hands, which were uncallused yet manly. "Dave, I need your friendship, your concern...your love. No one will ever replace you." She let him ponder her words, gave him time and space to study the incompatible parts of their lives.

Finally, he said, "I guess I should be happy with as much of you as I can get. I just can't bear to lose you entirely."

"You won't. I swear."

Dinner that night was a mostly silent affair. Dave looked as if he had only one wish—for Arturo Cristobal to vanish, leaving him alone with Analisa to share this Caribbean Shangri-La forever. Analisa even resisted Arturo's well-meant attempts to liven the scene with stories about eccentric divas with whom he had performed. By the time Emilia Jimenez served dessert, Analisa felt as if she was carrying a barbell on her shoulders. Exhausted and still in some pain from her head wound and contusions, she excused herself as soon as Emilia removed the last plate.

❦ ❦ ❦

At eleven on Saturday morning, Analisa, Arturo, and Dave followed Chief Inspector Madrigal to a dingy, windowless room inside Santa Catalina's main jail. Analisa shivered at the severity of the surroundings. Madrigal gestured toward a long wooden table whose chairs faced a room-wide one-way mirror. "You will sit over there, please."

Dave took the chair to Analisa's left. Arturo seated himself at her right hand. Together, they gazed into an empty, spotlighted room in which a low platform stretched left to right, from wall to wall.

Analisa expected six or eight people to line up
American-style, some of them suspects, others police per-
sonnel or building employees in a game of pick-your-perp.
Instead, the "suspects," both men and women, were led
into the room one at a time.

Speaking into a microphone on the table, Madrigal
instructed the accused. "Face forward...turn left...now turn
to your right. Face forward."

The process repelled Analisa. At the same time, this
somber jailhouse ballet fascinated her. The first five the
guards brought in bore no resemblance to her captors.
Each time, she whispered, "No."

"Next," Madrigal barked.

Analisa immediately recognized the sixth person in the
parade as Lupe Santana, the man pathologically determined to enslave her to a life of forced childbearing.
Images of his brutality countered any compassion she
might have felt.

Without hesitation, she announced, "That's him."

Arturo stiffened. He leaned forward as if about to crash
through the glass window and mete out his own punishment without waiting for the criminal court to do its job.
She laid a restraining hand on his arm.

"Note for the record," Madrigal instructed the police
stenographer at the end of the table, "the victim has identified one Guadalupe Santana as the man who held said
victim against her will and sexually assaulted her."

Analisa winced at "sexually assaulted." She gripped the
arms of her chair. Apparently, in Santo Sangre there was
little concern for the sensitivities of female victims. Dave
shifted in his seat. She wished he and Arturo hadn't been
allowed to witness this scene.

As they hustled Santana out, one of the jailers twisted
the prisoner's arms behind his back and clamped steel
handcuffs around his wrists. Several more men and

women followed Lupe, none of whom Analisa recognized as her abductors.

Arturo's fingers slid along the table to touch hers. She accepted the invitation and opened her hand to receive him. Last in the colorless procession came Marta. In less than forty-eight hours, she had aged considerably beyond her twenty-something years. Gone was the defiant look she had worn when Analisa last saw her in the back seat of the police car. She appeared defeated and as terrified as Analisa had been during her captivity.

When Marta stepped onto the platform, Analisa grappled with warring convictions and emotions. It would be so easy to deny that Marta was one of them.

"Recognize this one?" Madrigal said, hinting that he expected an affirmative response.

"Yes...no."

"Señorita Marconi." Madrigal barked her name but quickly softened his tone. "Take a good look, please. Either you do or do not recognize this woman as an accomplice in the crimes perpetrated against you."

Analisa guessed at conditions in the women's prison. Reality probably exceeded her harshest visions. And, who remained to care for Marta's child while his mother was in prison? "What will happen to her?"

"Neither you nor I have any say in that. My job as a policeman stops at these doors. So does yours as the victim. The court convicts and imposes sentence."

"Will she get a fair trial?"

Madrigal unleashed a humorless laugh. "With your testimony against her, does it really matter?"

"What kind of legal representation is available?"

"She says she cannot afford a lawyer. The court will appoint someone."

"A public defender?"

"We do not have that particular institution here, but something similar. Generally, the courts draw from a pool of young attorneys just out of law school who need experience and will work for minimal pay to get it."

"Can I hire someone to defend her?"

Madrigal sat back in his chair and stared at Analisa.

"You must think I'm from another planet," she said.

Clearly, Madrigal wanted to end this session and get on with his day. "It is highly unusual for the victim to pay for the criminal's defense."

She held his gaze. "I'm not your ordinary victim, Inspector. Is there a law against it?"

"As far as I know, it is legal. Now, may we continue with the identification? I need a definitive response. Is this the woman who abducted you and held you captive?"

Squinting blindly into the opaque window, Marta seemed to have grown more frightened and weary during the delay. She swayed slightly, as if unable to stand exposed much longer to the hot lights and invisible scrutiny.

Analisa wished Marta could see how reluctant she was to implicate her. She might as well be as naked as I was.

"Señorita Marconi?" Madrigal urged.

"Yes," she whispered. "That's her."

"Affirmative," he announced with a note of triumph.

The guards handcuffed Marta roughly, just as they had Lupe Santana. Before disappearing through the door, she peered at the window one last time. Analisa shivered at the wild-animal hatred visible in Marta's eyes. I had to do it, Marta. I had to. She had never experienced such sadness. Analisa laid her head on the table and wept. Not just for Marta, but for all of Santo Sangre's Martas and Lupes, men and women whose lives had started out like hers but, by some ill-crossed configuration of stars and planets, had turned out so differently.

Dave turned to console Analisa and offer support, but Arturo had already helped her from her chair.

"Come," Arturo said, "I must get you out of this terrible place." He slipped his arm around her waist and led her from the lineup room.

🐝 🐝 🐝

Monday afternoon ground to a sultry stop. The clouds hanging over the Cristobal estate were invisible to the naked eye, rising as they did from Analisa's dark mood. Part of her remained behind somewhere in the bowels of the Cárcel Central.

I'm the same person I've always been, she told herself. This experience hasn't changed me. No matter how hard she tried to convince herself that this was true, louder voices from some dark corner pronounced her "unclean."

"How about a dip?" Arturo suggested to his guests. "It will cool us off."

Analisa felt drained of all energy but agreed and went upstairs to change. She had never been particularly self-conscious about her body, but she discovered that, too, had changed. From her luggage she retrieved a conservative aqua-blue one-piece suit. Over it she put on a terry half-robe that was superfluous on this hot afternoon.

When she appeared on the verandah, the two men were already in the pool, treading water idly—and separately. Instead of tossing her robe onto a chaise lounge and entering the water, she moved unsteadily to the glass-topped table and sat in the shade of a market-style umbrella.

Arturo spotted her and waved. "Come in. The water will refresh your spirit."

"Later."

Dave encouraged her to join them. "Water's great."

"Not yet."

Dave exited the pool, grabbed a fluffy monogrammed towel, and dried himself off. Arturo emerged from the other end of the pool and headed slowly toward the table, letting the sun dry the wet crystals that beaded his athletic limbs.

Analisa reacted to both men. Her heart went out to Dave. Her body yearned for Arturo to take her in his arms and give her comfort, reassurance that she was still the same vibrant, unsullied woman he had met at the Embassy less than a week ago.

Dave sat down wearing his worried-friend expression. "You okay?"

She shrugged.

"What can I do to make it better?"

"Your being here makes it better."

He smiled and sat back, face to the sun.

Arturo joined them. "I thought a swim would do you good."

Analisa pulled her robe closed and tied it loosely in front of her. "Look," she began, "you guys have been really sweet. I couldn't ask for better care or more wonderful friends. I'm feeling stronger already, at least physically. I need to get on with my life." This is the second time in less than a year I've needed to get on with my life. The last time, she hoped. Although the men listened in silence, she knew what Dave wanted from her "getting on with it." She suspected, but wasn't sure, what Arturo hoped.

"I don't know how long Vice Consul Small will let me stay. I'll find out tomorrow. Arturo, I need your help with something."

He leaned forward, totally attentive.

"Hire the best attorney in Santa Catalina to defend Marta Lopez. I mean the best. Money is no object."

"Done."

"What about me?" Dave said. "What can I do?"

She needed Dave to do something, but he deserved to hear it in private. With a reassuring smile, she said, "Later."

❅ ❅ ❅

Analisa had showered and dressed for dinner when she heard a knock at her door. "Come in!"

"Room service," Dave joked.

"Last time I answered to that, it nearly cost me my life."

"Geez, that was pretty insensitive of me."

"It's okay. You didn't know."

"Well, anyway, I'm harmless." Dave moved to the wing-back chair facing the bed. "You wanted to talk to me. Is this a good time?"

"Sure." Analisa removed her sandals and sat on the bedspread, legs tucked beneath her. "Oh, Dave, this is going to sound so much harsher than I want it to." She paused, hoping to pack into her words, gestures, and gaze all the love she felt for him. "What I need from you is to...go back home." She avoided his eyes. "Keep me in your thoughts. Storm heaven with prayers for me. But go. Please."

He stared out the window. His eyes followed the curve of Chuchuán all the way to the top. His lips parted but remained wordless. Putting his elbows on his knees, he rubbed his eyes with his hands. His wounded expression told her he understood. "So it was love at first sight."

"What do you mean?"

"Nothing," he said. "Just something Arturo and I talked about the other night."

"I need time to see where this new relationship is taking me."

"You don't have to explain."

"Yes, I do." She went to him, kissed him on the forehead, and cradled his head against her body. "Because I love you."

Chapter 25

Analisa received clearance on Monday afternoon from both the U.S. Embassy and the local police to remain in Santo Sangre and even travel outside the capital.

"I'd say Los Dejados are out of business," Chief Inspector Madrigal told her.

On Tuesday, she and Arturo saw a reluctant Dave off to Miami. Saying good-bye at the airport was difficult for both of them.

"I don't know what to expect in the interior," she told him. "I'll do my best to stay in touch."

"I shouldn't have come?"

She hugged him tightly. "I'm glad you came. It's just that—"

He put up a hand to stop her. "Don't." A fading smile said he was doing his best to be noble. Dave had been involved in every major event of her life since high school. She wanted him to be part of her next and most important adventure. But here she was sending him away, knowing it was best, for him and for her. "I'm a big boy now. All grown up."

Unable to resist the opening, she said, "Not a pimply teenager any more?"

"I never was pimply."

"Seems I've heard that line before." She laughed and kissed him. "You're the best. I'll see you in Anaheim...soon."

Their relationship had taken a new and dramatic turn. The old days were gone. Every relationship has its seasons, she recalled her mother saying. She'd always love Dave, but this was the season for distance. It was time to loosen ties that had become so strong that less than a month ago they had explored, ever so cautiously, the possibilities and hazards of becoming one flesh, as well as one in spirit.

Dave passed through the gate and walked onto the tarmac where a twin-engine SSAir jet waited. He turned, waved to them, and ascended the movable stairway. Soon he was out of view.

Arturo put his arm around her. "Ready?"

"I want to watch his plane take off."

The jet taxied down the runway and gained speed. Only when it had lifted off and become a speck in the cloudless sky did she turn away.

🌻 🌻 🌻

"I'll need your help in getting ready for a trip to the interior," Analisa said on the drive home from the airport. Arturo kept his eyes on the traffic. "I want to get started before something else goes wrong. First, I need to figure out how I'm going to get from place to place using local transportation."

"I have given that a great deal of thought. Since the opera season is over, let me accompany you."

"Do you mean it?" Analisa's spirits brightened.

"There is nothing I want more."

The thought of traveling with Arturo offered comfort and security. He was fluent in the local dialect and "knew the territory." She also needed the practical wisdom and experience he had learned as a child on the cruel streets of Santa Catalina. Besides, everyone in Santo Sangre seemed to know his face—and voice. His celebrity status might open doors otherwise closed to her.

"How long can you travel with me?"

His look said "forever." His verbal response measured time with greater precision. "I have a concert in Madrid in three weeks. I will need a few days to rehearse. I can spend at least two weeks with you."

"Two weeks? That's a good-news, bad-news offer."

"It is the best I can do under the circumstances. If your search proves fruitless in that time, I hope you will return to Santa Catalina with me."

Despite the simplicity of her original mission, Analisa had never felt more confused. She had arrived in the country with nothing but time to conduct her search. No ties at home or anywhere else bound her to a schedule. Los Dejados had done their best to knock her off that course. Now, Arturo wanted to impose limits.

She shook her head. "I've come all this way to find the birth mother I haven't seen in over twenty years. How can I put a stopwatch on my search? When you leave, I'll continue...by bus. I'll even hitchhike from town to town if I have to."

"What about your safety? There are other dangers for a woman traveling alone besides Los Dejados."

"I'm already living on borrowed time. I—" Her throat closed as she struggled to fight back her emotions. "I should have died last February, but I didn't. Los Dejados could have killed me. They didn't."

"Analisa, I am offering to go with you, if you want me to."

She decided to accept and let the future take care of itself. "I want you to."

❧ ❧ ❧

Analisa quickly realized Arturo had been right. All the amenities Santo Sangre had to offer tourists ended at the outskirts of Santa Catalina. Once they were out of the city, paved roads became a memory, forcing him to slow his Land-Rover to a maximum thirty kilometers per hour.

The snail's-pace climb up the slope of the Chuchuán gave her an opportunity to view close-up the island's tropical landscape and wildlife. A mobile rainbow of wild parrots clustered above them, their chatter so cacophonous that it made normal conversation impossible. At times, the panorama of the shoreline and the turquoise sea beyond was nothing short of breathtaking. She was glad to be out of the capital, but memories of her recent ordeal cast lingering shadows. Twice since her escape she had awakened from nightmares. Once with the disgusting feeling that Lupe Santana's sweaty, naked body spread her limbs, his organ insistent, rough hands groping at her breasts. Another time, she awakened, choking from the stinging odor of chloroform.

In Arturo, Analisa found a compatible traveling companion. For long stretches at a time, he concentrated on the uncertain road and left her to contemplate her own thoughts.

At around two thousand feet above the sea, they came to a spot in the road that was free of the usual thick vegetation.

"Let's stop," she said.

Arturo pulled off the dirt road and got out.

Having grown up near the beaches of Orange County, Analisa considered the ocean a member of her family. She used to feel the same way about the "wild blue yonder," her father's favorite home away from home. As a teenager and college student, she had traveled with her parents across a large swath of the world—the British Isles, Western Europe, Australia, New Zealand, Hong Kong, and Taiwan, not to mention the U.S. from coast to coast, plus Alaska and Hawaii. What she saw below her was as beautiful as anything the world had to offer.

She leaned against the front of the Land-Rover, face to the sky. The sun, warm against her skin, commanded her tense muscles to adopt a not-to-worry attitude. "This place is growing on me."

"I hope it does. We are better people than we have shown you so far." Arturo returned to the driver's seat and started the engine. "We must keep moving."

As they continued up the mountain, he gave Analisa a short history lesson on her native land. "It's a story told about any number of nations. Fill in the blanks. The rich get richer by making sure the poor get poorer."

"There seems to be a thriving middle class."

"We have our doctors, lawyers, university professors, even the upper level civil servants."

"Opera singers," she added with a wink.

"Yes, okay," he acknowledged. "But not a middle class by American standards. But you are right. There is a level of society between the very poor and the oligarchs. Fifteen or twenty major families own virtually all the coffee plantations. They also own the hotels and casinos. Coffee and gambling keep the country going. Without tourism, Santa Catalina sinks into the Caribbean like a modern Atlantis and takes the rest of the country with it."

"And the middle class? What happens to them, in that event?"

"They join the ranks of the *campesinos*. So, whatever their private feelings about political realities here, their bottom-line allegiance is with the rich who drive the economy."

His blunt appraisal of local realities surprised her. "Sounds pretty bleak. What about you? I mean if it comes to a choice?" She touched his shoulder and felt him lean into her. "Forgive me. You don't have to answer that."

"I wish I had an answer. As you can guess from what I told you about my early life, my heart is with the poor and powerless. I can only hope they would always have my first loyalty."

Analisa eagerly soaked up everything Arturo told her about her birth country. "Talk to me about the political situation."

Arturo grunted. "And spoil a beautiful day?"

"I know what I read. I'd like to hear it from your perspective."

"For over twenty years, we were ruled by the infamous Raúl Montenegro. With the consent of the Families, of course. Our current president, Roberto Aguilar, isn't such a bad guy by comparison."

Analisa's curiosity ratcheted up a notch. "What did Montenegro do?"

"Being God at home wasn't enough for him. He took his divine role onto the world stage. When Prisoners of Conscience International, the human rights organization—"

"I know it. When I was in college, I used to write letters on behalf of political prisoners."

"Well, POCI lobbied to keep Western bankers from renewing development loans to Santo Sangre. To get revenge, old Raul hatched a harebrained plot to kill the children of the organization's leaders."

"How awful!"

"There were two murders before the whole thing unraveled, exposing Montenegro's stupidity. He resigned in disgrace."

Although horrified by the violent events of Santo Sangre's recent past, one aspect puzzled her. "If Montenegro was God here, why did he resign?"

"The Families are content to let their puppets believe they are divine, all-powerful, and immortal, but when God interferes with Mammon, guess who wins?

"Let's see. Does it start with 'M'?"

Arturo nodded. "POCI organized boycotts. The cruise ships stopped coming. Coffee exports fell. Montenegro had to go."

"They killed him?"

"He had enough friends to escape with his hide, if not his pride. Last I heard, he was living in style somewhere in South America and, if you can believe this, holding forth on the Internet. He has a venomous Web site on which he still rails against POCI and threatens to get even some day.

Anyone in the world can log in and get the latest dose of the old fart's bullshit. Pardon my language."

Arturo's survey of Santo Sangrían politics gave Analisa new insight into the passionate nature of her people. She understood why deep-seated wounds sometimes sought extreme solutions. Like Los Dejados, she thought.

When the first red-tiled roofs of Santa Teresita came into view, Analisa drew a deep breath to calm the jitters that twisted her stomach.

"I'm ready."

Arturo's right hand drifted from the steering wheel to the back of her neck. "Are you sure?"

She melted into his palm and let his fingers play among her curls. "Yes. I'm sure."

❁ ❁ ❁

Santa Teresita almost qualified as a town.

"The people here have a saying that hell is under their feet, inside the volcano," Arturo said.

Analisa wiped beads of perspiration from her forehead. "I can't argue with that."

Her tan safari shirt was a wet sheet that clung to her skin. The moisture provided a bit of relief, a tiny bit. After leaving Santa Catalina, she wished she hadn't worn a bra. Now that her shirt was practically see-through, she was glad to have it on.

Arturo parked outside a cafe just off the main plaza. It hardly mattered that the restaurant offered both "indoor" and "outdoor" seating, as the sign said. It had no walls. A flat, tin roof covered the indoor portion so that business went on uninterrupted when it rained.

Analisa chose the covered area because it offered relief from the oppressive mid-afternoon sun, if not the humidity. No one in the restaurant paid any attention to her.

Instead, it was Arturo who turned heads as the gushing owner escorted the visiting celebrity to a table.

"We will spend the night here," Arturo said.

"How long will it take to get to Piedras Blancas?"

"Two or three hours, depending on the weather. When it rains, the road can be treacherous."

A waiter took their order of *plátanos con crema*, local miniature bananas baked in honey and covered with the local equivalent of sour cream.

"In case you are wondering," Arturo said, "there is a small inn here. Nothing fancy, but it will keep us out of the elements."

The humid air turned suddenly more oppressive. "What if they don't have rooms for us?" Analisa emphasized the plural and wiped her sizzling cheeks with a limp wad of facial tissue that had made the trip in her breast pocket.

Arturo seemed to enjoy her discomfort. "The innkeeper has one of the few telephones in the village. I called ahead and reserved...two rooms." His fingers met Analisa's mid-way across the table. They felt wonderfully natural, as if his skin and hers were meant to touch and linger. "What are you thinking about?" he asked.

"Oh, Los Dejados...Marta Lopez . . ." Arturo's lips compressed; his mood darkened. She leaned closer. "What's wrong?"

"I was just thinking. Like all forms of resentment, this one festered, lying in wait for a leader to unify it, give it direction. Much of Latin America is ripe for this kind of sentiment. Of all places, it found its voice on my own tiny island." He turned her wrist over and massaged the soft underside of her forearm. Purple-blue blotches served as ugly reminders of her recent ordeal. "I want to say something, and I will put it as delicately as I can. You are still in danger here."

Analisa searched his clear mahogany eyes for his meaning. "That's not what Inspector Madrigal said."

"You may not have to fear Los Dejados," Arturo agreed, "but you are still an outsider—and a woman—traveling in unfamiliar territory, away from the big city and its security resources."

She raised her eyebrows. "Your 'big city' didn't offer me much protection last week."

"*Touché*. The danger here is more subtle. Be discreet in your inquiries. The people in these interior regions are suspicious of strangers who ask questions. For all they know, you could be from the Interior Ministry."

"Do I look like an undercover cop?" Analisa laughed. When Arturo scowled, she realized the inappropriateness of her remark. "I'm sorry. I don't always accept advice graciously. It's a pride thing. Used to drive my mom and dad crazy."

"That is the first fault I have discovered in you."

Analisa let the remark pass. It pleased her, though. "Go on."

"Don't start questioning people the minute you hit a village or town. Let them sniff you for a while. They will decide if and when it is safe to talk to you. Some people will take you to their hearts and offer help. Others will see a rich, vulnerable American and claim to be your mother, your brother or sister, or even your long-lost Tío Pablo." He had her full attention. "It's hard to know who is helping you and who is trying to rob you."

She sat back in her chair. "It's strange to be considered a foreigner. My parents did everything to instill in me a sense of pride in my native culture and language."

"I applaud them," he said. "I only want you to recognize how much your experience and environment have changed the genetic traits you received from your birth parents."

"I always thought I'd come back and be received as one of their own."

Arturo's smile assured her he spoke with respect and affection. "There is not a person in this restaurant who believes you belong here. In every way but the color of your skin, you are *una gringa* through and through. If you carry any label it is 'Made in Santo Sangre, Assembled in the United States of America.'"

Analisa's eyes moistened. Her experience with Los Dejados had clearly illustrated that the poor harbored feelings about international adoption that she would never fully comprehend. "You're frightening me. I don't want to be frightened anymore."

"Listen to me." His tone was neither parental nor patronizing. "As long as I am with you, no harm will come to you, not from me...nor anyone else. I promise."

They finished their meal in silence.

Chapter 26

Their stopover in Santa Teresita convinced Analisa it wouldn't be easy to find her birth mother. Everyone she and Arturo spoke to had a different version of where Martina might now be living. On the advice of the local parish priest, they kept to their original plan and moved from Santa Teresita to Piedras Blancas, farther up the mountain. Drawing a blank in that village, they followed one questionable lead after another.

Each day added a few squares to the quilt of information their discreet inquiries were assembling. Each day also reduced by one the time she had Arturo at her side.

"What is it you are afraid of?" he asked during one of their rest stops.

"How did you know?" The muscles in the back of Analisa's neck felt like twisted cables.

"I care about you. That gives me a measure of access to your feelings. Some of them, at least."

"It's not the people here I'm afraid of. I'm not even worried about being conned." She paused, groping for words to express her jumbled emotions. "I have an education, financial security, and a good future ahead of me. But ever since my parents died, I've had this overwhelming need to link my future with my past, my Santo Sangrían origins. If I don't find Martina, that connection will be broken. I'll always feel incomplete."

Her heart begged him to say he'd make it his life's work to see that she never felt alone or incomplete again. Instead, he closed his eyes and rested his head against the back of the seat. "I understand, Querida." He spoke softly, as if lost in the disorderly maze of his own thoughts. "I, too, have my demons."

She wondered what they were and if he'd ever share those tormentors with her.

❦ ❦ ❦

They got lucky in San Martín de Porres. A relative of
Martina's, a distant cousin, suggested that they try Volcán
Grande, a settlement on the eastern slope.

Buoyed by this news, Analisa gave herself permission
to relax for the first time in days. She decided to bank her
physical and spiritual energy, withdrawing each day only
what she needed to pay for its demands. Closing her eyes,
she let her body flow with the Land-Rover's incessant pitch
and yaw, which reminded her of the "Back to the Future"
ride at Universal Studios. Somewhere within, she found a
retreat from the vibration, a place of solitude in which to
rehearse possibilities.

What's the first thing I'll do if I find Martina? That was
easy. Analisa had trod that soil many times over the years.
I'll search her face for traces of shared genes. After that,
she'd play it by ear. Her next question involved Arturo.
What role did she want him to play in any eventual meeting between herself and Martina? She preferred to meet
her birth mother without anyone witnessing whatever
scene that encounter might create.

"Arturo," she said above the engine noise. "Is it too
much to hope we've hit the target this time?"

"Volcán Grande is a pretty small target, but let's think
positively."

"What if Martina's moved on from there, too?"

"Someone will know where she has gone. We will follow every lead, until—"

Analisa's confidence wilted. "Until you run out of
time."

"Let's hope that does not happen."

Analisa fought her way back from despair. "Now I
know why I need you with me. You're my emotional
compass."

The early evening sky put on a light show like none Analisa had ever witnessed. A multitude of progressively darkening, mobile shapes acted out the drama of the out-numbered Sun doing battle with the amassed forces of Clouds, Sea, and Night. Mother Nature selected one hue after another, splashing them in wild combinations across the expanse of her heavenly diorama, as if unwilling to lock in a final version.

Volcán Grande turned out to be not much larger than Santa Teresita. Analisa's heart sank when she discovered it was home to less than a thousand inhabitants. On the bright side, it wouldn't take long to determine if Martina lived among them.

Arturo parked in front of Mesón Antigua. "This is the only inn in town." He seemed uncomfortable, as if want-ing to reveal a secret but not knowing how to tell it. "There is something you should know about our...accommoda-tions. The inn has two suitable rooms, but—"

Analisa pursed her lips, then parted them in a half-smile. "Let me guess. Only one is available."

"You must be psychic!"

"We've been through that already," she said.

"Ah, yes. The parking lot at the Gran Palacio."

"I flunked, remember?" Analisa wondered what it would be like to share a room with him. Their feelings for each other had burst into the open ever so briefly before Los Dejados doused them. The task of outfitting them-selves for this journey had occupied the days following her escape and recovery. There hadn't been time to pay atten-tion to the mysterious new feelings she sensed in herself and was almost sure Arturo shared with her.

What do you want to happen if you spend the night together? Analisa didn't welcome the question. With her conscious side ignoring it, her intuitive self responded. The answer came in the form of a yearning that pulsed in her lower abdomen and sent splintered lightning bolts along her inner thighs.

Arturo took her hand, which defied the elements by suddenly turning cold. "We have our sleeping bags in the back, in case we need them."

"That's right," she said. "We have our sleeping bags."

🌿 🌿 🌿

The innkeeper beamed when Analisa and Arturo entered Mesón Antigua. "Bienvenidos, Señor Cristobal. You are just in time for the evening meal."

Invisible jet streams, originating from the kitchen, permeated the downstairs area with promises of a tasty supper. Even the small lobby's walls and furniture gave off local flavors of onion, garlic, red peppers, and roasting tomatoes. The aroma of fresh-baked tortillas blended with the spices in this culinary paradise.

Arturo signed the register, took the key to Room Two, and led the way up the tiled stairs. "The bathroom is across the hall." He put the key in the lock and opened the door. "The shower is next door. The water will be lukewarm at best."

"You've been here before."

"Once. Maybe twice."

She was curious about Arturo's previous visits to Mesón Antigua. Since he didn't offer, she curbed her inquisitiveness. Analisa scanned the Spartan furnishings. A chipped wash basin hid behind the door. A plain wooden night stand separated the unmatched twin beds, which also provided the only places to sit.

"We won't need our sleeping bags," she said, disturbed by the sinking feeling in her chest. With Problem One out of the way, she tossed her nylon carry-on onto the bed nearest the window, claiming it as her own. "The AAA

Guide Book might give this place one diamond. That would be a generous call."

Arturo dropped his bag at the foot of the second bed and lay down with an audible sigh of relief that another leg of their journey was over. "It has a watertight roof. Around here, that's more important than a good mattress."

"The man downstairs checked me out pretty carefully while checking us in."

Arturo stretched out full-length and rubbed a deeply tanned forearm across his eyes. "You are a woman men check out...carefully."

"Thanks for the compliment." She went to the sink and splashed her face with cold water. "How did you sign us in?"

"Not as Señor y Señora Cristobal, if that is what concerns you."

"The innkeeper knows you. Doesn't this hurt your...reputation?"

Arturo flashed an adolescent grin. "If he was checking you out as carefully as you say, it might enhance my reputation." When Analisa winced, he quickly added, "The moment I learned they had only one room, I explained we weren't married, but that we would consent to sharing a room only if it had two beds."

Analisa cocked her head in a "likely story" pose.

"If it helps, I did my best to imply that we are not romantically involved," he said.

She took a white cotton towel from the rack near the basin. "Straight-arrow guy, aren't you?"

Arturo raised himself on his elbows. "You do not like 'straight-arrow' guys?"

"I didn't say that." She laughed over her shoulder on her way out the door.

※ ※ ※

Mesón Antigua was more like a bed-and-breakfast inn than a hotel or motel. The daily room rate included three meals. Everyone ate at the same time, boardinghouse-style at a large mahogany table in the rough-plastered dining room. The cook offered no menu, just a plentiful *fare du jour*.

Following dinner, Analisa and Arturo circled the main plaza, then settled on a bench opposite the village church. At eight-thirty, the out-of-towners returned to their room.

After baking in the summer sun all day, Mesón Antigua's tile roof served as a heating unit for the upper floor. Analisa rummaged in her bag for a pair of shorts and a tee-shirt. Given the oppressiveness of the air, she preferred sleeping in the buff. Their shared living arrangement removed that option.

"I'm going across the hall to...well, you know," she said. When she returned to the semi-darkened room, Arturo was already in bed, lying on his stomach with only a sheet covering him. His face was turned away from her toward the wall. From the outline of his form, she noticed he hadn't shared her scruples.

She stepped out of her sandals and switched off the small shaded lamp on the night stand. Slipping into bed, she felt like a piece of lunch meat in a sandpaper sandwich. No matter which way she shifted or turned, the coarse sheets grated against her skin, chafing her knees and elbows.

"What did you do at Disneyland?" Arturo's disembodied voice came from far away. "When you worked there."

Wondering if he might be talking in his sleep, Analisa answered, "I was dressed like Alice in Wonderland. Worked the teacup and Mad Hatter's rides." She felt foolish talking to someone who might not recall the conversation when morning came.

"Short dress...pinafore?"

"You've been there?"

"Saw the movie. Must...have been cute...in that...little..." His words receded into measured, rhythmic breathing.

"Blue dress," she added, finishing his thought. "Good night, Arturo."

No response.

Analisa had never spent the night this close to a man. She didn't count camping trips with her dad. Often, seeking warmth against High Sierras temperatures prone to dip close to or below freezing even in mid-summer, they had pushed their sleeping bags close together inside their cozy igloo tent.

Tired as she was, sleep refused to come. She blamed the sheets. The real reason was her nervousness and excitement. Martina Aguilada could actually be right here in Volcán Grande. Analisa saw something romantic and slightly pathos-evoking in her situation. A young woman— orphaned in adulthood by a tragic accident—traveling from village to village in the land of her birth, tearfully begging the local inhabitants to provide her with some tidbit of information leading to her birth mother. Great movie plot. She saw the words, "Based on a true story," emblazoned on the big screen.

Reigning in her imagination, she focused on reality—or what might actually happen. What would it be like to meet the woman who had brought her into the world, then given her up? Some little girls collected dolls. Since childhood, Analisa had gathered a set of queries and stored them in a private internal repository. Face to face with Martina, she expected them to burst through the ruptured spillways of her heart.

After growing up with retellings of her adoption story from the Marconi point of view and from Don Ricardo's, she needed to hear it from her birth mother's side. She wanted Martina to confess, "A piece of my maternal heart was ripped out the day we made that long bus ride into Santa Catalina."

That defining moment in Analisa's life was now only a tattered rag of disjointed images. She had sewn them together with threads of make-believe in an effort to retain some small piece of her Santo Sangrían past.

In light of her recent involvement with Los Dejados, she was also curious about her siblings. What kind of lives had they lived while she enjoyed the privileges of growing up in America? *What if they're among those bent on forcing me into a life of child-bearing captivity? They might even be in jail in the capital at this very minute with their fellow Dejadistas.*

Visualizing her encounter with Martina, Analisa rehearsed the interrogation she had waited all her life to conduct. She balked at admitting that the purpose of this trip was to dump manure on Martina's doorstep. *What difference does it make anymore why she put me up for adoption?* But there was some truth in it. She felt angry and frustrated that an unstoppable clock ticked away Arturo's generous but rationed time. *Was it realistic to continue without him? I have to, no matter what.*

"Are you awake?" came a voice from the darkness.

Frightened, she clutched the coarse sheet with both hands and pulled it to her chin. "Arturo?"

When he sat up in bed, the wall behind him silhouetted his bare upper body. "What are you doing?"

She hesitated. "Was I talking out loud?"

"No. Just tossing and turning. The bedsprings woke me. Calm down or I will have to get someone up here to oil them."

"Sorry. I'll try not to move so much."

"Analisa, I'm joking. It's okay with me if you do somersaults."

They were quiet again until he said, "Analisa?"

"Yes?"

"Is there anything I can do?"

There was, but how to tell him without hurting his feelings? "Matter of fact, there is."

"Name it."

"I'd rather you didn't hang around too close to me tomorrow."

"Very well."

Silence rejoined darkness as the fourth presence in the room. It wasn't the peaceful quiet of a veteran couple, accustomed to spending all their nights together. This silence was alive, charged with energy in the form of needs and desires wordlessly transmitted from one to the other, as if by distant satellite.

"Arturo." Her call was barely audible.

"Yes?"

"It's important to me to be in charge of this process. I don't feel empowered when I have a bodyguard shadowing me."

"All right. You are in charge."

She had expected him to object. Instead, he had yielded to her that first essential beachhead.

"What I'm saying is, don't be too close, but—"

"Don't stray too far?"

"Exactly."

"I understand. You are in charge."

Analisa longed to touch him, to have him hold her through this anxious night.

Closeness.

Distance.

She struggled to find a middle ground between these opposites.

Chapter 27

When Analisa opened her eyes at seven, Arturo was already awake, lying on his side facing her. He looked serene, as if in his dreams he had seen a vision that still enraptured him. No sense of urgency stirred his demeanor. Naked beneath the thin sheet that covered only the lower portion of his body, he seemed content to do nothing other than gaze at her.

Analisa felt exposed—hair disheveled, teeth unbrushed, gritty eyes blinking in an effort to focus and accept the day. "Now, you've seen me at my worst."

"Let me tell you what I see." Arturo thought for a moment, as if a poet or songwriter, carefully selecting his words, keeping some, discarding others, combining the lucky ones into lyrical phrases. "Irresistible hair, yearning to be caressed, its fragrance inhaled. Lips mine respond to as if caught in a magnetic field, at once powerful yet sweetly gentle."

Analisa had no clue how to stop him. Nor did she wish to.

"A neck the most queenly swan would die for. Above all, I see the clearest, most pure and honest eyes in the world. They caution, 'Don't lie to me,' and I pledge I never will, that I will speak only the truth that is in my heart...and pray it will drive away all sadness and doubt."

His words stirred her with desire as nothing had before. She broke from his gaze and turned toward the open, screenless window. A voice urged her to forget Martina Aguilada. If you came here looking for family, it said, you may have already found all you need right here, in this man. When she turned toward him again, he stood between the two beds. During her mental and visual absence, he had magically produced a clean pair of khaki shorts and slipped them on. She felt deprived, having missed the transition.

"Words like that turn a girl's head." Her voice was distant, wistful.

He sat on her bed and touched a curl that had strayed to the outer edge of her pillow. "You got me started."

Searching his eyes, she found no hint of deception, only truth and love.

"No one's ever said those things to me before, not like that."

Since that night—when was it?—that she and Arturo had stood together on the empty stage of the Bellas Artes, Analisa had known at some primal level that they'd be together, alone like this in some romantic place. She also believed that love had its own seasons and order of events. In her present vulnerable state, the inevitable might happen too soon. Did it spoil love to make love before its time? Then, there was the shadow of recent events. Had she sufficiently recovered her sense of self to respond to Arturo freely, with wholehearted passion...without fear?

"I'm not the same as I was before. You know, Los Dejados and all that . . ."

Arturo frowned. "Damaged lily?"

"I wouldn't use that term, but yes, I suppose so. In some way."

"If you are asking, do I wish it had never happened? Of course." His voice hardened with suppressed rage. "I despise those people for putting your life in jeopardy. For hurting you. I despise them for hurting me. I cannot stand to imagine what awaited you had you not been so resourceful and courageous." His expression softened. "But if you are asking, can I still love you . . ?"

Analisa had to know the truth. Now. Before she took the next step along this road they traveled.

A quiet laugh emerged from some private chamber within him. "I didn't expect us to be having this conversation. Not this morning. Not for some time."

"Me either. But here we are."

Their lives had melded at a frightening pace, much faster than she was prepared for. Apparently, he felt it, too.

"All right, then." He took her hand and placed it over his heart. "Analisa Marconi, I love you. I feel more alive today than I have in all my life. I want to spend all my days and nights with you."

She had shed enough tears of grief in the past year to last a lifetime. Those she wept now were of a different kind. Their source was joy, from which she had become so estranged that she despaired of ever experiencing it again. "I thought singing made you feel alive."

Arturo embraced her, drawing her head to his chest. "I thought so, too. Now, I realize my whole career has only been the Overture. You have given me a reason to sing other than to make money and receive applause and adulation from my audiences. Act One of our opera is about to begin."

Analisa thrilled at his expression of love. Still, she couldn't yet imagine how she might fit into his world of theatrical performance and international travel. Based more on hope than on common sense, she took his head in her hands and pulled his lips down to meet her ready mouth.

For a long time, they lay holding each other on the narrow bed, Arturo on top of the sheet, she beneath it, her bottom tucked into his abdomen. Neither spoke. The flow of undammed, unpredictable words had ceased. Analisa needed time to absorb what had passed between them. Although she felt him grow hard against her body when she covered her breasts with his hands, he made no move to invite himself under the covers.

🌟 🌟 🌟

For over an hour, Analisa sat in the plaza on a splintery bench whose paint had long ago faded into distant memory. The broad, flat leaves of a fruitless mulberry protected her from the midsummer sun. She was grateful for the altitude of Volcán Grande. It took the edge off the heat and exposed the village to the soft caress of an occasional passing breeze.

Before assuming her "sniffing location," as Arturo called it, she had crossed the plaza and entered the empty chapel. No hymns filled the sanctuary and spilled out toward the plaza. The good people of Volcán Grande labored at their jobs, if they had work, or in their homes caring for their children. She envied them. They had somewhere to go, unlike her own uprooted self.

Having taken up her position, she waited. No one approached her, except two old men who walked by, scowling as if she had usurped their private, privileged places. She tossed a friendly "Buenos días" but resisted the temptation to engage in conversation. *Too soon. It's better to let them come to me.* The *viejos* sought out less-protected benches nearby and pretended to ignore her.

In her solitude, Analisa contemplated the events of the current year.

Graduation.

The plane crash and her parents' deaths.

Her rescue and seemingly endless rehabilitation.

The decision to return to Santo Sangre in search of a woman she had never really known and to whom she was linked by blood but not emotion.

Her thoughts drifted to Los Dejados, especially Marta. Then to Arturo. Dave. Back to Arturo.

"Señorita. Señorita."

Youthful voices called Analisa back to the plaza, to the leaden heat that had intensified as the morning progressed. A boy and girl studied her with the unquenchable curiosity of children. She guessed their ages at no more than seven or eight, although undernourishment might have kept their bodies from maturing normally. "I'm sorry. I must have dozed off," she said in Spanish. "It's very warm, isn't it?"

The boy looked at her with a puzzled expression. "You sleep with your eyes open, Señorita?"

Analisa burst into a childlike giggle. "Maybe I do. I never looked." She hoped the ice had broken and was glad she had waited for someone to come to her. She patted the empty seat beside her. "Sit down a moment."

"No, *gracias*," the boy said.

The girl asked her name.

"Analisa."

The child repeated the name, caressing each vowel, lisping slightly on the "s". "My name is Chacha."

"I am Federico," the boy volunteered. "Everyone calls me Rico."

"Where did you come from?"

"I live in the United States, but I was born in Santo Sangre."

"Have you come to live in Volcán Grande?" Chacha asked. Clearly, she found no logic in trading America's milk and honey for a life in their village.

"I'm not sure, yet." Analisa decided to make a gentle probe. "I'm looking for someone."

The children's smiles vanished. They stepped back, out of arm's reach.

Analisa upbraided herself for moving too quickly. "Please, don't go away. I'm not from the police or from the government. I promise." She told them about her adoption and how her parents had been killed. The children, caught up in her story, reversed their retreat. At the end,

Chacha's eyes pooled with shared sorrow. Rico wanted more information about the Bonanza.

"I'm trying to find my first mother, the one I was born to. It's very important to me. I've come a long way. I was told she might be living in your village."

"Someone adopted my baby sister," Rico said. "She lives in a place called Israel. I miss her. So does my mother. They used to send pictures." His voice trailed away. "Not any more."

"Was Analisa the name your 'here mamá' gave you?" Chacha wanted to know.

"No. I was born Isabella María Aguilada."

"Aguilada," Rico repeated.

Analisa detected a spark of recognition. "Do you know someone with that name?"

"The brick lady!" said Chacha, proud of herself, as if she had raised her hand in school and given the correct answer.

Analisa's heart skipped a beat. Slow down, slow down, she cautioned. You'll scare them away. Don't sound too interested. "The . . . 'brick lady'?" With a reassuring smile she added, "It would be fun to meet someone with the same name as mine."

The children moved away, and Analisa's spirits sank. I'm close. I know it!

When she didn't move, Rico gestured for her to follow. She rose from the bench and trailed the pair across the plaza. They stopped at a small stand. A youngish man of indeterminate age was busy on this hot morning selling the greenest tennis ball-sized oranges Analisa had ever seen.

Rico pointed to the man. "Aguilada."

Analisa studied the orange seller's face. As much as she wanted to discover herself in his features, he looked nothing like her. She turned to share her puzzlement with her guides, but they had disappeared into the dust of the plaza. She wondered if they had really existed in the flesh. Or

were they angels of God? Had the Lord sent them to move
her off the bench and forward on the road to herself? At
any rate, they had left her alone to deal with her namesake.

When he had satisfied his last customer, the man turned
his back and fished more fruit from a crate to replenish his
countertop supply.

"My name is...Isabella María Aguilada," she whispered
to his back.

At the sound of her voice, he raised himself slowly and
studied her face, her clothing. He seemed to be looking for
someone he once knew. "Isabella María?"

She nodded. "What is your name?"

"Jesús. Jesús María."

Analisa's body language urged him to complete the
appellation.

"Aguilada."

Stay calm! "My mother was Martina Aguilada. Do you
know her?"

"Isabella María?" he repeated, squinting into the bright
midday sun.

"Yes."

"From America?"

Chapter 28

"My sister?" Jesús María spoke without emotion, wary of some trick or deception.

"It's possible." Analisa needed affirmation that her search was about to end. "Martina?"

His jaw set. A fire of inner turmoil projected onto the screen of his eyes. "I am her son."

"Then, I believe I am your sister." She experienced this moment in eerie slow-motion. She wanted so much to embrace this stranger whose blood she almost certainly shared, but Jesús María's unwelcoming expression and rigid body cautioned against it. Her experience with Los Dejados reminded her that, for Jesús, years of want, perhaps even deep-seated loathing might contaminate their fraternal reunion. She had thrust herself into his life like an alien being. His reaction called for a cautious approach, discreet inquiry about his personal life.

"Be careful about accepting anyone as family too soon," Arturo had warned.

As if on cue, Arturo entered the plaza from the front door of Mesón Antigua. She signaled for him to join her at the orange stand.

"Arturo Cristobal, I'd like you to meet Jesús María Aguilada. My brother."

Surprise and a host of other cautionary feelings collaborated to banish the friendly smile Arturo had worn as he approached.

"Perhaps we should talk privately," he whispered.

When Analisa stood firm, he extended his hand to Jesús María. The orange seller hesitated, then met Arturo's hand without energy or commitment.

"I'd like to see Martina," she said.

Jesús María loaded several crates of fruit on his cart and pushed it away from the dusty plaza. With a motion of his head, he signaled for Analisa and Arturo to accompany him. They did, in silence, hand in hand.

Jesús María stopped several hundred yards up-slope from the village. They had arrived at a level area from which the vegetation had been cleared. The rust-colored earth beneath their feet reminded Analisa of the infield at Edison Field in Anaheim.

Jesús María pointed to a group of three women in straw hats who were conversing, with their backs to the approaching visitors. Behind them stood a crudely con-structed, dome-shaped structure, covered with layers of thick dried clay. A stream of boiling, smokeless vapors escaped via a tin chimney.

On the ground, in neat rows, lay over a hundred molds, a foot long and about six inches deep and filled with a wet mixture of sand and thick, red clay. The ruddy color of the women's legs made it clear they served as human mixers. Analisa recalled Rico's and Chacha's description, the brick lady.

Jesús María touched Analisa's forearm and pointed. "Martina."

Before she asked another question, he started back toward the village to resume his interrupted commerce.

Analisa and Arturo approached the women. She guessed the age of the oldest to be not more than fifty. Her skin and graying hair evidenced a life hard-fought on the volcano's outer skin. The other women were closer to Analisa's age, but physical labor and exposure to the ele-ments had treated them with equal harshness.

Analisa tried to speak, but no sound conveyed the thoughts bubbling inside her. She looked to Arturo with a plea for help.

"Buenos días, Señoras," he said politely.

"We've sold all our bricks for today," one of the younger women said. "If you want to place an order, we can have them for you day after tomorrow."

Analisa finally found her voice. "We haven't come to buy bricks." She took a deep breath. "I'm looking for Señora Martina Aguilada."

The trio eyed her with suspicion. Analisa smiled and did her best to look like a non-threatening American tourist. Inside, the possibility she had made a mistake and reached another dead end terrified her.

"I am she," the older woman said without moving forward.

Her coworkers edged protectively to her side.

"Señora." Analisa cleared the lump that had formed at the back of her throat, blocking her airway. "I have reason to believe...that I am...your daughter, Isabella María. I was born twenty-four years ago and placed in an orphanage in Santa Catalina at the age of four. I was adopted by—" The lump returned, this time the size of a golf ball. "An American couple."

The older woman stepped forward without changing her business-like expression. No glimmer of recognition darted across her eyes.

Had the woman heard her? "I believe I am your daughter," Analisa repeated.

"What do you want?"

The question's simplicity stung her. Martina was exactly right. What do I want? What do I expect from this woman? From this moment? Arturo slipped a steadying, encouraging arm around her waist. "I'd like to know you. I want you to know me."

Martina's leathery forehead wrinkled into a row of question marks. "Why?"

"My parents—my adoptive parents—are dead." Her mind numbed. In its absence, her uncensored tongue spoke her rawest feelings. "I thought I knew who I was. I lost that certainty when they died. My hope is that, in finding you, I will rediscover my true identity." She pointed to her chest. "Here. Inside."

The first flicker of emotion appeared at the corners of
Martina's mouth. She wiped her muddy hands on the sides
of her faded print dress. Callused fingertips grazed
Analisa's cheek and moved across her forehead, before
playing with a strand of curly hair. "Come."

🌽 🌽 🌽

Analisa and Arturo sat side by side in the stifling living
room of Martina's small house. The wooden slats of the
thinly upholstered sofa felt as hard on her bottom as gym-
nasium bleachers. On the way from the brick yard,
Martina had introduced the other two women as Analisa's
older sisters. Carolina del Rosario, the older of the two,
now sat on the floor close to her mother, her shapeless
dress pulled over her knees. Elena María disappeared into
the kitchen to prepare refreshments.

"Your father was very good looking," Martina said.
"You remind me of him." She reached over to touch
Analisa's chin and turn her face to a profile. "Same nose
and mouth, the same large eyes that made a woman
believe every word from his mouth was God's own truth."
Martina spoke so softly that at times Analisa had to strain
to hear her. "He had a wife in another part of the island.
Said it was a forced marriage. Her parents never liked him.
They accused him of beating her. His father-in-law swore
to cut your father's heart out if he ever came near his
daughter again." A wry smile parted Martina's lips. "He
never did, as far as I know."

Without a hint that anything remained of whatever love
Martina might have once had for the man, she described in
simple terms a life that had been a battle for survival, a
lonely struggle. Her on-and-off partner, now deceased,
had been more of a drain on the family's resources than a
help. A guttural quality invaded her voice, a poor imitation

of laughter. "All he was ever good at was getting drunk and making me pregnant."

Analisa tried to imagine herself knotted up inside Martina's womb, drawing nourishment—life itself—from her weathered body. Had she really sucked at those wrinkled breasts that rose and fell with her breath at the neckline of her plain dress? I am flesh of Claire Marconi's flesh, bone of her bone, she thought. Spiritually and mentally, if not physically.

"I had the older girls and Jesús María. Then, you came along. Our life got worse. We survived by selling tortillas in the plaza first at Santa Teresita, then here." Her voice trailed off when Elena María entered the room carrying a tray of glasses and a lemonade-type drink.

Hearing this story filled Analisa with a sense of her birth mother's dignity and nobility. We Aguiladas are survivors. Must be a family trait. Plain as Martina's environment was, she had finally achieved a stable place in local society, no longer living on the edge of starvation. Elena set the tray on the floor and took her place cross-legged next to her sister.

Martina continued. "One day, I heard of a man in the village making inquiries. He was looking for fatherless families with too may children to feed. The next day, he arrived at my door—I did not live here then. A nice man, very concerned about us."

"Don Ricardo Valenzuela," Analisa said.

Surprise flashed across Martina's face. "How do you know?"

"He helped my parents—my American family—adopt me."

"Then you know the story."

"I know their side of it."

Analisa's rising emotions made it hard for her to formulate and express her thoughts. "I'd like to hear yours."

Arturo rested his hand on her knee and massaged it gently. His touch gave her strength.

Martina hesitated, as if asking herself if she wanted to revisit a place from which she had long ago moved on. "Don Ricardo said, 'If you want to offer one of your daughters for adoption, bring her to the capital.' He gave me his address and the address of a Señora Dorada, a foster mother. He promised to take good care of my child until he found a family for her."

"My child," not "you," Analisa reflected, keenly aware of the emotional separation between Martina's four-year-old Isabella and the grown-up woman sitting on the sofa in her living room. Analisa had waited all her life for this moment. "This is hard for me." A wave of bitterness threatened to contaminate her words. She pushed it away. "What I don't know is . . ."

"Why I chose you?"

Analisa rejoiced that she didn't have to say the words herself. She repressed an urge to leap across the room and throw her arms around Martina. Instead, she composed herself and said, simply, "Yes. Why me?"

"Perhaps I should not say this in front of Elena María and Carolina del Rosario. I have never spoken of this to anyone." She leaned forward and lovingly rested her hand on Elena María's shoulder. "I chose Isabella María...you...because you were different. When you dropped out of my womb, I said to the midwife, 'Where did this one come from?' I knew your father. I had borne you in my body and given you life. No doubt about that. But you were a stranger. By the time you were two, I knew you did not belong to me. You were like a little caged bird who needed to be set free to find your true home in the world. When Don Ricardo came, I...opened the cage."

Analisa ripped a tissue from her pocket and dabbed at the corners of her eyes. When the tissue became a sodden wad, Arturo offered a clean white handkerchief.

"All this time, I thought . . ." Analisa's words evaporated in the dense humid air.

"That I valued you the least."

Analisa nodded.

"Well, now you know," Martina said.

"Now I know."

Martina explained that the turning point in the Aguilada women's lives had come the day an Australian businessman arrived in Volcán Grande. He announced his plan to form a banking cooperative just for women. "Señor Roper believed men were less reliable. 'A woman will do whatever it takes to feed her children,' he said. He made the first loans from his own funds for us to invest in businesses of our choice. He made us the bank's directors. I saw the need for a brick yard to supply building projects in the region." Pride forced a smile across Martina's craggy features. "My business succeeded. I repaid my loan and purchased new materials. Now I own the brick yard...and this house."

Analisa's heart reached out in gratitude to this woman who had unlocked and shared her precious store of intimate memories. She was convinced that, in the telling, Martina had reconnected with her, too. Harder to gauge were the feelings of Elena María and Carolina del Rosario. And Jesús María? Why hadn't he joined them?

Suddenly, the walls closed in on Analisa. She longed to get out of Martina's house, back to the inn or the church. She needed space to assimilate this information in private. She grabbed at Arturo's sleeve and moved toward the door. "May I come again?"

Martina shrugged. "Tomorrow if you wish. We will be making bricks all day." No parting kiss. No family embrace.

Neither Analisa nor Arturo spoke as they made their way back towards the center of Volcán Grande.

Chapter 29

By the time Analisa and Arturo reached the edge of Volcán Grande, the sun had fallen well past its zenith. The temperature and humidity hadn't noticed.

"The Aguiladas had no idea who you are," she said.

"It was wonderful to be a fly on the wall, not the center of attention."

"Is it that difficult? Celebrity?" Uncertainty about how she might someday fit into his world layered the question with personal significance.

"Sometimes." He thought for a moment. "Too often." Then he brightened. "By the way, the innkeeper informed me this morning he has a second room available tonight."

Analisa stopped in the path and they faced each other. "What did you tell him?" She shaded her eyes to monitor his reaction.

"That I must discuss it with you first," he said, not prompting her to decide one way or the other.

"What do you prefer?"

"I want what is best for you, whatever will make you happy."

Analisa accepted his embrace and pressed her head to his chest. At this moment, she felt richer and more fulfilled than at any time since her parents' deaths. She had come to Santo Sangre seeking answers from Martina. Mission accomplished. In fact, she had received more from Martina than she ever expected. In Arturo, she had found that previously elusive other half of herself. She stretched to meet his lips, which he opened in welcome.

"Tell him we won't need the second room."

❦ ❦ ❦

Once they were back in their room at Mesón Antigua, Analisa's body turned to lead. She lay on the bed and closed her eyes.

"I need a shower and some fresh clothes," Arturo said. "You probably need some time by yourself."

She marveled at how accurately he read her in so short a time. With great effort, she raised her weary body, resting on her elbows. "Thanks for being there today."

A golden smile crinkled his face, making her realize there had been little laughter in their day. The day's not over, she reminded herself. "Is there a public telephone here? I'd like to tell Dave about Martina."

Arturo's smile slid behind a passing cloud. "I have my cell phone. Use that."

"What's the matter?"

"Nothing. I love you, that is all."

Analisa savored the words. They felt sweet and silvery. She memorized each syllable and instructed her memory to keep them fresh and available forever. "Do you still wonder about Dave and me?"

"I need to know more about how he fits into your life."

Analisa sat up and pushed her back against the wooden headboard. She had always heard that Latin males were jealous of their women. She detected not the slightest hint of this vice in Arturo's straightforward question.

"All right. Let me tell you about David Gallego." Analisa related the history of their relationship, her vision of him at the crash site, and the indispensable role he had played in calling her back to the world of life, laughter, and hope. "Dave's a constant in my life. Always will be. I wouldn't be alive if it weren't for him."

"Then I am indeed grateful to him." Arturo sat on the edge of his bed, idly fingering the ripples on the bedspread. An uncomfortable silence filled the charged space between them. It was clear he had more questions.

"But?" she prompted.

"Were you in love with him? Are you?"

"'No' to the second question," she said without reservation. "I'm not in love with Dave. Was I ever? Yes, in some fashion. I suppose I thought he was safe to love when I was younger. He epitomized the unavailable, unattainable clergyman. By the time I left for college, loving him had stopped being safe. It took on all sorts of dangerous overtones, requiring major life choices neither of us had the will to make. Loving each other was okay. Being together was impossible. Not as husband and wife. And, any other way was unacceptable."

"Dave loves you. Is he still 'in love' with you?"

"Persistent fellow, aren't you?"

"Everything about you is important to me."

She loved being important to Arturo. "Is Dave in love with me? That's tougher. I believe he is." The admission startled her. "Gosh, I've never said that aloud before, to anyone. In some ways, I know Dave better than he knows himself. That part of his life is very painful. Priesthood and work versus marriage, children." A deep sadness gripped her chest. "He wants it all."

Analisa felt as if she had stumbled into a secret room inside Dave's heart. She had discovered the source of the melancholy that often hid behind his warm, inviting eyes.

"I have never understood why that is not possible for priests," Arturo said.

"Me either. Neither does he." She had a strong urge to put her arms around Dave, to comfort him and tell him what a good man he was. But her friend was a sea and a continent removed.

"Will he remain in the priesthood?"

"I sure hope so. He's a priest through and through. A good one. The best, in fact. Any more Dave questions?"

"Just one. If he left the ministry, would it make a difference to you? To us?"

"That's an easy one." A broad smile sprang fresh from the center of her being. "No. I love Dave. I love being with him. That's no secret. But my heart soars only when I'm with you. Do you believe me, Arturo?" When he took her hands, she gazed directly into his earnest eyes, which shone like polished ebony.

"How can I not believe you?" he said. "What did I ever do to deserve your love?"

Her gentle laughter broke the heaviness of the moment. "You don't deserve me. I'm a gift. So are you to me."

"Then, we are meant to enjoy what we have and spend the rest of our lives puzzling how it ever came to be."

"I like the sound of that." She leaned forward and kissed him. Her cheek grazed his late-afternoon beard spreading a warm, at-home feeling throughout her body.

"Did I really say, 'The rest of our lives'?" he teased.

"You did and I'm holding you to it." The reality of how her life had changed in the few short days she had known Arturo caused her to become serious. "I never believed love could happen this fast. Not to me. Usually, I need to think things through, plan before I act. That's what I did when I was weighing basketball scholarships. I decided on St. Mary's and selected international business as my major."

"How good are you?"

"At what?"

"Basketball."

"Damn good!" she said. "At least, I was before my knee got all smashed up."

"I'd like to see some of your moves."

"I haven't held a ball in my hands—a basketball—since the accident." A warm rush crept up her neck and set her face on fire.

Arturo drew her to his side. She resisted. "Go take your shower," she said. "I told you I'm a thinker. It's time to reflect on what's happened today."

❦ ❦ ❦

Analisa went downstairs, out into the plaza, and soon found herself facing the open doors of the old wooden church. She slipped inside, hoping to find it deserted. It wasn't. She sat in a rear pew and watched a mother and daughter light candles at the flowered shrine of the Virgin Mary. When they left, some inner force called her to the gaudy shrine. She knelt on the worn wooden priedieu, shifting her weight to ease the burden on her bad knee.

The statue of a brown-skinned Mary holding her infant Latino son was too saccharine for Analisa's taste. Still, she focused on the Madonna's glassy eyes, which seemed to gaze back at her with motherly concern.

Thank you for helping me find Martina. I thought I'd know what to do next, but I don't. Analisa felt rudderless, in danger of drifting off in whichever direction the strongest wind might take her. She weighed her options. Do I get on a ship and go back to the States?

Do I return to Santa Catalina with Arturo, become part of his entourage?

Should I stay on in Volcán Grande to be close to Martina and her family?

Reflecting on this third possibility, Analisa envisioned herself calf-deep in the rusty muck of Martina's brick molds, lifting heavy blocks from the firing kiln, and selling the finished products to local builders. The image wasn't totally disagreeable.

This is the life I was born to. It's probably what I'd be doing right now if Martina hadn't set her "little bird" free.

Set free. Analisa had based all her adolescent rage against Martina on a wrong assumption. If only I'd known her story from the beginning.

Uncaged. Her father often spoke of the mystery of a Divine Providence that united the three Marconis in a seemingly predestined union—the memory so vivid, she heard her father speak and saw again how his eyes misted over in the telling, no matter how often he repeated the tale.

With her heart both aching and rejoicing, Analisa brushed away a falling tear with the back of her hand. She glanced over her shoulder, sure her parents hovered near-by within the empty sanctuary's twilight shadows.

It had taken two powerful loves to make her the person she was today. The first, Martina Aguilada's. That brave woman had responded to a message whispered in her soul that Isabella María was not hers to keep, but was merely on loan to her. The other love was that of her parents who had gladly offered Martina's tiny bird a welcoming perch.

Finally, she prayed for Arturo. And for the two of them. She asked the Virgin Mother to guide them along the unmapped paths ahead. Rising stiffly from the hardwood kneeler, she genuflected and turned to leave. Halfway down the center aisle, she turned abruptly to address Mary again. "I'm going to sleep with him tonight," she said aloud. "What do you think of that?" She waited for her echo to fade into the incense-laden air. No words of con-demnation bolted from the heavens. Nor did any rise in protest from within.

Her heart sang along with the joyful trills of native song-birds as she strolled back to Mesón Antigua. Her body felt lighter than it had in days.

Chapter 30

"Feel better?" Arturo asked when Analisa returned from her visit to the chapel.

She flashed a broad grin. "Much."

Having showered, he stood at the sink vigorously drying his thick black hair with a not-so-absorbent towel. He had changed into a different pair of shorts but wore no shirt. "Are you ready for some supper? I told the innkeeper we plan to dine out. He looked offended. I think his wife is the cook. He suggested that little place across the plaza."

Analisa moved behind him. She slipped her arms around his broad chest. His skin, moist from the shower, felt clean and soft. When she kissed him between the shoulder blades, he stopped toweling his hair. "Are you sure?" he said.

"Yes. You?"

"I want you so much, I could take you right now and not concern myself with the consequences."

"But what?"

"I respect you too much to make love to you until I know we are in this together," he said. "No turning back."

She inhaled his scent and, with her fingers, traced tight, feathery circles around his nipples. "You're supposed to be the impetuous artist."

"Passion I have in abundance. Enough for both of us," he said to her reflection in the mirror. "I'm learning from you to plan ahead."

"We can't see the future." She pressed her lips to his back and wet her tongue with the moisture from his flesh. It failed to quench her thirst for him.

Arturo turned around. Finding the lifeline in her palm, he traced the crease with a finger before pressing her hand to his lips. "I need to know you will be with me always, wherever life takes us."

She made her choice. "I'll be here."

"So will I."

Despite Analisa's solemn vow to this man who had so unexpectedly won her heart and lifelong loyalty, David Gallego refused to leave her alone with Arturo. His presence at this intimate scene made a crowd of three, consuming precious oxygen in the already stuffy westside room. She recalled a conversation she'd had with Dave one evening in his upstairs suite in the rectory. It took place during Christmas break. She forgot what had triggered it, but the subject of marriage drifted into their rambling discussion.

Dave climbed up on his soap box and expounded, "The Church has always taught you don't need a priest to get married. The wedding ceremony is only a confirmation of the fact that a man and woman are already married. They were wed before God when they committed themselves to each other for life. If they haven't made that commitment, nothing they say or do during the ceremony—not even their vows—can make them husband and wife."

"What about witnesses?" she had countered.

"A technicality. Society and the church need to document marital unions. Look, Analisa. What if you were cast ashore on a deserted island with a man? You were the only survivors of a shipwreck. If you decided to commit your lives to each other as a married couple, who would witness your union?"

She dismissed this argument at the time as another of Davé's liberal theological opinions. Today his words made perfect sense. She and Arturo had become one in spirit—before God—by exchanging lifelong vows over the wash basin in their stifling room at Mesón Antigua. Any future marriage ceremony would only confirmed what they had already pledged.

Arturo's mouth covered hers. His determined tongue searched for its mate. In his arms, Analisa felt dizzy, ungrounded, suspended in space, yet more alive than ever in her life. He carried her to the bed—his bed—the one farthest from the open window, where the sounds of their lovemaking would be least likely to disturb—or entertain—others at the inn. She considered the choice of beds symbolic. She wanted to be in his bed, forever, to make it their bed.

A steamy rain drummed on the roof, forming an impenetrable curtain outside the open window and buffering any sounds emanating from their room. Arturo unbuttoned her damp shirt and laid his face against her chest. "You smell like a garden."

"More like an overripe melon," she quipped.

Tasting her, he vowed, "From now on, I will eat only overripe melons."

Her eyelids closed, resting. She retreated inside herself to prepare for him a place of hospitality and comfort, a home. He raised her slightly and reached behind to unhook her bra, which she tossed across the room. When his mouth covered her right nipple and a portion of her firm breast, wild sensations beamed to every part of her body.

The night of the Fourth of July resurrected itself from Analisa's memory. She recalled the distant tingling sensation Dave had aroused in her when he slipped his hand beneath her sports bra. Arturo's touch, the play of his mouth and tongue, was infinitely more satisfying. Best of all, no cautionary voices demanded that she halt him in mid-flight...or do anything but enjoy and rejoice.

He unbuttoned the top of her linen pants and slid the zipper down. She helped him remove her undergarment. Fully exposed to him for the first time, Analisa felt free, like a three-year-old who strips off her clothes because she finds them an encumbrance to play.

Arturo hesitated before removing his shorts. He was like a camera, filling himself with images of her before satisfying other overwhelming desires. She nudged him over on his back and straddled him. "No rush," she breathed. "Dinner can wait."

"Breakfast, too."

Arturo's warm penis throbbed in anticipation against the outer walls of her most secret place. Not even Lupe Santana, with all his superior physical power and evil intent, had been able to gain entrance. Now, she willingly offered the key to Arturo Cristobal...to keep forever.

Never before had Analisa experienced such uninhibited pleasure. Even when her greatest high had been running up and down a basketball floor, a clock always marked the limit of play. She had to keep one eye on the defense, the other on the minutes' digital descent. She had promised to visit Martina and her sisters again. But that was half a day removed from the present moment. A lifetime.

She massaged Arturo's shoulders, all the while letting her lips roam without planned itinerary over his forehead, eyes, chin, and along the side of his neck down his chest. No part of him escaped her attention. The lovers rolled onto their sides facing each other, laughing giddily. He found the enlarged nub of her clitoris, by now so wet that his fingers glided lightly and with ease across its circumference—left, right, up, down and around—in rhythmic repetition, until her back arched with delight. She dug her fingernails into his flesh and bit his shoulder to keep from screaming her pleasure to all the guests in the inn. Finally, her orgasmic waves stilled, leaving body and spirit at rest, like the surface of a woodland pond on a summer day.

Analisa invited Arturo to enter. "I want you to experience what I just felt."

When fully inside her, he lay still, breathing heavily and repeating softly into her hair, "I don't want this to end."

"It won't," she assured him. "We've just begun."

They remained that way for a long time, savoring their closeness. Periodically, he jerked and made a guttural sound as his not-understanding organ pulsed deep within her, demanding permission to release. She did her best to delay his climax by not moving her pelvis, only clutching him against the length of her body.

"I like the way we fit together," she said.

"I thought I had everything before," he breathed. "I had nothing...until now."

Analisa hadn't realized the erotic power of words. Each time Arturo whispered his love into her ear, her lower body responded with an involuntary tremor. Inevitably, delay became impossible, despite their best efforts. Explosion was imminent.

"You might become pregnant," he said.

"I know."

"I want our children, but I am concerned for you."

Analisa clung to him, unwilling to let go. "I'll give you all the babies you want...but later."

With superhuman effort they disengaged, letting the sweat-soaked sheet absorb his semen. They repeated their lovemaking as often as it was physically possible for him to regain potency. Each time with greater passion and intensity. Each time with the same agreed-upon conclusion.

When the sun brought the first rays of daylight into their room, Analisa felt a wholeness she had never before experienced or even known possible. With the light, a post-deluge breeze made its lazy way through the open window, dispelling the slight chill of the nighttime dampness. She lay in Arturo's embrace, softly kissing his eyelids, envious of whoever else might populate his dreams.

"I'm hungry," he said when he finally awoke.

"Impossible. I feel devoured."

His smile was proud, triumphant. "Would you like some supper?"

"My darling, supper time came and went hours ago."

He laughed. "Why didn't you call me?"

"You were busy. Don't you remember?"

"I don't ever want to forget." She leaned over him, letting her pencil-point nipples graze his chest. "When we made love the first time, I thought about Dave."

Arturo raised a questioning eyebrow.

"That's not what I mean." She explained what Dave had said about marriage and the moment when two people are united in God's eyes. Arturo thought for a moment. "I don't think they preach that in St. Catherine's Cathedral."

"Or at my parish church," she said. "Not even Dave."

"But it makes complete sense. You are my bride, my wife, my partner until death separates us."

"And may God delay that for a long, long time."

"Amen!" he said, with the full tonal emphasis of his operatic baritone.

They consummated their marriage again, unsure of how many times they had done so since exchanging vows only hours earlier.

Chapter 31

"Dave, it's Analisa." She had waited until it was at least six in the morning on the West Coast. "Hope I didn't wake you up."

"Are you kidding? I had an early sick call. You sound so far away."

"I am." Very far, she added to herself.

He hastened a humorless, "How are you doing?"

"Great." She tried not to sound as great as she felt as she told Dave about finding Martina.

"How's Arturo?" Dave asked.

"Fine. He's with me." In fact, her back pressed against him in the small floor space between the beds in their room. His open palms rested lightly on her waist. She took his right hand and slid it to her breast, letting his touch ignite fresh recollections of the night just past. When he snuggled closer, a chill coursed along her limbs to the tips of her fingers and toes.

"What's Martina like?" Dave wanted to know.

"Turns out she's quite the business woman. Makes and sells bricks with two of her daughters...my sisters." The word sounded awkward. She had always thought of herself as an only child. "They live simply, but they own a small piece of land and a house. They're quite proud of their accomplishments."

He said he wished he were with her.

"I know." It was the only honest thing to say.

"How did they react when you showed up out of nowhere?"

"Not quite like the father of the Prodigal Son, but they were kind, very hospitable. I was finally able to get an answer to the big 'Why?'. . . . She said she saw in me, even at that young age—" Saying the words brought tears of gratitude for her own good fortune and sadness for

Martina's painful choice. "A 'caged bird' that needed to be set free."

"That's beautiful. When are you coming home?"

Analisa hesitated. She wanted to say she was home, that she had found her life in Arturo's arms. "I don't know if I am," she said, being deliberately vague.

"Ever?" A note of panic chilled his voice.

"Sometime, sure. There are things I need to settle here first."

Silence.

"I'll keep in touch, Dave."

"Promise?"

"Yes." It wasn't as solemn as the vow she had made to Arturo last night, but it was one she'd certainly keep. She had no intention of disappearing from Dave's life. She almost told him she and Arturo were married but didn't want to get bogged down in a theological-legal discussion. "Dave, I can't explain myself right now, but I want to thank you for a special gift you gave me."

"Gift? I don't get it."

"Something you said to me once. It's complicated. Look, I've got to run. You'll hear from me."

"I love you, Analisa."

"I'm counting on that."

She pressed the End button on Arturo's cell phone and handed it back to him with a worried expression. "That call's going to cost you a lot."

He kissed the back of her neck. "We can afford it."

She turned and idly ran her fingers across his temples until her hands joined behind his head. "Don't you love the sound of 'we.'"

"Yes. I think I am going to like being a 'we.'"

The full realization that she was a wealthy woman hit her. "Every dollar I spend of my parents' life insurance money reminds me of the price they paid for my financial independence."

"Somehow, I do not believe you will honor their memory by feeling guilty the rest of your life."

"You're right."   Analisa kissed him, tenderly at first, then with accelerating passion.   "My dad especially would be really pissed."

❦ ❦ ❦

The nighttime showers had left scattered puddles in the graveled plaza.   The trail to Martina's brick yard was another story.   The squish of volcanic dust-turned-mud made Analisa's sandals not only useless but a hazard.   She rolled her pants legs up to her knees and removed her shoes.   Immediately, traction improved as the soles of her feet met solid ground beneath the wet, mobile earth.   The warm brick-colored mud oozing between her toes felt sensuous to skin still charged from a night of lovemaking.

As she walked, she replayed every moment of their embrace.   The recollections caressed her body just as Arturo had.   Lost in daydreams, she rounded a large outcropping of volcanic rock and froze.   In front of her, positioned like a forbidding sentinel at a military roadblock was Jesús María Aguilada—her brother.   Although thoroughly startled, she did her best to hide it.

"Good morning, Jesús," she said in Spanish.

His response startled her as much as his unexpected presence.   "You are neither welcome or safe here."

"Why?"

"Do you think Los Dejados are dead because their leaders have been unjustly arrested?   We are many...and everywhere.   Our cause will prevail."

"We?   Our?"

"News travels quickly up the slopes of Chuchuán. What I did not know was that our new *coneja* was my own little sister."

"I'm no one's *'coneja,'*" Analisa growled. "I never will be. Does Martina know about this?"

He shook his head.

"Elena María? Carolina del Rosario?"

"They are with us."

"Why do you hate me so?"

Jesús scanned her appearance. "Look at yourself."

The answer lay in the contrast between his long-worn jeans and washed-to-holes tee-shirt and her own designer casuals; the purity and softness of her cheeks versus his sun-cracked, prematurely aging face; her smooth hands and his callused palms and work-torn fingernails.

"If you had been anyone else," he said. "I would have grabbed you yesterday and taken you to one of our houses in another part of the island."

Analisa stood firm. "Not without a fight. Besides, I have friends in the American Embassy and the police."

He brushed aside her bravado with the gesture of shooing a fly from his face. "I would not do this for anyone else. For the sake of my mother, I give you a warning. Leave Santo Sangre. If you do not, I cannot be responsible for what happens."

This renewed encroachment on her freedom and safety enraged Analisa and frightened her. What did it mean for Arturo, the idol of the island? What did it mean for them? Were they star-crossed, a latter-day Romeo and Juliet? Historic hatreds had nothing to do with them or their love but threatened to rip them apart. She shoved her way past Jesús. "Get out of my way! I'm going to see Martina."

Jesús grabbed her roughly by the arm. "You have only today. Be gone from Volcán Grande by tomorrow or—"

"I know. You won't be responsible. What about your sisters?" She no longer said "my." "Will I be safe with them?"

"We have agreed. Out of respect for our mother. You may have this one last visit." He released her arm and strode away. A few feet down the path he stopped and returned to where she stood. "That man you are with," he sneered.

"You know him?"

"No, but he is Santo Sangrían. Therefore, he is an enemy of our cause," Jesús said, disgust for her companion clearly evident. "As long as you are together, he shares your peril."

Arturo's safety was as important to her as her own. Would his position in Santo Sangrían society and in the hearts of the populace protect him from the Martas, Lupes, Jesús Marías, and others like them? She doubted it. Be they few or many, Los Dejados had set themselves on an insane, vengeful course that ruled out reason but not murder.

"I'll leave tomorrow and be out of the country within a few days."

Jesús let her pass. As she did, he uttered a low, "I regret this."

Puzzled by this contradiction, she studied his face. A deep sadness for him filled her heart. She stepped forward and kissed him on the cheek. "I don't hate you. If you had been the 'caged bird' Martina set free, I might be blocking your path and threatening you right now."

His black eyes swam in a pool of confusion. "Isabella María," he whispered. "You have grown up...you are very beautiful." He looked around to make sure no one overheard him. "You were my favorite. I was sure I would never see you again. I wish things were different."

Analisa took his rough hands in hers and brought them to her lips. "Then you don't hate me for being adopted?"

"It was not your doing."

"Do you hate your—our mother?"

"I can never forgive her...or any of the women who sent their babies away in the arms of greedy attorneys who turned them over to wealthy, sterile foreigners."

"Does she know how you feel?"

No answer.

"Does she know her son and daughters are Dejadistas?"

He broke away from her grasp. "We share our bitterness only among ourselves."

"Did you know Lydia Vitale?" Analisa refused to utter aloud the disgusting nickname they had given their past and future captives.

"No."

With that, he turned and started back down the trail. As she watched his back, Analisa wondered if he was following some shrouded internal trail as well. How will he deal with his ambivalence, now that he's come face to face with a real live *coneja*?

☙ ☙ ☙

"I must leave Volcán Grande tomorrow," Analisa told Martina. "Arturo must return to Santa Catalina...on business."

Elena María and Carolina del Rosario exchanged knowing glances at the news. Martina rested her chin on the long, iron paddle she used in the brick oven. Her eyes reflected neither sadness nor joy. "I see."

Since Analisa's feet were already muddy from the trek to the brick yard, she volunteered to tromp around in the mixing vat. The three professional brick makers looked on in amusement as she danced in the thick, reddish ooze. The four of them spoke only occasionally as they labored side by side the rest of the day. Pretending that Los Dejados hadn't turned her life upside down again, Analisa acted as if it was perfectly normal for her to be there. She wondered if Martina knew more about her children's anti-adoption activism than they realized?

During a water break, she asked Martina, "Do you wish I hadn't come?"

Martina looked away toward the crest of the volcano. "It was easier living with my loss when I had only your empty cage to remind me. From now on, I must carry the image of you as grown up, prancing in my brick molds, laughing and trying to be one of us. But I will remind myself that you are not one of us. You never were. You never can be. For that reason alone, it is best for you to fly away again."

"I'll never be completely away. No matter where I am, I will never forget you." Analisa laughed. "And mixing mud for your bricks."

"That gives me joy."

"There's something else. I am in love with the man you met yesterday. We will be married. It may seem strange, but—" Analisa always thought she'd say these words in the sanctuary of her parents' home on Wilhelmina Street. "May I have your blessing?"

Martina laid a rough, mud-encrusted palm on Analisa's head. "You have my blessing. But promise you will not return to Volcán Grande...ever."

"Not even with your grandchildren?"

"Not even."

It surprised Analisa that she didn't feel rejected by her birth mother. Martina's simple wisdom, her seeming ability to know what was best for both of them moved her deeply. "If that's what you wish, I promise." She asked if she could write and send pictures.

Martina nodded. In her first real display of affection, she took Analisa's face in her hands and planted a wet kiss on her forehead. "You are a grown woman now. Go. Make a life for yourself far from this place." With her thumb, she made the sign of the cross on Analisa's forehead. "And may God go with you."

Analisa accepted Martina's anointing as a sacrament of familial love. The earthy symbols of sticky mud and a mother's touch had also healed her of her life-long blindness. In the glare of the afternoon sun, she saw herself as a little girl in hand-me-down sandals and a dirty dress. Martina returned to her work, helping her "real" daughters slide bricks into and out of the fire.

Analisa stood alone, up to her calves in mud. Slowly, her hands took graceful flight. Like a pair of white-crowned Caribbean doves, they followed the gentle curve of the volcano as it rose from beneath her feet and soared into the clouds.

"I am Isabella!" she cried.

Chapter 32

In the late afternoon, Analisa hosed off her feet and legs at the brick yard and washed her face in the rain barrel. But the red earth of Santo Sangre clung to her, as if recognizing one of its own. She needed a long, hot bath but tubs weren't among the amenities at Mesón Antigua. She'd need several soapings to get down to her natural olive complexion and sun-streaked curls again. She hoped the water at the inn would remain at least lukewarm until she looked like herself again.

Sweaty and emotionally weary, she trudged back to the inn. Although most of it was downhill, the return journey seemed much longer than her morning trek to Martina's brick yard. Her body ached all over from using muscles she hadn't exercised since the crash, not even during rehab. The throbbing in her right knee reminded her she had no business using her legs to stir Martina's mud cakes.

Arturo was sitting in the lobby reading a week-old copy of *La Prensa Diária* when Analisa entered from the plaza. He laughed out loud at the specter before him. Jesús María's numbing ultimatum kept her from finding humor in her appearance. They embraced, and he kissed her on both smeared cheeks, then full on her gritty lips. "We need to talk," she said. "Upstairs."

He kissed her again. "We will do more than that...upstairs...after we have cleaned you up."

Analisa rushed ahead, taking the steps two at a time. Arturo closed the door behind him. "Why are you trembling, *Querida*?"

"Martina's children," she panted. "Dejadistas...Jesús María confronted me on the road to the brick yard."

"I should have gone with you!"

She recounted their conversation and her brother's mandate. "We will both be in danger if I stay in Santo

Sangre. I can't do that to you. This is your home, your country. You belong here. I don't. Not any more. Martina said so herself."

Arturo sat on the bed, their bed, solemnly assimilating her news. Analisa sat on the other bed, no longer hers, facing him.

"He ordered me to get out of the country, or else," she continued. "Last night, I let myself believe I'd found a permanent home here with you. I was wrong. Los Dejados stole my freedom once. They tried to rob me of my very identity, but I was spared."

"Your own wits and courage saved you."

"I have no doubt they can do it again, with or without Lupe Santana." She reached across the void and held his hand. "Arturo, I'm frightened."

His dark eyebrows arched. "You do not have a corner on the fear market."

"What do you mean?"

"I am frightened too. For you most of all." He hesitated, as if his next words were reluctant to vibrate his vocal chords. "For myself as well."

"For yourself? You always seem so calm, so in control." This was a new side of Arturo, one she hadn't seen yet. She had come to rely on him for strength when her own failed.

"A survival technique I learned as a boy living on the streets. My motto was, 'Never let them know how scared you are.'"

"What is it you are afraid of?" she asked.

He pulled her into his lap and held her tightly against his chest. "A week ago, I had not dreamed of making my permanent home anywhere but here in Santo Sangre. Today, I have no home you do not share with me. Before I met you, all I feared were the twin black holes at the center of my being."

"'Black holes'?" Analisa didn't understand. She watched like a distant observer as an inner battle waged within him.

He took a deep breath, as if hoping that the oxygen filling his lungs might bring with it courage to proceed. "One is poverty. The other...being homeless again."

"Your demons?"

He nodded. "My two-headed monster."

"But, you're one of the most sought-after baritones in Europe and Latin America."

"Fear drives me to accept every invitation to perform, even though it keeps me on the road much of the year."

"I thought it was the love of singing, of being in the spotlight, the favorite of critics and opera fans."

"That is the face I show to the public. The possibility of awakening one day with no voice at all terrifies me." He snapped his fingers. "Poof! What happens to me then?"

"But that's not—"

"Rational?"

Analisa regretted the implication. "That was cruel. I'm sorry."

"Are our deepest fears ever rational? Despite the outward appearance of my home, I live a rather simple, unglamorous life. I do not patronize the clubs and casinos here or in the cities where I perform. I invest conservatively, but one never knows."

"And you're still a bachelor."

"Yes. The only women I seem to meet are singers and—what is the American word?—'groupies.' I find most singers too self-absorbed. And I quickly learned that the hangers-on wish only to bask in my celebrity." He paused. "I do not mean to give the impression that I have been pure as an angel—"

Analisa put her fingers to his lips. "I don't want to know about before...not who...or how many. Only now and the future are important."

"You're right, of course."

Analisa was silent for a long time. Arturo's inner fragility surprised her. It also made him more human, more accessible. She'd be more than a wife to him, his guardian angel, keeping watch at the gate of his soul. Armed with the sword of unconditional love, she'd drive anxiety away from his doorstep.

"Well," he said, "now that you know my Achilles heel, so to speak, what do you think of me?"

"I love you all the more." Analisa touched his cheek which burned with emotion. Encircling him within her embrace, she said. "Let's hold each other...and be scared for as long as we need to. Then, we'll conquer our demons together, one by one."

❦ ❦ ❦

Arturo was stretched out on his back with his eyes closed when Analisa returned from her shower. She let her robe drop to the floor and snuggled in beside him. For a long time, they clung to each other.

He pushed a strand of her hair aside and kissed her eyelids. "When I first met you at the Embassy, I saw my whole future flash before me with absolute clarity. You were right there at the center of it. All I had to do was enjoy it, a day at a time. Right then, I knew I had to see you again. I had to convince you we were meant to be together. I wanted you to know me as the person I am inside."

"I wanted it, too."

"That first night, on the stage of the Bellas Artes, I felt a flicker of response from you. It gave me hope. Then, as quickly as you had come to me, you—"

"Vanished."

He winced at the memory. "I thought I had frightened you away. I berated myself for moving too fast, for being too aggressive. Whatever your opinion of me, I had to hear it directly from you. I went to the Gran Palacio with the heat of our first kiss still on my lips. When I learned what had happened to you, I became desperate."

The time had come for Analisa to explore a mystery she had lived with since the day Eric Small introduced them. "How long have we known each other?"

"Forever."

She laughed softly and ran her fingers across his temples, loving the feel and fragrance of his skin and hair. "I mean, when did we first meet?"

"It's hard to believe, but it has been less than two weeks."

Analisa rested her head on Arturo's chest. The rhythmic drumming of his heart against the side of her face had a calming effect. They were alive and together—a good starting point for the future. "Was that the first time you saw me?"

"Yes. I am sure of it, except—" He hesitated a moment. His eyes brightened as if a spark had suddenly linked two separate realities in his brain. "I had a dream once... Sometime after the first of the year. January. February. I cannot remember exactly."

"What sort of dream?"

"I was standing in the snow, but I was dressed in tropical clothes. I hate snow. Some people were in trouble. Two of them seemed to have died. The third, a young woman—I did not see her face clearly—was barely alive, but near death." He stared at the ceiling, as if projecting his memories onto the cracked plaster. "For some reason, I knew she was Santo Sangrían..."

Excitement built within Analisa as she awaited the conclusion. "What did you do?"

"Nothing, really. I smiled and encouraged her to choose life, not death. The dream ended. I have not thought of it since. Why is it important?" She related her vision of Dave and the stranger at the crash site.

Stunned, he said, "I knew I had seen you before! I told myself it was impossible."

"Nothing's impossible."

With only an occasional word, by the slightest ministrations and touches to sensitive places, they lost themselves in each other's arms. Neither felt an urgency to rush satisfaction. Analisa's senses tuned to his scent, touch, taste, his words that seemed to float through the window from a distant place. She had no recollection of how he— or she—had removed his clothes or how they had joined her robe on the floor between the beds. Nor could she account for how she had come to be lying on top of him reveling in every throb she felt inside her.

This is what "making love" means, she realized. It's different from last night—not less satisfying—just different. And in its own way, more satisfying. Last night, they had been careful not to get pregnant. This time, they discarded all caution.

"Leave it in God's hands," she heard a voice whisper from another part of the room. "Be fruitful, multiply."

"I hope I do conceive," she breathed into Arturo's ear. "I want more of you than you can physically give me. Sex is so...fleeting, however long we delay our pleasure."

"In God's hands, then," Arturo echoed, as if he had heard the same angelic voice.

They rotated positions so that she now lay beneath him. With her hands on his buttocks, she urged him deeper inside. She longed to share with him the complete mystery of her self, without reservation. When the moment of climax arrived, Analisa felt disembodied, as if floating above the bed, gazing upon herself in Arturo's arms. Her spirit chanted the danger-defying mantra, "I am safe. I am home. I am safe. I am home."

❁ ❁ ❁

In the afterglow of their union, Analisa felt soft and mellow, as if all her muscles had turned to warm honey. At
this very moment Arturo's seed might be speeding toward
a rendezvous with its mate deep within her receptive
womb. She wished it Godspeed, happy hunting.

"We must think calmly," he said.

"I can do anything calmly now."

"We will leave in the morning. Right after I call Chief
Inspector Madrigal."

"The police?" She didn't understand.

"We must report the incident with Jesús María and his
sisters."

A frown chased away the perfect harmony she had felt
in every part of her being. His words jarred her back to the
moment, to her need to face their renewed danger. "I can't
do it."

"You must," Arturo said, suddenly impatient. "If not for
yourself, do it for the next unsuspecting adoptee who sets
foot on this island."

"Martina's children are probably just sympathizers.
Jesús María told me he never saw Lydia Vitale."

Arturo's eyes flashed with annoyance. "And you
believe him?"

"Yes!"

Analisa paused to let them both cool down. The one-
ness they had achieved had rapidly disintegrated. Is this the
pattern of all human intimacy? she wondered. Can lovers
tolerate only so much baring of body and soul? When it's
over, are we compelled to pull back from the brink of self-
annihilation? And does unconditional love somehow
understand that prolonged and perfect union is an impossible goal?

God had provided conscience as a guide to human
behavior. Had Nature also built into the human spirit an
instinctive referee whose role was to step in and say,

"That's close enough! Stand off, lest you lose your sense of self, your inevitable separateness"?

"All right," she said. "Call Madrigal. Tell him we've been approached by a member of Los Dejados. Tell him whatever you want, but please don't give him any names. They let me go for their mother's sake. I'm begging you to do the same." She recalled the trio of women working hard and proudly at their business. "For Martina."

The veins at Arturo's temples relaxed. "All right. But not for them...or for Martina. I will do it only for you."

Analisa circled his neck and held him close to her trembling body. "Thank you."

Arturo accepted her embrace but continued building his defenses. "I must also provide for security at my home. I will hire personal bodyguards to accompany us whenever we leave the estate."

Analisa shook her head. "I don't want to live like that. It would be like living within the Embassy compound— high walls, guns, all-night patrols on the perimeter." She wasn't being argumentative, just truthful. "There has to be another way. I won't live as a prisoner in my freedom, especially not in my own home. I want my normal life back."

Arturo seemed to have fled to some inner retreat to digest her protest. "Do you trust me, Analisa?"

"With all my heart."

"Then, we will find your other way."

They clung to each other as sunset faded into night, no longer two frightened children—one a tiny bird not wanting to be caged, the other a street urchin surviving by his fragile wits. Although answers eluded them, conviction that a benevolent Providence guided their decisions assigned courage as a companion to their anxiety.

Chapter 33

It was late afternoon the next day when Analisa and Arturo arrived back in the capital. Within a half-hour, Chief Inspector Madrigal's car passed through the Cristobal mansion's electronically controlled gate. Arturo led him into the music room where Analisa waited.

"So wedding bells are ringing, Señorita Marconi?" the Inspector said. "¡Felicidades!"

Analisa blushed. "Thank you. I can hardly believe it myself."

The Inspector gave her hand an affirming squeeze. "I am delighted for both of you. You must know, Señorita, that you are breaking every female heart in Santo Sangre."

Unwilling to pursue that line of conversation, Analisa invited him to take a seat on the white leather sofa. She took his order for a sparkling water over ice.

"So, Los Dejados are still alive and well," Madrigal said. "My optimism was premature. I was sure we had killed that rabid dog. Apparently, they have more support in the countryside than we gave them credit for."

Analisa's thoughts were on Jesús María and his sisters. "It isn't a crime to be a sympathizer, is it? Where I come from, you can't be arrested for what you believe."

"Our laws are not so generous as yours. You were threatened in Volcán Grande by some...unknown person." The arch of his left eyebrow told her he respectfully doubted that part of her story. "In light of the previous assault against you, that in itself was a crime. The Attorney General now considers mere affiliation with Los Dejados worth five years in prison. Enough time for them to contemplate the foolishness of their decisions and actions."

Analisa gasped. "Five years!" She worried about Martina. And the brick yard. Arturo went to her side and laid a supportive hand on her shoulder.

Madrigal set his glass on the coffee table in front of him. "The law is the law."

"What about Marta Lopez?" Analisa asked. "Has she had a hearing?"

"She has. The attorney you hired made her sound like the Virgin Mary." Clearly, Madrigal saw no humor in the comparison. "She is guilty as the Devil, but the judge seemed quite moved by her lawyer's emotional appeal. It might go well for her. Right now, she is looking at five to ten years."

Analisa's heart sank. "You call that 'going well'?"

"She deserves that and more."

"I'd like to see her. Is that possible?"

A rippling frown told her what the inspector thought of her request. "If you wish, I can arrange it."

She stood firm as a California oak. "It's what I wish."

"Be at the Cárcel Central tomorrow at two in the afternoon. I will meet you there." He rose from the sofa and shook hands with Arturo. "Now, I must go."

They escorted the Inspector to the circular driveway. "Thank you for coming," Analisa said. "We'll meet you at two o'clock."

Inspector Madrigal started his car and shifted into first gear. "I wish everyone in Santo Sangre was as forgiving and kind-natured as you, Señorita."

"If they were," Arturo said, "you would have to find a new line of work."

"My wife would like that! No danger of it happening, I'm afraid. By the way, the off-duty officers you asked for are already watching your estate. The teams will maintain round-the-clock, low-profile surveillance. Do not worry if you cannot always see them. They will be on guard, I assure you." With that the Inspector pulled away from the entryway. He paused to let the electronic gate swing open, turned left, and disappeared from sight.

❧ ❧ ❧

That evening, Analisa and Arturo soaked for a long time in his double-sized Jacuzzi. Bubbles tumbled over their naked bodies, massaging away the tension that gnawed at them. When their skin began to wrinkle, they quit the tub. She accepted the soft, full-body towel he offered and let his hands play freely within its folds. Every inch of flesh he touched sent sensuous messages to her brain until a shadow fell across her desire.

"I feel...awkward," she said.

"What is it, *Querida*?"

"It's not you. It's just...everything here belongs to you. There's nothing of me. Being together felt different when we were on neutral ground. It's a woman thing, I guess. The need to make her own nest."

"Listen well, Analisa Marconi." Arturo placed his hands on her shoulders and peered directly into her soul.

"The only thing in this entire house that means anything to me is you. It is all replaceable. If it burned down tonight, I would mourn none of it as long as I had you in my arms."

She led him to the bed and pulled the covers over them. Languid from the hot bath, she let him minister to her awkwardness.

Hours later, Analisa opened her eyes. The only light was the red glow of Arturo's digital alarm clock. She hadn't yet spent a full night in his bed, yet she already knew he had claimed the left side as "his." The right was "hers," until death forced one of them to sleep alone again.

"Awake?" he asked the darkness.

"Uh-huh."

"Let's get away from this island."

"It's your home," she said.

"It was yours, too."

"I didn't have a choice."

In the darkness, Arturo's fingers traced a path from her temple to her chin. "I doubt that, but this is no time for metaphysics."

The ensuing silence weighed heavy as the muggy night air. She was still awake when his voice interrupted her brooding. "This whole Los Dejados situation has helped me face something that has been pushing its way to the surface for a long time." He had her full attention. "When Martina said she opened your cage and set you free to find your true home, her words pierced my heart. I realized we had more in common than either of us knew. We'd both flown away. You to America."

"How did you escape?"

"My flight was more social than geographic. I left behind the poverty and abuse of my childhood. Perhaps it is time to complete my journey, with you as my North Star, my guide." The words echoed from a frightened boy, making it on his own in the unfriendly midnight streets of the capital.

Analisa reached out to him, letting the tips of her fingers serve as her eyes. She rubbed away tight furrows from his forehead and loosened the grip of unhappy memories from his compressed lips. "If only I could soothe your heart," she whispered.

"You have...God knows, you have." He pressed her closer to his body. "I have a condominium just south of Tarragona on Spain's Costa del Sol. I use it as a retreat when I sing in Europe. It overlooks the sea like this place, but it is much smaller. I believe you would be happy there."

Analisa clung to him, feeling safe, regardless of the dangers that might still lurk outside the walls of his estate. "I'll be happy any place on earth where we're together, even if we stay right here. Give me a month and I'll have enough of myself in this house to turn it into 'our' home, not just yours."

"I have no doubt about that, but I cannot live here any longer—not in this house, not in this city or this country—knowing you might be in danger."

They exchanged few words the rest of the night. Breathing the air of new possibilities, they expressed their unity through intimate touches and such hungry kisses that they'd bear the brands long into tomorrow.

❧ ❧ ❧

Analisa and Arturo met Chief Inspector Madrigal at the entrance to the women's section of Santa Catalina's Cárcel Central. She shivered when they stepped out of the afternoon sunshine and into the jail's dank interior. Madrigal handed her a document bearing an official-looking stamp and his signature.

"All is arranged, Señorita Marconi. Present this at the main desk. They will need to see your passport." He started to leave, then turned, his expression grave, concerned. "Don't expect to like anything you see here. In Santo Sangre, prisoners forfeit all rights at the prison door. They retrieve them only when the court pronounces them innocent or after they have served their sentences, if condemned."

A surly guard slumped over the information desk, his on-duty *siesta* suddenly interrupted by the man and woman standing before him. He checked Analisa's documents and gave her a Visitor badge. Pointing to a steel-barred door at the end of a dark hallway, he said, "Press the button and wait."

When Arturo started down the hall with her, a large bear-like paw attached itself to his wrist. "No men allowed. Just her."

An equally disagreeable, droopy-eyed guard visually strip-searched Analisa before allowing her to pass through the barrier. She felt as assaulted by his lust as she had by Lupe Santana's.

Without taking his eyes off her bare knees and calves, he unlocked a door and ushered her into a brightly lit, windowless room. It had the gagging odor of stale urine and no memory of its last coat of paint. A dozen plain wooden tables rose like high desert plateaus from the dusty floor. About half were currently occupied by visitors and inmates.

"No touching. No passing objects of any kind," the guard warned.

Madrigal had been right. There was nothing and no one in here Analisa liked. Only her desire to see Marta kept her from fleeing this place and never looking back. She thought of Jesus' gospel words, "I was in prison and you visited me," and chose a table close to the wall. With nothing else to do, she studied the film of condensation that drew Rorschach-like patterns on the crumbling plaster. She imagined the dampness as resulting from the ocean of tears shed by brokenhearted mothers and loved ones.

Privacy was no more important than cleanliness or comfort. She sat alone for about ten minutes listening to soft, mournful murmurs emanating from nearby tables. When she heard the metallic click of a key turning in the lock at the opposite end of the room, she took several deep breaths to fight off a wave of lightheadedness.

Marta entered and, with her, the shrill sounds of women's voices, some screaming obscenities, others weeping or moaning in pain. Her round features fell slack along her jaw. Life had vacated her eyes. Spotting her visitor, Marta turned to retreat back through the door, but the matron had already locked it behind her.

Analisa gestured an invitation to join her. Left with no other option, Marta approached the table and sat down.

Analisa didn't know what to say to someone who was alive
but not among the living. It hurt her to see Marta in the
role of captive. "How are you?"

Marta turned her face away.

"They tell me your attorney is a good one."

Without looking at her visitor, Marta said, "Why did
you do it?"

Why? Analisa's exact question to Martina. Why do
people do the things they do? She had found her answer.
Marta deserved hers. "When we were...together," Analisa
began, "you talked about being my sister, *mi hermana*.
You made me realize that the difference between us was
the thin line of fate. For that, I am grateful."

For the first time, Marta engaged Analisa. "Fate," she
echoed across the gap that separated them.

"I found my birth mother. And a brother and two sisters." Analisa calculated the risks involved in her next
statements and the potential danger they posed for her
Santo Sangrían family. "All but my mother are Dejadistas."
She spoke their names. "Do you know them?"

Marta shook her head. "There are far more of us than
anyone suspects."

"My brother threatened me but let me go for his own
reasons. I fear for them." She glanced around the room, at
the guard, the inmates, their visitors. "I don't want them to
end up here."

"There is nothing you can do for your brother and sisters," Marta said without emotion. "Nor do they want anything from you."

"Maybe not. But I can do something for you if you will
let me."

"All I want is to get out of here."

Analisa strained forward. "I'm trying, believe me. The
attorney is working hard on your case."

Marta became agitated, like a cornered animal longing
for freedom. "I mean...out of this country. With my son."

Another bird who wants to fly away, Analisa thought. "Where do you want to go?"

"Anywhere. With you?" The glacier thawed and Marta's tears pooled into small puddles on the table top. She swiped at them with her fingers.

"What about Lupe?"

"Lupe!" Marta spat the name with a growl of contempt. "See what loving him got me. He does not have a good lawyer to plead his case. He will never see the outside of a prison again."

"You don't know that for sure." A feeble attempt to offer hope in a hopeless situation.

"What difference does it make? I cannot live with him. I, too, had dreams...once...long ago. I wanted a better life. In my bitterness, I closed my eyes to what was happening." Like a blind woman groping for her cane, Marta reached across the table in search of Analisa's hand. The guard took a step toward them and raised his hand in a warning gesture.

Analisa withdrew her hands to her lap. "We aren't sup- posed to touch."

"Forgive me. I do not want to get you in trouble." Marta lay her palms flat on the table. "I am not an evil per- son, despite what I did."

"I wouldn't have hired an attorney...I wouldn't be here now if I thought you were an evil person," Analisa assured her.

"Will you write to me?"

Analisa put a trembling hand over her heart. "I prom- ise you this. I'll be waiting outside the gate the day you are released. If it is humanly possible, I will get you and your son out of Santo Sangre."

"You will be waiting?" Marta's voice was childlike, trusting, but wary from a lifetime of empty promises, too many broken pledges.

Analisa felt closer to this woman than to either of Martina's two daughters in Volcán Grande. "I'll do even better than that. I will set aside funds for the care of your child. My attorney, Don Ricardo Valenzuela, will see that whoever cares for the boy will get money each month to provide for him."

Marta seemed unable to comprehend what Analisa had just told her. "Why are you doing this?"

Analisa managed a wan smile. "I'm just being a good sister."

A light went on in Marta's eyes. "¿Hermanas?"

"Sí. Hermanas." Analisa glanced across the room in the direction of the guard who was opening the door to let another visitor in. With a quick movement, she leaned across the table and kissed Marta on the cheek. "Ten cuidado, mi hermana."

"Take care yourself—" Unable to continue, Marta rose and signaled the guard. At the door, she turned and mouthed something Analisa interpreted as, "Now, I have something to live for."

After she had gone, Analisa sat alone at the table. Sucking in a deep breath from the airless environment, she tried to pull herself together. Finally, she left the room to rejoin Arturo—and the human race.

Outside the prison walls, she gulped hungrily the precious air of freedom.

"You really promised to meet her when she gets out of prison?" Arturo's tone wasn't accusatory. Quite the contrary. "Your compassion and forgiveness amaze me."

"Let's go home."

"I like the sound of that word. I have always referred to the place I live in as my house or my estate. Without being conscious of it, I have never thought of it as my home. It never felt like a real home. Not until you crossed its threshold."

"Yet you're willing to give it up?"

"I told you. Home for me now is with you. Wherever we are together."

✹ ✹ ✹

Analisa went for a swim, feeling the need to purge herself of the spiritual and material grime of that chamber of horrors called Cárcel Central. Lapping freestyle, she gradually shed her mental fatigue. She prayed for her new sister-in-spirit to survive her prison experience and come out whole and prepared for whatever the future held for her. As if to engrave her jailhouse pledge on her soul, Analisa clenched her teeth and chanted with every stroke of her arms, I'll be there, Marta. I'll be waiting.

Arturo was poolside when she emerged. He reached down with one hand and helped her onto the warm deck. "You swim with a vengeance."

She pressed a towel to her face and dried her dripping limbs. "Let's go upstairs."

Arturo didn't argue.

✹ ✹ ✹

Emilia Jimenez had supper ready for them when they entered the dining room just after six o'clock. Their bodies still glowed from lovemaking. Analisa wore shorts and a tank top and felt as if she'd never be cold again.

Emilia fussed around her and smiled approvingly at Arturo before retreating to the kitchen. Each time she emerged, she behaved like a mother whose son had brought home a girl she, too, loved.

After supper, Analisa joined Arturo for coffee on the verandah. It was time to make specific plans. "What will become of Emilia?"

"I have instructed my attorney to set up a trust fund. She and her family will be well provided for whether she decides to work again or not."

"I like your idea about going to your condo in Spain after the concert," Analisa said. "We both need some distance from all that's happened."

"I am glad you agree."

"There's just one thing. I haven't been in an airplane since the day my parents died." She hoped he wouldn't argue, as a shrill inner voice did, that her fear was silly and immature.

He sipped his coffee and watched the under-surface spotlights dance with the rippling rhythm of the blue water. "What was it like to fly with your father?"

"I loved it! I felt like an eagle, soaring above the clouds, not a care in the world."

"Martina was right, then, wasn't she?" He laughed. "You are part human, part bird."

"I never thought of it like that."

As if measuring his words, he continued deliberately, "Now a tragic accident has grounded that winged creature, even though you know you still have the desire to explore what is beyond the next hill."

"A poet!"

"Still a bad one?"

"Pretty good, actually. At least you're improving." Analisa let this exchange circulate within her. Her brain checked out the idea, first with her nervous system, then her heart. She waited to see if the thought of flying again, with Arturo at her side, produced any of the usual somatic symptoms—racing heartbeat, cold sweat, darkened vision, and that lightheaded feeling that made her feel as if she was about to lose consciousness. All she felt was excitement to begin her new life.

"I can do it," she whispered.

They sat, holding hands and enjoying the onset of night.

"What about California?" Arturo asked. "And Dave?"

"I want to—" She carefully avoided the expression, get married. She already considered herself permanently and sacredly vowed to Arturo. "If it's okay with you, I'd like to have our wedding celebration in my parish church...with Dave doing the honors."

"Of course." Arturo looked away, concerned about something.

"What is it?"

"How difficult will this be for Dave?"

Analisa leaned back in her chair. She envisioned Dave officiating at their wedding. "He'll be fine. I know him...probably better than anyone. I've been a safe, healthy outlet for him. He's been as intimate with me as a priest can be without violating his commitment."

"He is fortunate to have a friend like you. I realize that more every day I spend with you."

"I owe so much of who I am to Dave. There's a part of my spirit you'll always have to share with him. Can you accept that?" The rhetorical question required neither affirmation nor denial.

Arturo grazed the skin of her upper arm with the backs of his fingernails, then kissed her bare shoulder. "If any other woman were to give me that line, I assure you I would run from her as fast and as far as my legs would carry me. When you say it, I am not frightened. Nor am I jealous of the love you reserve for Dave."

"My love for him isn't a piece I withhold from you. From now on, what I give to Dave I will draw from our love. I love him more because you love me." She threw her hands up and laughed. "God, I sound like my old philosophy professor at St. Mary's! I don't know if what I'm saying makes any sense or not."

Arturo contemplated her treatise on love's energy source. "At some level I understand. I'm not sure why. It just seems right."

Analisa changed the subject. "When do we have to be in Madrid?"

"Next week for rehearsals. The concert is a week from Saturday. On Sunday, we will go to the Catalonian coast. I have never felt a greater need for a vacation."

"It'll be our honeymoon."

"I never expected to have my honeymoon before the wedding ceremony."

"We've lived a lifetime in the days we've known each other, haven't we? Neither of us expected any of it." Analisa curled up in Arturo's lap like a little girl. She rested her head on his shoulder and cuddled close to him. "I'm looking forward to spending the rest of my life getting to know you."

He shrugged. "There is not much to know."

She kissed him tenderly, then again with far greater passion. "I doubt that very much, Señor Cristobal."

Chapter 34

Opera lovers in Madrid—even the critics—fell in love with Arturo Cristobal. As the final encore, which he dedicated to "my beloved Analisa," he sang her favorite, "Il Prim' Amore." Throughout the rendition, he looked directly into her eyes, drawing the audience's attention to her box just above the right corner of the stage.

After the concert, their hideaway on the Costa del Sol provided their first real opportunity to enjoy "being" together.

Ten days later, they were in California. Arturo had gone to Los Angeles to discuss plans for a spring concert with the Los Angeles Philharmonic at the Dorothy Chandler Pavilion.

Analisa met Dave to discuss plans for the wedding, which they had set for the first Saturday in October. She sat on the sofa in his upstairs study, shoes off, bare feet and legs tucked under her. Selecting Scripture readings and music for the nuptial Mass took less than half an hour. Dave appeared in no hurry to send her home. She yearned to reach out, spirit to spirit, to let him know that nothing had changed between them.

"I can't tell you how much your coming to Santo Sangre meant to me," she said.

"Neither wild horses nor an irritable pastor could have kept me away." In his high-backed rocking chair, he moved slowly back and forth like the pendulum of a metronome. "I imagined every possible scenario connected with your trip, but you fooled me. Twice. I didn't foresee Los Dejados. And—" He picked up her marriage license. "I never expected this."

"You're not the only one."

"If I hadn't spent time with Arturo, I'd be very worried about you right now. I..."

She waited patiently while he searched for words to express his feelings.

Dave bit his lower lip. "I knew you'd find someone and get married sooner or later. Somehow I thought you'd always be living close by. Now, you're going off to live in Spain. It won't be the same without you."

Analisa watched him struggle to restrain tears that signaled the depth of his feelings about this new turn in her life, and his. "You've got to visit us."

"I don't know. Three's a crowd, and all that."

"Not in a family. I can't imagine having one you aren't a part of."

She knew he wouldn't come. He was already disengaging, cutting the cord that had bound their lives together for almost a decade. If their relationship was to continue, she'd have to take the initiative—visit, send cards, e-mail, an occasional phone call.

"You wanted a new family," he said. "Marrying Arturo is a good start."

"And I found my true, best self in the process."

"Congratulations. That's more than I can say."

She was a senior in high school when she first became aware that Dave expended megawatts of energy keeping the lid on a deep and festering grief. That year he made the transition from parish priest to her closest friend.

"It hurts me to see you like this."

"Not the Father Dave of your teen years?"

"No."

It wasn't like him to wallow in self-pity. He forbade her to do it during the interminable weeks of her hospitalization and rehab. She felt his pain now, as he had shared hers then. They fell silent, each lost in thoughts of past times shared, good and bad. Because of his dark mood, Analisa hesitated to let him in on her latest news. Finally, she trusted him to deal with it.

"I'm pregnant," she said.

Shock flickered behind his outwardly loving, priestly expression. Disappointment followed. She had become so proficient at reading his eyes that he always said it was no use trying to hold something back from her.

"Next spring," she added, anticipating his question.

"I didn't think—"

"That I'd sleep with a man without being married to him? Dave, Arturo and I are married."

He stopped rocking and planted his feet on the carpet. "Civil ceremony?"

"You know I'd never do that."

He twisted in the chair and swung his right leg over the polished arm. "I don't get it."

She reminded him of the conversation in which he had expounded his theology of the-moment-when-the-marital-union-is-sealed. "I believed you. I'm a married woman. In October, Arturo and I will make our private vows public and ask this community to bless us and join in our happiness."

Dave looked out the window as if searching for that improbable place on earth where all the pieces of his life came together and made him a whole person. He exhaled a deep sound whose origin had to be some primal place within his psyche. "I envy you. Part of me wants what you have so much I can taste it."

"It can't happen until all of you wants it."

"That's the trouble. I want everything." He closed his eyes and slumped against the back rest, sagging like a man with an elephant on his chest. "Life lets us have only part of what we desire. So, we pick and choose, knowing we may never—will never—experience some of its possibilities."

"How do you live with it?"

Dave's gaze drifted to the window and beyond. "Yesterday's gone. It'll never come back. Tomorrow?

Who knows about tomorrow? Today is all I have. It's what I have to deal with and account for."

"You said once in a homily that today's a gift. That's why we call it—"

"The present." Dave's tears flowed freely. "God, I'll miss you!"

Analisa knelt by the side of his chair and rested her head against his shoulder, aware of a new instinct, one she identified as...maternal. Probably, she thought, because of the child she and Arturo had conceived and whose life she now nurtured. She grasped his hands and held them tight. Kissing him tenderly on the forehead, she let her lips linger on his flesh to emphasize her love and concern. "What will become of you?"

Dave sighed. "With God's help, I'll just...keep on keepin' on."

A spark of hope burned some of the sadness from his eyes. Analisa longed to see the burden lift from his heart, as well.

❧ ❧ ❧

"Inspector Madrigal, this is Arturo Cristobal." He spoke in rapid-fire Spanish. "I'm calling from California. Anaheim to be exact."

"Have you been to Disneyland?" the Inspector wanted to know.

"Not yet, but Analisa's home isn't far from the park."

The policeman expressed the desire to take Laura and their new baby to Disney World in Orlando some day. "And when is your big day?"

"First Saturday in October."

"That may become a national holiday here."

Arturo wasn't sure if Madrigal was serious or joking. "If it does, the children will at least remember me for getting them out of school for one day every year. I'm calling about Los Dejados, Marta Lopez in particular. What is the status of her case?"

"Both the Lopez woman and Lupe Santana were tried and sentenced yesterday," the Inspector said. "The court will hear the remaining cases next week."

"And the outcome?"

"On the advice of her attorney, Señorita Lopez pleaded guilty. She threw herself on the mercy of the court, as they say."

Arturo knew the risk of taking such an action. But judges in his country were known to be open to "suggestions." With Analisa's money to work with, Marta's attorney had some extra bargaining power.

"The judge was lenient. Two years."

"Analisa will be pleased. Knowing her, she will put the release date on her calendar and be there at the gate, as she promised." Arturo hesitated. "What about that...Santana fellow?"

"Against the advice of his attorney, Señor Santana fought the charges all the way, spouting his anti-adoption philosophy from the witness stand. It didn't play well. Fifteen years. In my opinion, that fellow deserved a life sentence."

Arturo thought of all that Analisa had suffered at the hands of Lupe Santana. "Me, too." He asked for the mailing address of the women's prison and wrote it down. "Thank you for the information, Inspector."

"Give my best wishes to the bride-to-be."

"I will. Thank you. Goodbye."

"Two years!" Analisa sighed. They sat on the covered patio of her home, enjoying the warmth of the late-summer day.

"Madrigal said she got off lightly," Arturo said. "It could have been much worse. I hope she appreciates what you did for her."

"She wants to make a better life for herself. If I'd stayed to testify on her behalf, she might have received an even lighter sentence."

"I doubt it. Besides, we'll have another chance to help her when she gets out."

Two years in that miserable place, Analisa reflected. It would be an eternity for me.

Arturo took her in his arms and kissed her. "Los Dejados sentenced you to life in prison without parole. I don't feel one bit sorry for any of them."

A cold shiver rippled through Analisa's body.

❀ ❀ ❀

On a gentle spring evening on the east coast of Spain, Arturo called for the midwife. Analisa's labor was anything but gentle, but she forgot those anxious, painful hours the moment Isabella Claire Cristobal sang her first note.

Motherhood gave Analisa a new appreciation of how Martina Aguilada must have felt when giving up her youngest daughter, caged bird or not. "What tremendous love she had for me," she told her husband. Contemplating the miracle of new life sucking at her breast, she couldn't imagine parting with her Isabella...for any reason.